"Too shock. Andrew was married."

Diantha kept her voice lowered in order to mask her mounting alarums.

Devlin flicked open his snuff box with his thumb-nail. "Of course, he is, Miss Atwood. I know my memory is shockingly bad, but yours is far worse if you don't recall the ceremony at St. George's Hanover Square."

"I don't mean that!" she said, laughing despite her worries. "I received a call this morning from a Mrs. Tribbet of Topping Green. She told me a preposterous story that Andrew had married her daughter a month ago and had the wedding certificate to prove it."

The viscount inhaled a pinch of snuff. "A very old trick, my dear. It's a hoax to extract money from the unwary."

"That's what I had supposed, too," Diantha agreed. "But she didn't ask for any money. All she wanted was Andrew to return as her daughter's lawfully wedded husband."

"The request for money will come later. Depend on it, my dear," he assured her.

"I do so hope you're right, Lord Devlin," Diantha answered.

"Heaven help us, so do I, Miss Atwood. So do I."

Books by Clarice Peters

HARLEQUIN REGENCY ROMANCE
CONTRARY LOVERS
THE MARQUIS AND THE MISS
11–VANESSA
23–PRESCOTT'S LADY
53–THE HEART'S WAGER

Don't miss any of our special offers. Write to us at the following address for information on our newest releases.

Harlequin Reader Service
P.O. Box 1397, Buffalo, NY 14240
Canadian address: P.O. Box 603,
Fort Erie, Ont. L2A 5X3

BELLE OF
PORTMAN SQUARE

CLARICE PETERS

Harlequin Books

TORONTO • NEW YORK • LONDON
AMSTERDAM • PARIS • SYDNEY • HAMBURG
STOCKHOLM • ATHENS • TOKYO • MILAN

For the real Diantha,
who read my first Regency years ago and liked it

Published January 1992

ISBN 0-373-31165-6

BELLE OF PORTMAN SQUARE

CHAPTER ONE

THROUGH THE HALLOWED portals of St. George's, Hanover Square, had passed many a reluctant male and none more so than the tall, black-haired gentleman now slowly mounting the front steps on this late April morning in 1817. Viscount Devlin was not the bridegroom, that distinction falling instead on the shoulders of his boon companion, Mr. Andrew Atwood. A confirmed bachelor, Devlin nonetheless felt a definite urge to quit the scene where so many men before him had taken the fatal plunge into matrimony.

"Courage," he murmured under his breath as he entered the church.

From the silence of the guests assembled within, he concluded the nuptials were under way and quickly slid into a vacant spot in a nearby pew. No opportunity to look for Roddy and Emily who had promised to hold a place for him. His tardiness was a result of not only the crush of traffic, but also a hard night's play at Brooks's which rendered him unable to rise before eleven. He stifled a yawn now and suffered a withering glare from a stout matron sitting in the pew in front of him.

From his position in the back of the church Devlin counted three Patronesses present, including Lady Jersey, who had predicted that Esmeraude would one day be a duchess. Oddly enough it was Andrew, a mere gentleman, who had won Esmeraude's hand.

Indeed, the match between Miss Esmeraude Lowell and Mr. Andrew Atwood had fuelled the prattle boxes during most of the Season. The bride was a diamond of the first water and an heiress who had had her choice of a dozen wealthy noblemen, while the bridegroom—though of impeccable lineage—was acknowledged to be impoverished, with a taste for the gaming tables of Watier's.

Devlin's thoughts on the dangers and pleasures of the green baize tables halted upon the arrival of another latecomer. A young lady dressed entirely in blue burst through the side doors in a rush, catching herself guiltily as she realized the ceremony was going on. Automatically, Devlin put up his quizzing glass.

She was quite tiny, not five feet tall, with raven-coloured tresses peeking from under a hat and a rather self-possessed air. As she searched for a seat, Devlin slid farther into his pew, indicating the space now made available to her.

Her eyes brightened as she took her seat. "Thank you," she whispered. "I'm very late. I had a devilish time getting here. One of my team lost a shoe on the way, and I was obliged to stop and have it repaired."

"Surely, your groom?"

"I drive alone," she told him, and seeing the surprise on his face added in a challenging fashion, "I always do."

That challenge in her dark eyes amused him, but before he could delve further into her abilities handling a rein, the matron in the pew in front turned around.

"Shhhh!" she hissed.

Meekly the two of them fell silent, but he recognized the ready laughter in the eyes of the young lady. A spirited creature. Intrigued, he promised himself he would talk to her later and learn her name.

"Do you, Esmeraude, take Andrew to be your lawfully wedded husband?" The minister's voice droned on, and Devlin yawned yet again. His pew mate smiled. The neck of the matron in front had turned decidedly crimson.

The sound of the organ announcing the welcome end to the ordeal of the wedding brought the viscount to his feet, where he discovered he towered a good foot higher than the young lady in blue. He intended to speak to her as soon as they left the church, but before he could follow her out, the crowd's surge carried her away from him.

"Blast and botheration!" he said, pushing his way towards the exit.

"Have you lost someone, Devlin?" Lady Jersey turned at the sound of his voice. The ostrich plume on her hat tickled his chin.

"Good morning, Sally. No, I haven't lost anyone. Though it's goose to guineas that someone will be lost in this crowd."

"As long as it's not me," the Patroness said, accepting his escort down the stairs. "Why do I come to these weddings?"

"Because you are the fairy godmother, of course," he said with aplomb.

"Fustian!" She tapped his knuckles playfully with her fan but did not appear too displeased by his comment, which acknowledged her powerful position in London society.

He left Lady Jersey with a circle of admirers and was taking another quick glance about for the lady in blue when he heard his name called by his friend Mr. Roderick Bridger. That sturdy-looking gentleman stood off to the side with his pretty blond wife, Emily, who looked very *enceinte*.

"There you are, Dev. Andrew wagered a monkey you wouldn't even show!"

"Always happy to see someone else get hitched, Roddy. You know that," Devlin drawled, smiling over at Emily.

"You're the last one, Devlin," Emily said shyly. The three men, Devlin, Roderick, and Andrew had been dubbed the Bachelors by the Bow Window Set nearly half a decade ago for their avowed intention never to wed. Now Devlin was the only bachelor left of the original trio.

"Not for long, I vow," Roddy said with a grin. "Emily was just telling me about her cousin."

The viscount shot his friend a thundercloud look. Too late. Emily seized the opening and spoke with enthusiasm about her cousin Dorothea: twenty-six, possessed of liveliness, intelligence, and not just in the ordinary way.

"I'm sure she's not," Devlin agreed, smoothing his cravat tied flawlessly in an Orientale and vowing vengeance on Roddy's head. Suddenly all thoughts of revenge vanished when he spied his pew mate from the church talking with the newlyweds in the distance.

"Roddy, who is that female with Andrew and Esmeraude?" he demanded when Emily paused for breath, her catalogue of Dorothea's virtues at a temporary halt.

Roddy looked over his shoulder in the direction his friend indicated and then punched him lightly on the back. "That's Diantha, you gudgeon. Andrew's sister."

"His sister? Do you mean the bluestocking?" Devlin ejaculated. "The one who dislikes Society and social occasions?"

"Yes. I suppose she felt duty bound to appear," Roddy suggested, "since Andrew was getting married. As a rule she spends most of her time at Portman Square, doing whatever it is bluestockings do."

"Indeed?" Devlin murmured, continuing to take Miss Atwood's measure through his glass. Blondes were the current rage, but Devlin personally preferred brunettes, and Miss Atwood filled that category to perfection with her head of raven curls falling to her shoulders, her creamy complexion and large laughing eyes. As befitted her inches, her figure was petite but surprisingly curvaceous.

Frowning, the viscount dropped his quizzer. What in heaven was he thinking of detailing the charms of Miss Atwood in such a manner? His taste in females had never run to bluestockings or the sisters of his friends or for that matter any young innocent. Mrs. Whorley, an amorous widow currently enjoying the viscount's patronage, was all that he required in a female.

Emily pulled Roddy away to talk to another couple also facing parenthood in the near future. Devlin wondered just how much longer he would be obliged to stand in the April wind.

"Not enjoying the festivities, Devlin?" The bride's uncle, Lord Feberman, an acquaintance from White's, paused for a word.

"On the contrary, I was admiring the celebrations greatly, sir," the viscount replied. "Weddings are best appreciated from a distance."

Lord Feberman's double chin shook with a hearty laugh. "Ranks of bachelors appear to be thinning from your set, Devlin. Last one left, aren't you?"

"Yes," Devlin agreed. He was rescued from Feberman's twits by Esmeraude and Andrew, the bride looking radiant, and Andrew so genuinely happy that Devlin felt an unfamiliar pang in his breast. He identified it after a moment as envy, an emotion he stifled by ruthlessly recalling the many charms of Mrs. Whorley.

From several feet away, Diantha Atwood chatted amicably with Esmeraude's father, all the while wondering who the black-haired gentleman she'd shared a pew with could be. Quite probably one of the Lowell clan, judging by the way he smiled down at Esmeraude. Although no expert when it came to judging manly attributes, Diantha was obliged to admit that the specimen she saw was exceedingly good-looking, with jet-black hair worn thick and cut in the fashionable Brutus and broad shoulders which filled the entire breadth of his coat of Bath blue superfine.

As she turned to ask Mr. Lowell about the identity of his kinsman, Esmeraude's mother seized her in a tearful embrace.

"My dear Miss Atwood, such a happy occasion," she said, looking anything but as she dabbed at her eyes with a damp handkerchief.

"My daughter Mrs. Andrew Atwood. I'd never have believed it," Mrs. Lowell said. Diantha's lip twitched.

"Now then, my dear," Mr. Lowell said gruffly. "Andrew will do fine by Esmeraude." He glowered. "Or else he'll answer to me."

"My brother will make you proud of him, sir," Diantha said.

Mr. Lowell cocked a craggy brow. "I hope so. All I ask is that he stay away from the cardrooms. Don't know if I should have allowed the match. But Esmeraude would cry..." he said, looking uncomfortable as he led his wife away.

Diantha smiled as she recognized the signs of a doting father. Her own father had been equally devoted.

"Di! What are you doing back here in the crowd?" Andrew, clucking his tongue, rescued her. "You'll get trampled."

This reference to her lack of stature won a smile from those nearby.

"No one will trample me," she replied. "I have a hat pin," which she duly showed to him. "With it I am impervious."

He laughed and hugged her exuberantly. "Dear Di. I wish you were as happy as I am today!"

She stood on tiptoe to kiss his cheek. "Dear Andrew. I am, truly!"

He tugged her hand. "Come, Roddy tells me that Devlin is perishing to meet you."

"Devlin?" All laughter vanished from Diantha's sparkling eyes, and she pulled away from her brother. "You must be jesting. I don't wish to meet that insufferable man."

Andrew's smile faded, and he raked his fingers through his sandy hair. "Now, Di, don't say such things. I wish you would just meet him. You'll like him. Most people do."

Diantha laughed, but there was no mirth in the sound. "How could I like such a man?" she demanded hotly. "Before Devlin encouraged you, you never set foot into a cardroom. But then with his assistance you racked up so many debts that I feared you would be up the River Tick. I'm just glad poor Papa didn't live to see you become a gamester," she said before noticing her brother's abashed expression. She felt instant remorse. "Oh, Andrew, I am sorry. I didn't mean to pinch and scold you on your wedding day, of all days."

He brightened at once. "I know you didn't, dear Di. You are the best sister one could ask for. That is why I am so eager to introduce you to *all* my friends.

"Will you meet Dev, then, Di?" he asked.

Seeing the hopeful look in his eyes and knowing that she would probably have to meet the viscount some time, she finally consented.

"Very well," she said, feeling driven to the wall. She followed Andrew through the crowd in search of the viscount, though the mere notion of meeting devilish Devlin made her lips curl involuntarily, giving her what Andrew teasingly dubbed her Medusa look.

Dear Andrew. She really could not fault him for falling in with the viscount. Andrew's temperament had always been agreeable and impressionable and he had needed male companionship when their father had died three years ago. One of the richest peers in England, Devlin could afford to laugh off the loss of a thousand pounds at Watier's one night and a thousand pounds at the races the next, but her brother had very soon found the depth of his purse substantially less than the viscount's. The very tidy competence their father had left had quickly evaporated. A true friend would have steered Andrew into safer waters.

On several occasions, the brother and sister were stopped by the crowd of well-wishers, as guests demanded to know where Andrew was bound on his honeymoon. Just as inevitably they became separated. Diantha did not repine. At least now she would not have to meet Devlin.

The plunge into the thick of the crowd had tired her, and as the crush of bodies pressed closer, Diantha found herself requiring air.

"In need of rescue?" a voice asked. She looked up into the blue eyes of the black-haired gentleman from the church.

Blue eyes, not black.

"I seem to have misplaced Andrew," she said hastily, becoming aware that she had not answered his question.

"Esmeraude has him," he replied, from his vantage point of a foot taller. He led her quickly through the crowd, using his broad shoulders to clear a path for her.

Large people had an advantage, Diantha thought, not for the first time in her life. She would have gladly traded some of her lustrous curls for a few more inches in stature.

"I am obliged to you, sir," she said now. "For nearly a moment I was in the liveliest dread that I might faint, something I assure you I am not in the habit of doing!"

He smiled. "You are most welcome, Miss Atwood."

She looked across at him, a situation possible only because he was on the lower of two steps. They were nearly eye to eye.

"You know my name!"

"Roddy told me," he said.

"Pray, what is your name, then? I should like to thank you properly."

"Devlin. My family name is Horwich and my Christian name is Oliver, but luckily my friends do right by me and call me Dev."

Diantha's mouth opened and closed. "You're Devlin! You can't be!" she exclaimed.

Her reaction surprised him. "I assure you I am Devlin, your servant, Miss Atwood."

"If you were my servant I would turn you out," she said without thinking.

Devlin blinked. "Harsh words, Miss Atwood," he said mildly. "What pray have I done to make you so despise me?"

"I have heard about you, my lord."

"Really? Well, I have heard of you."

A look of confusion suffused her face. "Heard about me?"

"Yes," he said, pleased at this hit. "Your residence in Portman Square. A veritable hotbed of ferment, or so some I know call it. Of course I do not pay heed to the gossips, and I would advise you not to, either."

Diantha coloured at his words. "Hotbed of ferment! That shows how little you know of what you speak!" she said indignantly.

"My thoughts precisely," he said in dulcet tones.

With a furious glare, she turned and stomped down the steps. He watched her go, smiling involuntarily at her deliberately dignified exit and hoping no one would trample her to death.

"Dev, 'pon rep I'm glad you're still here," Andrew said, approaching from the other side.

"Not a sentiment your sister shares, Andrew," the viscount replied, indicating Diantha's retreating back.

The other man winced. "Oh, good Jupiter. Have you locked horns with her already?"

"Yes. She seemed to hold me in considerable dislike. I confess to complete bewilderment."

Flushing slightly, Andrew pulled his friend into the church. "Dev, I want to explain. Di didn't mean any offence."

"I think she did," Devlin replied. "But I don't hold it against you, Andrew. One can't be responsible for the freakish whims of one's sisters. My own sister in York . . ."

"She holds you responsible for introducing me to the greeking establishments," Andrew said, dismissing Devlin's sister with a wave of his hand. "I mentioned your name once with regard to them and from that she concluded that you were taking me to every hell in Town. She blames you for my losses. I told her you had nothing to do with them, but she won't listen. She's a very stubborn creature."

"So I noticed."

Andrew peered out the door, making certain that they were alone. "Dev, I must confide something in you. Will you promise not to repeat it?"

"My dear boy, are we bran-faced Eton brats sharing secrets?" Devlin asked, laughing aloud.

"This is important," Andrew protested. "Whatever Di accused you of, you and I know she's wrong. I can't explain fully to her without revealing how I fell so far into debt."

Devlin darted a quick, thoughtful look at his friend. "I have wondered that myself. I know they don't play for chicken stakes at White's or Watier's, but the sums you're rumoured to owe—"

"It wasn't all my doing, Dev," Andrew said quietly. "Most of the sum was owed beforehand by my father."

Devlin lifted an eyebrow. This was news indeed. Andrew's father, Thaddeus Atwood, had been a veritable pattern-card of respectability.

"It's not something I can discuss with Di," Andrew said, skirting around a stone pillar and sitting in a pew. "She dotes on Papa's memory so. But he was well into the suds by the time of his death three years ago. I didn't know how scorched he'd been until it all passed to me. There was little inheritance left to speak of. Fortunately, Diantha inherited that house on Portman Square from my aunt, and my mother left her an annual income."

"I had no idea," Devlin said, leaning back against the pillar.

"Oh, I don't repine for myself. Poor Papa. He kept testing his luck in order that there would be a substantial inheritance for me. He simply got deeper into debt. The estates were mortgaged to the hilt which I discovered only after he died. He begged me sometime prior to his death not to tell Diantha about the debts. But I am duty bound to settle them.

"And perhaps I shouldn't be so hard on Papa. For faced with so many debts, what did I do but sit down to cards in the vain hope that I could win part of it back? I couldn't, of course."

"Why didn't you tell me?"

"I didn't want anyone to know. And you mustn't say anything to anyone, particularly Di, even though I cannot like it that she thinks badly of you."

"Under the circumstances I shan't take offence."

"I'll tell her everything when I get back," Andrew said. His face brightened. "And now that I'm married to Esmeraude, I can pay off the debts."

"Such are the advantages of wedding an heiress," Devlin said drily as Andrew rose from the pew. "Does she know?"

"Not about Papa. She thinks the debts are mine." He grinned. "She's convinced that she's reformed me. But I do love her, Dev!"

"Of course you do." Devlin clapped him on the shoulder as they walked out into the sunshine.

"There is one thing I must ask of you, Dev. Will you watch Diantha for me while I'm off to the Lakes with Esmeraude? Just to make certain that she doesn't fall into the briars? Until I get back."

"Your sister might not wish my looking after her," Devlin warned.

"Lud, that's the truth!" Andrew laughed. "But that doesn't signify. She needn't know you are watching over her."

The viscount shook his head. "I have a feeling that when the matter concerns your sister, everything signifies."

CHAPTER TWO

UPON RETURNING TO Portman Square, Diantha made immediately down the long corridor to the music room, where she found her friend and companion, Susan Kirkpatrick, practicing a new composition at the pianoforte.

She paused in the doorway, enjoying the music wafting out.

"Bravo!" Diantha clapped when the last note faded.

Susan turned, smiling. The sunlight streaming in from the bow window made her look like a Dresden china doll, pink cheeked with blond hair plaited on her crown.

"Diantha, are you back from church so soon?"

"Yes, and you will never believe whom I met at the wedding." At once she confided with relish details of her impromptu skirmish with Devlin.

"Good heavens, Di!" Miss Kirkpatrick's fingers crashed down on the keyboard, and she lifted her delicate brows in astonishment. "Turn him out like a servant. Do tell me you are roasting me and that you didn't really administer such a set-down to Lord Devlin."

"Of course I did," Diantha replied, pulling off a blue kid glove with nonchalance. "Why do you look so surprised, goose? I always warned you I would do so if my path ever crossed his."

"Telling me is one thing, but telling him quite another," Miss Kirkpatrick replied in her quiet way. Her forehead puckered ever so slightly at her friend's audacity. As a rule Miss Kirkpatrick was as placid as she was pretty.

"It wouldn't do to be at cross points with him, Diantha. His consequence is enormous."

"I don't care about that."

"Yes, I know," Susan said with a fond smile. She turned the topic to the more agreeable one of Andrew's wedding. "I suppose the wedding was very grand and Esmeraude looked beautiful?" Susan had been unable to attend the ceremony at St. George's owing to a lingering and persistent cough.

"Oh, yes," Diantha said. She laid aside her gloves, took a deep sniff of the bouquet of red roses on the small ormolu table and went over to sit next to her friend on the pianoforte bench.

"Do tell me all the details," Susan begged.

"The church was crowded, and I arrived late," Diantha replied, explaining about the bay losing a shoe. "Esmeraude was radiant and Andrew very handsome." She laughed. "Oh, botheration. You know my head for details. You should have been there to tell me all about it. How irksome that your cough has worsened this week. Do you think we ought to send for a physician?"

"Never!" Susan declared. "You know what quacks doctors are. Besides, a doctor will only turn me into an invalid again. My invalidish days are over, thanks to you." She reached out and squeezed Diantha's hand.

Bosom bows back in their Derbyshire board school, the two ladies had crossed paths again in London a year and a half earlier. Diantha had been shocked at the change in her friend. Always a frail child, Susan seemed to be hovering on the edge of her death-bed, swathed in great blankets and lap rugs, and a seemingly endless amount of medicines and potions to swallow.

Her brother, her only relation, lived in Edinburgh and had dispatched her to London in the company of her former governess, Miss Bonaventure, in order to seek advice from a specialist. By the time Diantha had renewed her friendship in London, Susan was heartily bored with doc-

tors and medicines. Sympathizing with her plight, Diantha
tried to amuse her, inviting her to Portman Square, which
always bustled with activity. Miss Bonaventure, a devoted
chaperon, was at first sceptical but soon realized that
Diantha was no flibbertigibbet.

Within a fortnight all symptoms of illness disappeared.
Susan's colour was much improved, her stamina better and
her appetite keen. Miss Bonaventure was thoroughly won
over, convinced that Diantha's friendship was the only tonic
Susan had needed.

After more weeks of these restorative measures Susan
descended the Adam staircase one morning to announce
that she was not swallowing any more potions and intended to stay on at Portman Square if Diantha would have
her.

With Susan contributing a portion of her income to the
household, the plan suited Diantha, as well. The two
friends prevailed upon Miss Bonaventure to stay on also,
and she soon found her own duties to perform which in-
cluded identifying loose screws and coxcombs and sending
them away before they could dangle after either Susan or
Diantha. Both ladies in vain assured Miss Bonny that at
five-and-twenty they were considered by most gentlemen to
be on the shelf.

The only thing Susan, an honest soul, did not like about
the arrangement was the Banbury tale she was obliged to
spin in her letters home to Edinburgh. Her brother still laboured under the impression that she remained in London
enjoying the excellent care of Dr. Angus Brewster, a physician Susan had never even met.

Everything had gone along swimmingly for the past year
and a half. Susan's strength was now near the equal of
Diantha's. But then a month previously the stalwart Miss
Bonaventure faltered, struck low by the inclement London
weather. Diantha overrode Bonny's protests and dispatched her to Brighton to take the air and rest.

"Do you think Devlin is handsome?" Susan's question summoned Diantha from her brown study. An image of two very blue eyes under a crown of jet black hair flew into Diantha's mind. Were a squarish jaw and aquiline nose considered handsome traits in a male? she wondered.

"Women would find him so, I think."

Susan tilted her blond head slightly towards her friend. "Was he civil? Or odiously starched up?"

"His manners were impeccable," Diantha said truthfully. "Indeed, when I didn't know he was Devlin I thought him charm itself. That shows how mistaken I can be. Do you know he suggested that our gatherings here were a veritable hotbed of ferment?"

Susan laughed. "How absurd. As though we were Bonapartists as well as bluestockings. The war's over anyway. And I wish there were more ferment afoot than Mr. Cumbert's dreary poetry, which he read me this afternoon."

Well acquainted with Mr. Cumbert's dreary poems, Diantha was delighted to have missed him.

"You will have an opportunity to hear his latest verse on Tuesday," Susan said.

Diantha clapped a hand to her mouth. "Oh, Susan, you didn't say he could read then, did you?"

Susan hung her head. "You know I can't say no to people the way you can, Diantha," she said lamely.

"My dear, you must practice, as faithfully as you practice your scales every day. You shall stand in front of the looking glass in your bedchamber and say: 'No! No! No!'" She beheld her friend convulsed in giggles. "I am very serious I assure you. You will feel much stronger for it."

"Well, I am sorry about inflicting Mr. Cumbert on everyone again," Susan said when she finished laughing. "But I truly didn't have the heart to refuse him."

"I daresay no real harm will result from Cumbert's reading," Diantha said, ending the tête-à-tête on a note of optimism.

WHEN TUESDAY ARRIVED Diantha discovered that Mr. Cumbert's poetry was even worse than memory served. More insipid doggerel was impossible to imagine, and the poet's pretensions did little to endear him to an audience who stared in mute horror at him in Diantha's Long Gallery. Even Sir Philip Forth, the ton's leading moralist and a member of the Clapham Sect, could be seen shaking his pocket watch.

Although Diantha was the hostess, she did not feel obliged to be bored to an early death and left the Long Gallery in the middle of a long and tedious ode. Clearly her duty lay in the refreshment room. Once Cumbert loosened his hold on his audience, they would be ravenous.

Yielding to temptation, she made a plate for herself, carrying it across the hall quickly to her library. She closed the oak-panelled door behind her and leaned back against it for a moment. Here she was safe. The book room with its leather-bound tomes was the one place where she felt most at home. Books never ruffled her feathers the way people did. They were never in a temper or feeling out of curl. She gazed up at the shiny brass Egyptian sphinx in the middle of the great mahogany bookcase, then put down her plate of food on the ivory and ebony inlaid table, intent on finding something suitable to read. Infamous to confess to such a habit, but she did so enjoy eating while reading.

Over the years she had amassed a fine collection of books and pamphlets. Her latest achievement was a movable library stairs which had been installed only in the past week on the recommendation of Lord Sylvester.

As she ascended the stairs they rolled first to the left and then to the right, before connecting with the small track that lay midway between the ceiling and the floor. The sensation was the closest thing she could imagine to what flying must be like. Her eyes scanned the titles on the spines of the books.

Now what would best enhance her refreshments? The Meditations of Marcus Aurelius? Caesar's campaign against the Gauls? Byron? She paused. Yes, of course. He was the perfect author for the consumption of lobster patties. By all accounts he had a prodigious love of lobster patties and sweets before vanity caused him to embrace a diet of biscuits and soda water. She placed the volume of his poetry against her hip.

Ah, she passed Mr. Shakespeare's Quartos. She had a particular fondness for his comedies. She placed several against the Byron and readied herself for the descent. As she did so she noticed for the first time that she was not alone in her library. One of her guests lay with his coat off, stretched out on the crocodile-legged couch below her.

A just woman, Diantha did not begrudge him his escape from Cumbert, but to lie on her couch bespoke a certain familiarity. Unfortunately, with his back to her, she could not identify him properly. However, she could see that he was at least six feet in length, possessed of a broad pair of shoulders and an unruly shock of black hair.

As she gazed down at him, he turned over. Feeling rather guilty at being caught watching another sleep, she swung the controls of the stairs. But her mastery of them was still imperfect, and she miscalculated the turn, bumping too hard against the solid mahogany shelf.

"Ouch!" she exclaimed, as she lost her balance and to her horror found herself toppling down towards the couch below.

"Oof!" Devlin, for it was the viscount who reposed on the couch, awoke at once as he received Diantha on his chest.

"Where the devil did you drop from?" he demanded, his nose nearly tip to tip with hers.

"From up there," she replied distractedly, pointing to the rococo ceiling. She attempted to wrench free from his arms, which held her tight against his unbuttoned waistcoat. She was out of breath and flushed from the fall and mortified at landing on him.

"Any broken bones?" he asked, brushing a strand of hair back from her eyes.

"No," she said, pulling away from his touch. "What about you?" she asked with as much dignity as she could muster.

He grinned at her as he swung his legs off the couch. "Just the wind knocked out of me. It's fortunate you're so tiny."

Eyes flashing, Diantha drew herself up to her full height of four feet and eleven inches. For a moment she wished she were a hundred stone and that all of it had landed on his head.

He stooped and picked up the volume of Childe Harold which had landed near the couch. "Byron, eh?"

"Yes, Byron," she said, prepared to defend her choice of reading material.

"Whatever his faults, Byron won't put you to sleep," Devlin said with a twinkle in his eye.

She hid a smile and began to gather the Quartos strewn about on the Aubusson carpet.

"Allow me."

His greater height lent Devlin a clear advantage, and he soon had the volumes back in place on the mahogany shelves. Not only his height commanded notice, Diantha realised on this her second meeting with him, but all the rest of him, as well, including his snowy-white neckcloth exquisitely tied and the Hessians' champagne buffed to an eyeblinding gloss.

"I beg pardon for waking you in such a frightful fashion," she said. "You must have thought it a nightmare."

"Yes," he said, pausing as he inserted one long arm into the sleeve of his coat. "Actually, we're both lucky. You could have killed me."

"Killed you? That's absurd. You have undoubtedly sustained far heavier blows in one of your mills at Gentleman Jack's," she replied.

"No one at Gentleman Jack's would have hit me with a copy of Mr. Shakespeare's work. A weighty tome. If it had landed on my head, you would now be speaking with a corpse."

"Those were Quartos, my lord, not the Folios. More probably they would have landed on your foot," she said, undismayed by the scenario he had envisaged. "And those Hessians seem sturdy enough to endure a blow or two!"

He threw back his head and laughed. "Served with my own sauce! I shall have to tell Hoby that when next I order a pair of boots." He paused, his eyes focusing on the plate of food on the table. "Is that yours?"

The colour rose in her cheeks. "Yes, I sometimes eat while I read," she explained.

"I daresay you and I both could do without Mr. Cumbert's poetry?" he teased. "Then why in thunderation are you inflicting him on your audience?"

"Because I felt sorry for him."

"I'd save my sympathy for his audience. Surely being so small you wouldn't be needing all that food," he said, casting a wistful glance at the plate.

Diantha could not help smiling. "Have some if you wish."

"Thank you, I shall," he said, popping a lobster patty into his mouth. "I had a devilishly small breakfast."

"A habit that is common to many," she said, glad to have a neutral topic to discuss. "But breakfast is actually the most important meal of one's day. You should partake of the usual English breakfast—an assortment of meats, eggs, breads, kippers."

"I'd liefer not hear about all that," he said, holding up a hand in supplication.

"Why not? Are you foxed?" she asked curiously.

"No. Merely suffering a bout of envy. My chef quit my employ last week to return to France. I've yet to find an adequate replacement. These lobster patties are delicious. My compliments to *your* chef."

"Thank you. And lest you eat them all up by yourself, I shall take one," she said, taking a seat on the couch and preparing to share what was left on the plate.

He sat next to her and chuckled as she ate.

"You find my eating a lobster patty amusing, sir?" she enquired, wiping the corner of her mouth with a napkin.

"No, of course not. The eating of lobster patties is a deadly serious matter," he said gravely and won a choke of reluctant laughter from her. "What I find amusing is that we should be sitting here side by side so amicably after our last somewhat stormy encounter."

"Yes," she agreed. "I never thought we would meet again."

"Oh, I had no such qualms about that," he said, keeping his eyes steadily on hers.

She felt a definite jolt in the pit of her stomach, which she blamed on eating much too quickly. Or maybe it was an after-effect of her fall.

A fall which Devlin broke.

She swallowed hard and looked away from him. Her throat was dry. She should have brought some lemonade with her.

She was acting like a ninnyhammer. She had made plain the other day that she held him in dislike.

But if so why had she shared her plate of food with him today? an inner voice quizzed.

Well, she couldn't be rude to a guest under her own roof, she argued back.

"I beg your pardon?" he said, puzzlement evident on his handsome face. "You spoke?"

"No. Did I?" she asked quickly.

He rubbed his chin. "Something about a guest under your roof."

"Yes. That accounts for our amicable meeting today."

"Ah." His blue eyes glinted with amusement. "You agree with the ancients, then, about the custom of hospitality. Even the Greeks of old dared not slaughter a guest.

Though now that I ponder the matter you nearly did me grave injury with that copy of Shakespeare.''

Her lips twitched.

"The library stairs are a new purchase, I take it?"

She nodded. "Lord Sylvester recommended them. In fact he is the designer. He's a member of the Academy. Are you acquainted with him?"

"Indeed I am. Sylvester told me about your habit of inviting all London to your Open Day and assured me that you would not mind if one more person came through your door."

"Prettily said, my lord," Diantha murmured. "But why are you really here?"

Her thoughtful query brought him up short. Because your brother bade me keep an eye on you, you beautiful witch, he wanted to tell her. It seemed a simple favour to grant until the moment Diantha landed on his chest, knocking the wind out of him with her soft curves and mesmerising eyes.

"Perhaps I am trying to better my intellect," he said.

She shook her head so hard that her curls bounced. "What an outrageous whisker. You don't care a groat about intellectual matters."

"How do you know so much about me?" he demanded.

"Your exploits are chronicled in our daily papers."

"You know better than to believe everything you read," he chided. "I wouldn't judge a book by its cover."

"But the cover's the best part," Diantha blurted out without thinking, then flushed scarlet, gazing up to the nymphs gracing her ceiling for help in extricating herself from this coil.

She was saved by Susan's sudden entrance into the library.

"Di— Oh!" Miss Kirkpatrick halted in confusion, observing her friend alone in the library with the viscount. "I didn't know you were with someone. I just thought you *should* know Mr. Cumbert has finished his reading."

"Heavens, he'll think me wholly rag-mannered if I don't congratulate him," Diantha said, seizing upon this excuse the way a drowning man would a log. "Lord Devlin, may I present my good friend Miss Susan Kirkpatrick?"

Devlin smiled and bowed over Susan's hand. "Charmed to see you again, Miss Kirkpatrick."

Diantha gazed from one to the other. "Do you know each other?"

"I don't believe so," Susan said.

"I was with Roddy and his charming wife when Emily chatted with you at Hookam's last week, Miss Kirkpatrick. We were not formally introduced then, but I am happy now to put a name to so charming a face."

"Oh, Hookam's. Now I remember," Susan said.

Diantha digested this information carefully. Had Devlin come to her Open Day because of Susan? To be sure, that made more sense than developing a sudden passion for Mr. Cumbert's poetry.

Thinking of the poet recalled her to her duties as a hostess, and she ushered them out of the library. Devlin paused in the hallway in front of a vase on display.

"Ming dynasty?" he asked.

"Yes," Diantha said, a hint of pride in her voice. It was the prize of her collection.

"Superb," Devlin said, admiring the tall tapering slope of the neck and the rich porcelain glaze over the blue and white colours.

"Actually, my father acquired it," Diantha told him. "He was a fine collector and a most excellent father."

Devlin polished his quizzing glass. "Yes, so I've heard," he said carefully.

By this time Mr. Cumbert's newly liberated audience streamed out of the Long Gallery, glazed expressions upon their faces. Diantha hastened to shake hands and to soothe the frayed nerves of her guests.

"Next time Cumbert reads, warn me," Mr. Hugo Fanshaw muttered under his breath.

Mr. Fanshaw was a young playwright inclined to dandyism. He was currently penning his latest work, a moral piece on government through the ages with the help of Sir Philip Forth. Diantha had agreed to present the play, but after inflicting Cumbert on everyone, she knew she had best delay Fanshaw's presentation.

"Diantha, there you are." Lord Sylvester approached. His red hair and freckled complexion gave him a schoolboy demeanour. "I have never heard such rubbish in my life."

"Do be fair, Sylvester. Cumbert listened to your explanations of your various inventions without protest."

"But that's different! That's interesting!" the young inventor protested. "And how are the library stairs working out?"

"They have a tendency to pitch its rider to the floor," she told him, not wishing to think about her recent accident. The more she thought about the incident the more embarrassing it appeared. What *had* she been thinking to stay closeted there so long with Devlin? She must find Susan and warn her not to say anything about finding them alone in that way.

"Of course I shan't say a word," Susan said later when everyone else had gone. "But it's not usually like you to worry about conventions."

"It's not conventions I find worrying. It's Devlin," Diantha confided with a pensive look in her dark eyes.

CHAPTER THREE

HIS UNPRECEDENTED appearance at Diantha's Open Day and a round of calls on tradesmen on St. James Street made Devlin late for his afternoon call on Mrs. Whorley, his current chère amie. The widow who lived in Grosvenor Square was not pleased to be kept cooling her heels by the viscount, even if he happened to be the most generous patron she had ever had.

"Where have you been, my lord?" she asked as soon as Devlin strode into her blue drawing room. The toe of one shoe tapped against her prized Wilton. This shoe, Devlin noted, was much larger than one Miss Atwood would wear. But then Mrs. Whorley was taller and wider than Andrew's petite sister. Indeed Thalia was almost equal to the viscount in height and, except for the colour of her brown hair and green eyes, built along the lines of a Valkyrie with her weight distributed generously to hips and shoulders.

"I beg pardon, Thalia," Devlin said, putting down his Malacca walking stick, "but I was detained by Hoby. I needed a pair of Hessians sturdy enough to sustain a blow from Childe Harold."

Mrs. Whorley threw him a look of utter bafflement from her Egyptian settee. "Child? Whose child is this Harold? Surely not yours!" she asked.

The viscount smothered a laugh as he thought of the reaction of his intimates to any byblow of his making an appearance in London.

"A private joke, my dear."

"I see nothing humorous in it," she said trenchantly.

"I don't suppose you would," he agreed. Despite her real beauty and amorous appetites, Mrs. Whorley always suffered from a deplorable lack of humour.

He fortified himself with a pinch of snuff from his Sevres snuff box and began the always tedious task of coaxing her out of the boughs.

"I am sorry to be so tardy. But you know how tailors can be."

Mrs. Whorley did know how tailors could be and also milliners and glovers and modistes. The curt remark on the tip of her tongue withered as she remembered the very large amount owed to Fanchon, London's leading modiste, for the apricot silk she now wore. As usual she had directed the bill to be sent to Devlin.

"You are forgiven, Devlin," she said magnanimously.

"Good," the viscount said, pleased that the reminder about tailors had turned the tide for him. "Do you still wish to accompany me on a drive?"

"No, there will be too many people at the Park at this hour."

"Curious. I thought the entire purpose of driving to the Park at the fashionable hour was to be seen by as many as possible. Would you rather drive somewhere else? Perhaps Somerset House?"

Twirling a limp strand of hair round a finger, Mrs. Whorley paused and stared at him aghast. "Good heavens, Devlin, whatever would I want to do at Somerset House?"

"There is an exhibition of landscapes, I believe."

"You know how I loathe the country. Why would I wish to look at pictures of the countryside?"

"A good point." The viscount inhaled another pinch of snuff. He was beginning to feel heartily bored. His brief slumber on Diantha's couch had revived his spirits, but these few minutes with Mrs. Whorley brought back a cloud of ennui.

"Then what is your pleasure?" he asked, feeling restless.

Mrs. Whorley lifted her lips archly and walked over to him with a definite sway to her hips.

"Let us go upstairs," Mrs. Whorley said huskily.

The viscount stroked her hair, which he found now a bit plain when he remembered the unruly curls Diantha Atwood boasted.

"Oliver?"

Devlin wracked his brains for a way to distract Thalia, finding and rejecting several choices. With anyone else he could offer to show her the new bay he'd bought at Tattersall's or propose an excursion to Hookam's. But Mrs. Whorley did not consider horses a fit topic for polite conversation, and she rarely read except for copies of *La Belle Assemblée*.

The cloying aroma of her perfume enveloped Devlin in a fog certain to give him the headache. Mrs. Whorley's thin lips drew closer. Devlin eyed them with dispassionate interest. Miss Atwood's, he remembered from the library couch, were a delicate red akin to a rose. Thalia's, on the other hand, were so deep a hue that he suspected she must have applied a cosmetic. They were as red as rubies. *Rubies*. He jerked away from Mrs. Whorley so violently that the kiss she was about to bestow on him landed on his ear.

"Oliver—" she said with some exasperation.

"Pray forgive me, Thalia." He pecked her on the cheek, still thinking of rubies. "I'm such a clumsy lummox."

Rubies were his ticket out of her drawing room.

"Do you or do you not wish to go upstairs?"

"Not yet."

One eyebrow rose autocratically. "And why not?"

"Because you and I are going for a drive."

"I have already told you that I don't want to drive in the Park. And I won't look at any dreary pictures of hillocks or streams," she warned.

"Yes, I know. They put you in mind of the countryside which you loathe. But what pray tell do you think of rubies for viewing?"

"Ru—?" Her eyes flew wide. "My dear Ollie."

He winced, not liking his Christian name of Oliver at any time and particularly despising the diminutive Ollie from her lips.

"Rundell told me the other day a new shipment had arrived from India. We shall have to inspect it."

"And pray what must I do to earn it?" she asked coquettishly as she drew her arm through his.

"Just make a promise never to call me Ollie again," he said from the bottom of his heart.

A HALF HOUR LATER Devlin stood at the bay window in one of the anterooms reserved for only a select few of Mr. Rundell's clients, seemingly absorbed in his view of the street below.

Across the room behind a glass-topped sandalwood display case sat the ascetic-looking Mr. Rundell. The jeweller was showing the latest of the ruby shipment from the Orient to the eager Mrs. Whorley, who pelted him with questions as soon as she entered the room.

Mrs. Whorley's knowledge of jewels was no surprise to Devlin who could remember three well-pursed gentlemen who previously enjoyed her favours. Wholly entranced by the red gems lying on the velvet cloth in front of her, Thalia appeared to have forgotten Devlin's presence in the room.

Almost as though I didn't exist, Devlin thought. He shrugged philosophically. He supposed any other gentleman of rank would suit Thalia's purpose just as well as he, provided that gentleman boasted a fortune and a willingness to squander it on her.

This revelation might have smote a lesser man to the core, but the viscount was made of sterner stuff. Theirs was not a love match. From the start of his affair with Thalia he knew she saw him as a convenient way to pass the time, while he saw her... He paused, shifting his view from the dome of St. Paul's back to the lady in question. Just what *did* he see in her?

Protection against the Marriage Mart, an inner voice reminded him.

That was it. The widow provided a convenient buffer from the marriage-minded mothers who seemed to plague the ton. But if so, why was he suddenly entertaining thoughts of giving Mrs. Whorley her congé?

Abruptly he walked away from the window. As he closed the distance between them, Mrs. Whorley emitted a piercing scream.

"Oh, no, that pinches," she shrieked as Rundell fastened the gold clasp on the ruby-and-diamond bracelet she was trying on. "Get it off me this instant, fool. This instant, do you hear?" she demanded, striking the jeweller on the shoulder with her other hand.

"There is no need for fisticuffs," the viscount said at once, taking up the cudgels in the defence of the jeweller. "Have you sustained any injury, Mr. Rundell?" he asked quietly.

"No major damage, my lord," Rundell replied, mopping his brow and vowing to himself to let his assistant handle Mrs. Whorley if she ever darkened his door again.

"You haven't asked if I have sustained an injury, Oliver," Mrs. Whorley scolded, holding her hand out to Devlin. "Do you see that red mark? It came from the bracelet. It's much too small."

"So it would seem, or perhaps your wrist has got larger." The viscount inspected the wrist with desultory interest.

Mrs. Whorley snatched her hand back. "Don't be ridiculous, Devlin. What a thing to say. My wrist hasn't got any larger. None of me has," she said mulishly, conveniently forgetting her weakness for bonbons.

"Sorry, my dear. If that bracelet is too small, we can always find a larger one."

"I was just about to suggest that myself," Rundell said.

"No," Mrs. Whorley said. "I don't like bracelets, anyway."

The viscount's eyes met Mr. Rundell's.

"I have a brooch," the jeweller said. "Of rubies and diamonds." He found it in the display case and laid it on the velvet cloth. "Would you care to pin it on, my lord?" he asked.

The viscount's lips twitched. He didn't blame Rundell for his wariness. If Thalia had hit poor Rundell for pinching her wrist, what might she do if he stabbed her with the brooch in a vital spot?

"With pleasure, Rundell." Devlin picked up the brooch and examined it under the glass the jeweller handed him. Shaped like a tiger, the brooch consisted of a dozen flawless diamonds and an equal number of flawless rubies in an antique gold setting.

Devlin pinned it onto the right shoulder of Mrs. Whorley's apricot silk and stepped back.

"Exquisite, my dear," he pronounced.

Mrs. Whorley examined herself in the looking glass which Rundell offered. Most females would have been cast in alt at wearing such a stunning piece. Without question the brooch dazzled the eye, and it didn't pinch the way the bracelet had. But her heart was set on the ruby-and-diamond necklace she had glimpsed earlier in the case.

"I don't know," she said now, turning her head petulantly to the right and then to the left as she gazed into the mirror.

"Well, I do," the viscount declared. "The rubies match your lips to perfection."

"Perhaps," Thalia said, putting down the mirror. "But I don't like brooches. I find them insipid. No one ever notices a brooch next to a necklace." She darted a quick glance at Devlin, who had a faraway look in his blue eyes. She felt a moment's hesitation. Perhaps she had miscalculated. It wasn't too late. She could still take the brooch. She fingered it absent-mindedly. It really was the most magnificent brooch she had ever seen. But the necklace was even more magnificent.

"A necklace, is it?" Devlin asked.

"Yes, a necklace," Mrs. Whorley said eagerly. "Do look at this one here, Dev." She pulled him towards the case and pointed. "I don't believe it would be much more expensive than the brooch."

"Then what a good thing you don't work here, Thalia," he said affably. "Because the necklace, if I'm any judge, would be three times the worth of the brooch. We shall take the brooch, Mr. Rundell."

"Very good, my lord." The jeweller looked relieved that the decision had been made.

"No, we will not." Mrs. Whorley stamped her foot. A rather large-boned appendage, all in all, the viscount decided. "I told you I didn't want the brooch."

"Don't be idiotish, Thalia," the viscount said, recognising too well the avaricious glitter in Mrs. Whorley's eyes and no longer willing to indulge it. He unpinned the brooch from her dress. It would serve as a farewell gift to her.

"You are a beast, Devlin."

"Don't be a widgeon. The brooch is pretty. You will not get the necklace from me."

"Then perhaps some other gentleman will buy it for me," she said, tossing her head angrily. "Hewitt and Sir Arthur Long have been sending me letters asking if they may call. I've said no before because I am loyal to my friends, Devlin, but..."

"You need not utter a word more, my dear. I had no idea you felt this way. By all means feel free to tell them to call. You may receive them starting this very second."

Mrs. Whorley felt a rush of alarm. She was not getting any younger, and Devlin was the most generous of patrons and usually so obliging.

He handed the brooch to Rundell. "I'm sorry, Rundell, we shall not be requiring the brooch, after all. I apologise for taking up so much time for naught, but perhaps I shall make it up to you with a future purchase." He turned to Mrs. Whorley. "As for you, madam, I think it time I escorted you back to Grosvenor Square."

The ride back to Mrs. Whorley's residence was silent, both the widow and the viscount lost in thought. Mrs. Whorley's mind teemed with strategems to win Devlin back. She knew he was in a ticklish mood, but she also knew what restorative measures could be applied successfully in the privacy of her boudoir.

"Do come in and have some tea," she invited when he pulled his carriage to a halt on her flagway.

"I think not," he said. He jumped down from the seat and offered her a hand.

She stepped down and kept her hand in his. Her nails slightly grazed his palm.

"Oh, Devlin, don't let this stupid quarrel put things at odds between us. I didn't mean what I said about Hewitt and Long."

"It hasn't put things at odds, my dear. In fact it has put things to right. I bid you adieu and good luck with Hewitt and Long."

Agitated, she put out a hand on his driving cape and tugged him back. "Ollie, you can't mean that."

He removed the grasp on his cape. "I also asked you never to call me that. But I don't suppose it matters any more. I don't think we shall be hearing much of each other in the future," he said. He climbed back into his vehicle, thinking their parting had been all in all a propitious stroke of good fortune for him.

GOOD FORTUNE WAS NOT on Miss Diantha Atwood's mind during the days which followed. On Wednesday the bills for Quarter Day arrived, and she spent Thursday scrutinising her accounts. This task was followed by one even more tedious, and a further strain on her precious sight, namely reading Mr. Fanshaw's complete epic.

When Susan found her Friday evening ensconced by the fireplace with sheafs of paper at her feet, she immediately protested Diantha's plan to read the entire masterpiece.

"I won't," Diantha promised. Such a Herculean attempt was beyond her abilities. "Just enough to get the flavour of the work. He is calling tomorrow for my opinion. He must have the muddiest hand in the kingdom." She held up a sheet of paper with the lines crossed and recrossed over the page.

"Give me some of the pages to read," Susan volunteered. "We needn't read every scene, I presume?"

"Every other scene," Diantha agreed, and in this fashion their evening passed. Later, after she bade good night to Susan and retired to her bedchamber, Diantha thought about all the other ways there were to spend a Friday evening.

Within a stone's throw of her own residence, balls and routs were probably under way with beautifully gowned ladies dancing, laughing and flirting with handsome gentlemen. Never before had she felt the slightest inclination to join them. She received invitations practically every week and usually refused them. Now she felt a yearning to attend one.

Would Devlin be at a ball? she wondered as she put the lit taper she carried down on the dressing table. Quite probably that depended on his own cook's progress in the kitchen. She smiled to herself as she shook her hair free. Too restless to sleep right away, she walked to the window and gazed out at the dark star-studded night. She felt an uncharacteristic longing in the inner recesses of her heart. Longing for what? her practical mind quizzed. The ballrooms with their bustle and excitement? She often got a migraine from the noise. The laughter and good will? Portman Square resonated with laughter. She and Susan had been in whoops this evening over Mr. Fanshaw's dreary masterpiece. The flirting? That would depend entirely on whom she was flirting with.

She walked slowly back to her bed and climbed in, drawing the coverlet over her shoulder. She blew out the candle by her bedside and lay back, her hair fanning out on the down pillow. She was just tired. A touch of the grippe, perhaps. That would explain her listless mood. She would feel better in the morning.

SATURDAY MORNING, however, held no respite for Diantha. Eager to hear her verdict, Mr. Fanshaw called while she was still partaking of her morning meal. Since Susan was taking a tray in her bedchamber, Diantha was obliged over a plate of ham and sausage and muffins and eggs to tell the playwright that the epic was still too long, and she could only stage it for one night.

"One night! Oh, very well. But you can't be serious about cutting any more of it. If you noticed I left out anything having to do with the Egyptians and the Turks."

"Oh, did you?" Diantha asked, wiping her mouth with a napkin. She had assumed that those were the scenes that Susan had read for her. "But perhaps if we abandoned the ancients and just started on the eighteenth century."

"The eighteenth century?" he gasped. "Then you would cut the Greeks, both Sparta and Athens, all mention of Aristotle and Pericles and I suppose exclude the Romans, as well?"

"It is a good deal to ask of you," Diantha soothed, returning to her shirred eggs. "Take out whatever civilization you must. If you want to perform it here it just has to be shorter."

Emerging from his sulks, the playwright departed with the manuscript.

As soon as Diantha finished her breakfast, the housekeeper bustled in with the menus for the coming week. Diantha was still absorbed in inspecting them when she heard the sound of raised voices outside in the hall. Hoping it was not Sylvester preparing to test another one of his inventions under her roof—an experiment on combustibles had shattered her chandelier a month earlier and she had the bill from the glassmaker to prove it—she left the breakfast parlour and discovered her butler trying to turn away an unwanted caller.

"Is something amiss, Hughes?" she enquired.

"No, ma'am," Hughes, as wooden as a statue, replied with stately dignity. "This person was just on her way out."

"Person, indeed." The caller, a female dressed in a vivid purple dress and matching hat, emitted a scornful laugh. "I'm every bit as respectable as anyone. And I'll be talking to Miss Diana Atwood if I have to sit here till kingdom come."

Hughes sent an apologetic look at his employer.

"I am Diantha Atwood," Diantha said, laying careful emphasis on her first name. "Pray, won't you come in and tell me what this is all about?"

The woman cast her a suspicious look. "Are you really her? You seem a mite young."

"I assure you I am she," Diantha said, leading her into the blue drawing room. "And you are?"

"Mrs. Tribbet." The woman gazed about the room, appearing satisfied by the tasteful black lacquer Chinese screen and the Etruscan armed chairs. She settled herself in one of them with a flourish.

Diantha sat across from her on the satinwood sofa, thinking that the woman must have fifty years in her dish at least. She certainly used a good amount of rouge and colouring. Her strawberry blond hair was so unusual a colour that it had to be a wig.

"Now, madam," Diantha said politely, "if you would state your business, please."

"I'm here because of that brother of yours," Mrs. Tribbet replied.

Whatever Diantha had expected, it was not this. "My brother?" What could such a female want with Andrew?

"What business do you have with my brother?" she asked, deciding to be blunt.

"Private business," Mrs. Tribbet said with a sniff.

Her answer baffled Diantha even more. What private business could lie between such a female and Andrew? The possibility that perhaps Andrew and this female had had a liaison flew into her mind, almost sparking a fit of the giggles.

Andrew had never dabbled much in the petticoat line, and she was sure he would never have dallied with this particular petticoat.

"Then I do not see how I can be of any assistance," Diantha said quickly, determined to draw this interview to a close. "My butler, it seems, was correct. You come calling and yet refuse to state your business. Under the circumstances, ma'am, I shall have to ask you to withdraw!"

"Not so fast!" Mrs. Tribbet said, alarmed at this dismissal. "I've come to find Mr. Andrew Atwood. You can tell me how I can reach him."

Diantha was sure she could do no such thing. The very thought of inflicting Mrs. Tribbet on anyone. "I don't know my brother's whereabouts," she said truthfully. "He is travelling and I have no idea how to reach him."

"Travelling." Mrs. Tribbet put down her tea cup. "That's all he has been doing since his marriage."

"Yes," Diantha said. "Do you know Andrew well?"

"As well as I could anyone who married into my family."

Diantha had been listening politely, thinking how she could best remove Mrs. Tribbet from her drawing room without too obvious a scene, but now she hesitated. If Mrs. Tribbet were a relation of Esmeraude she must be accorded every civility.

"Maggie is going into a decline," Mrs. Tribbet said. "That's why I came here."

A frown knitted Diantha's brow. "Maggie? Pray excuse me, ma'am. I don't mean to be stupid, but I don't entirely understand. Who is Maggie?"

"She's my daughter and your brother's wife!" Mrs. Tribbet declared with some satisfaction.

CHAPTER FOUR

"MY BROTHER'S *what?*" Diantha exclaimed.

"Wife." Mrs. Tribbet's eyes glittered as she pronounced the word. "They were wed on the twelfth of March, and he hasn't been back to Topping Green to see her since. Now I'm not a woman to begrudge him a lark or two, but my Maggie is wasting away. She is an angel, and I won't have her heart broken. Your brother must do his duty by her!"

"This is preposterous," Diantha said, rising angrily from her sofa. "I've heard quite enough of your incredible story," she said, holding up a hand to silence Mrs. Tribbet.

Anticipating Diantha's exit, Mrs. Tribbet lunged towards the door.

"My good woman, get out of my way," she ordered. "Or I shall summon my servant with orders to fetch the Runners."

"You must listen to me," Mrs. Tribbet implored, wringing her hands. "It's no trick, Miss Atwood. Your brother stumbled upon my daughter Maggie as she bathed in the stream near our house in Hertfordshire. Being a gentleman and seeing that she was a lady, he did the right thing under the circumstances. He found a minister in the next village and married her. Maggie is a great beauty. Some say she takes after me." She preened momentarily.

Diantha recoiled as if struck. "Mrs. Tribbet, I'm sure this Banbury story you have spun is most entertaining to you, but I warn you that I am not amused. Nor will my brother be when he hears that you have been slandering him."

"Slandering?" Mrs. Tribbet looked affronted. "No word against him have I spoken. I merely want him to return to my Maggie. Married her and took off a month ago. And we've not seen him since. What is Maggie to do? She's his wife." Mrs. Tribbet dug into a faded velvet reticule. "Here's the proof." She waved a document under Diantha's nose. "A marriage certificate. All proper and signed by a minister it is."

With trembling fingers Diantha took the document in her hands. The certificate did look official. Could it be possible? No, the story was absurd!

"Convinced?"

"Not a jot," Diantha said as she handed it back. "I bid you good day."

"It is genuine," Mrs. Tribbet protested. "And I'm determined that he do the right thing by my Maggie. So you tell that brother of yours to come back and see her in Topping Green. Do you hear? I shall return," she said grandly and swept out of the room.

Diantha sank back on the sofa, her mind spinning like a catherine wheel. What an addled notion Mrs. Tribbet had about Andrew. Her brother would never marry an innocent from the country without informing Diantha. Or would he?

She wouldn't find the answer staring at her Chinese screen, she told herself. Since Andrew wasn't in London to question, she must find out from one of his cronies. Roddy, perhaps. She nodded briskly. Yes. Roddy would know what to make of this ridiculous situation.

Feeling better now that she had a plan of action, she ordered her curricle to be readied, and a half hour later drove to the Cavendish Square residence of Roderick and Emily Bridger. As she ascended the steps, preparing to sound the brass knocker the door suddenly opened, and Devlin emerged, nearly knocking her flat.

"Oh."

He caught her quickly before she toppled from the top step.

"I always seem to be catching you off balance, Miss Atwood."

"So it would appear, my lord," she replied, rendered a trifle giddy by the near loss of balance as well as by his tall, magnificent figure swathed in a multicoloured driving cape and a high-crowned beaver felt.

"Have you eaten?" he asked.

"Eaten?" she asked, taken aback by his question. "Well, I've had breakfast, if that's what you mean?"

"Kippers and muffins and eggs and ham by that distinguished chef of yours?"

"Yes," she said a little guiltily. "But what are you doing, my lord!" she exclaimed, becoming aware that he had closed the door of Roddy's residence and was leading her back down the steps. "I have matters to discuss with Roddy."

"I daresay you may," he agreed, "but it's not an auspicious time. The entire household is at sixes and sevens."

Diantha frowned. "Why?"

"Can't you guess?" A mischievous look glinted in Devlin's blue eyes.

"No," she said, confused.

"The babe came early."

All thoughts of her mission to Roddy flew out of Diantha's mind. "The babe! Oh, Devlin! You should have told me immediately. Is it a boy or a girl?"

His forehead knit in a frown. "Actually, I don't know."

Her brows flew up. "Devlin, you don't know?"

A wry smile touched his lips. "It's true. Roddy and I were preparing to lunch at White's when he got word of the babe's early arrival. I accompanied him here, since he was so giddy with excitement that he would undoubtedly have turned his carriage over. I assure you that anything you tell him now will have to be repeated in a week's time."

"Oh, dear," Diantha said. "I did so wish to ask his advice." Now what was she to do?

"Perhaps I could be of assistance," he drawled. "I assure you, under this frivolous exterior lies a useful brain. What is the problem? A tipsy footman who must be dispatched? I know a female's distaste for such unpleasant scenes."

Diantha laughed. "I haven't come all the way here because of a drunken footman. Besides I have never fought shy of dismissing a servant who is not up to the mark."

"Then perhaps you should come with me and fire my chef," he said wistfully. "Let's get out of this wind, shall we?" He led her towards her vehicle. "Is that your carriage? What an excellent sprung framework. And your team looks like a prime pair."

Diantha beamed, pleased at the praise from so knowledgeable a nonpareil as Devlin.

"Since I drove Roddy home in his rig, I am without transport," he went on. "Would you oblige me by giving me a ride?"

"To be sure. What is your destination?"

"Anywhere, as long as I'm not obliged to eat anything under my own roof."

She smiled as he handed her up. "Is your cook still a hardship?" she asked when he had settled next to her against the velvet squabs.

"The worst penance imaginable. I almost cracked a tooth on a loaf of bread he baked this morning."

She gathered the reins in her hands and set her team off with a flick of her wrist. "Why are you so pudding hearted, sir? I should think that you would have no difficulty bidding him goodbye?"

Devlin sighed. "A want of dash, I'm afraid, Miss Atwood."

"You are just like Susan. The two of you lack willpower."

"We do?"

"If you cannot fire a man who is starving you to death, what would you call it?"

"Sheer cowardice," he said promptly.

She laughed. "You must stand in front of a mirror and practice saying, 'You're fired.' What is his name, pray?"

"George."

"George, you're fired."

"George, you're fired," he repeated dutifully.

She sighed. "If you say it like that he'll be with you until your dotage. You'll be skin and bones by then. Shall I drop you back at White's?"

"If you do, I won't be able to help you with your problem."

She chewed on her lower lip. "It's actually not my problem, it's Andrew's."

"Andrew?" He pushed back his beaver felt. "Then you must allow me to help."

"You have helped enough with Andrew, don't you think, my lord?" she asked in a tone of quiet reproof.

Devlin was silent as the curricle rolled over the cobble-stoned streets. He would have to let her think what she did of him. He'd promised Andrew. He broke the silence by asking where she was preparing to take him.

"Or am I being kidnapped?"

"Kidnapped?" She shifted her gaze from the road to his face and became mesmerised by the twinkle in his eye.

A shout from a coachman recalled her to the real hazards of driving in London, and she narrowly avoided a collision with the carriage thundering towards her on the street. Her ears reddened at the insults the other driver hurled her way.

"Pay him no mind," Devlin drawled. "That was a nice piece of driving."

"Thank you." She should have kept her eyes on the road, but it was difficult when she had such a handsome passenger.

"I am taking you to Gaston's," she said in answer to the question which had sparked the near accident.

"Gaston's?" The viscount frowned. "Is he an acquaintance of mine?"

She smiled. "Gaston is a chef. A most superior one. He came to Portman Square to demonstrate his dishes a fortnight ago. He has since opened his own restaurant."

"I hope he is a better practitioner of his art than Mr. Cumbert was of his," Devlin replied.

With the viscount asking questions of the passersby, Diantha found Gaston's restaurant on Piccadilly. She was persuaded by Devlin to join him in a brief luncheon.

The small restaurant teemed with customers, the air redolent of the odours drifting in from the kitchen. The cook himself, a smiling Gallic soul, emerged to kiss Diantha's hand, promising a veritable feast. He was as good as his word.

"That was an excellent meal," intoned the viscount, taking a swallow of the equally excellent claret.

"Gaston is a genius." she agreed.

"Now that the meal is completed, let's turn to your problem," he said. "My offer of assistance stands."

Diantha stared down at her plate. A pity Roddy was so preoccupied. It was easier to ask for his help than Devlin's.

"I don't think there's anything you can do about it, my lord. Today I received a great shock. Andrew was married."

Devlin flicked open his snuff box with his thumbnail. "Of course he is, Miss Atwood. I know my memory is shockingly bad, but yours is far worse if you don't recall the ceremony at St. George's Hanover Square. True, you were a late arrival, as was I, but we did see the exchange of vows."

"I don't mean that!" she said, laughing despite her worries. "I received a call this morning from a Mrs. Tribbet of Topping Green. She told me a preposterous story that Andrew had married her daughter a month ago and had the wedding certificate to prove it."

The viscount inhaled a pinch of snuff. "Let me guess what she looked like, your Mrs. Tribbet. A female well past her youth, coarse, loud, painted."

He cocked his brow at her.

"It seems unkind to put it that way," Diantha said.

"A very old trick, my dear. I'd wager a pony that Andrew didn't even look at her daughter, if she even has a daughter. As for that wedding certificate, it won't be worth the paper it's written on. It's a hoax to extract money from the unwary."

"That's what I had supposed, too," Diantha agreed. "I am no green girl and have cut my wisdoms. But the odd thing is, she didn't ask for any money. All she wanted was Andrew to return as her daughter's lawfully wedded husband."

"The request for money will come later. Depend on it. Did she know Andrew was absent from London?"

"Yes, that's why she came to see me."

Devlin shook his head. "No, Miss Atwood. If Andrew were in London, she wouldn't play this trick, believe me."

Diantha felt reassured by his words. They comforted her like a warm blanket on a cold night. Maybe it was Devlin himself, so strong and commanding.

"I feel like a perfect paperskull," she said now. "I did think at first it might be a trick. I vow, the mere thought of bigamy overset me. Esmeraude's family are so high in the instep. If Mr. Lowell ever got wind of this—"

"The fat would be in the fire," Devlin agreed. "However much I like Esmeraude and I do, her father can be mightily starched up."

"I do thank you for helping me with this problem of Mrs. Tribbet."

"My dear Miss Atwood, you supplied me with the acquaintance of Gaston! It's the least I can do for the assurance of one solid meal a day!"

Much relieved, Diantha took Devlin back up in her carriage and deposited him at his residence on Mount Street. As she drove off, she was unaware of the piercing scrutiny of another female standing nearby.

Mrs. Whorley had been waiting for several days for Devlin to do the right thing and come to his senses. When he had not responded to her handwritten pleas for forgiveness, she judged it time to take a second look at the situation. Devlin would not just throw her over.

Struck by the sight of the viscount stepping down from a curricle driven by another female, Mrs. Whorley felt her face turn choleric. The friendly exchange of goodbyes further fuelled her ill temper. Who was this upstart? Mrs. Whorley forgot all about bearding the viscount in his den and started after the vehicle driven by the unknown woman. However, the tide of traffic was against the widow, and she lost the curricle in the Berkeley Square area, never having got a good look at the woman.

Thalia pulled her redingote tighter against the April wind, no longer in the mood to confront the viscount. First she must find out who her replacement was. As she pondered the matter, a smile broke out on her face. She knew exactly how to go about it. She'd hire someone to watch Devlin's comings and goings. She knew several people with ties to the East End who could put her in contact with the sort of individual who would for a fee be only too pleased to assist her.

UNAWARE THAT HE was the target of much speculation, the viscount went about his daily routine of visits to Manton's Shooting Gallery and Cribb's Parlour. On Friday morning, however, he received urgent news that a prime Arabian was for sale at the bankrupt estates of Lord Mayerling. Half an hour later, he was on his way to Hertfordshire and by noon he had inspected the horse and done the thing, purchasing the Arabian from under the nose of the Earl of Ludlow who arrived ten minutes late.

With this task successfully concluded, he was on the verge of returning to London when he recalled that the village of Topping Green lay only ten miles to the west. This was the village which Mrs. Tribbet had given as her residence. Impulsively, he decided to pay a visit. He wasn't quite satisfied with Diantha's account of her and wanted to learn more about the game Mrs. Tribbet was running. After promising Andrew to keep an eye on Diantha, he felt it prudent to investigate further into Mrs. Tribbet and her threats.

Once in Topping Green, he easily found directions to the Tribbet residence, a shabby grey-stone house with an overgrown garden. As he reined in his mount, a woman emerged: painted, with a coarse air about her. He had no difficulty recognizing her from Diantha's description.

"What can I do for your lordship?" Mrs. Tribbet asked, dipping a quick curtsey to the most elegant swell she'd ever seen.

"I've come on the matter of Mr. Andrew Atwood," he informed her, speaking from astride his horse. "I should like to advise you not to annoy his sister in the future."

"Annoy, is it?" Mrs. Tribbet huffed, lifting her chin. "It's I who should be annoyed. That there gentleman married my angel and has not come back once to see her. He's a blackguard."

"Your angel is out of luck, my good woman. Do take heed and stay away from Miss Atwood."

"Maggie will have what's rightfully hers," Mrs. Tribbet retorted. "She's a good girl, and he married her willingly."

Devlin wrinkled his nose in distaste and threw down a bag of coins at her feet. "I warn you, madam, that is all you will ever get. Do not play this game again. Or I shall have to take drastic steps."

Mrs. Tribbet stooped and picked up the bag of coins. "You don't scare me."

"Then you are even more foolish than I thought," he said cordially, and prepared to take his leave. But as he started down the road, he suddenly halted. Coming his way and headed straight for the house was a vision of ethereal loveliness.

"Who is that?" he asked.

"That, my lord," Mrs. Tribbet said with great satisfaction, "is my Maggie!"

"YOU MUST FORGIVE my mother," Miss Tribbet said a half hour later as she and Devlin strolled in the small Shakespearian gardens behind the house. "She had no right to call on Andrew's sister. I already spoke to her about that. All I can do is wait and hope that he will return to me."

"You patience is astounding," Devlin said, leading her towards a small stone bench. Miss Tribbet was definitely cut from a different bolt of cloth than her mother, with a head of guinea curls, striking brown eyes and—there could be no denying it—an angelic countenance. "Your husband disappears, and you merely wait for his return."

Miss Tribbet plucked a rose off a nearby bush. "You call him my husband, but actually he wasn't a husband in that sense of the word. Forgive me for speaking so plainly."

"It's you who must forgive me," Devlin said gently. "I know the situation must seem awkward to you."

"Awkward and peculiar," Miss Tribbet said with composure. "I know it sounds odd. But you must consider that our marriage was a ceremony of necessity."

"Necessity or not, I find it hard to believe that Andrew would marry a woman like you and forget all about it. He'd be daft."

"Did Mama explain how Andrew and I met?" Miss Tribbet asked, twirling her rose idly between her fingers.

"She said something about your bathing in a stream?"

Miss Tribbet coloured. "It was actually my fault. There is a stream some miles away which is not really known to many people, except the villagers here about. I've always enjoyed swimming there and thought of it as my special place. Last month we had a bout of terrible weather, followed by a glorious few days of sun. I didn't think anyone would be about, so when the opportunity came, I went bathing. When I came out of the water to dry myself, Andrew was there, equally astounded to see me. My position was undoubtedly compromised. So being a gentleman, he married me.''

"Was a minister lurking in the bushes, too?"

She laughed. "No. Andrew found one the next day who performed the ceremony post-haste."

"Did his offer of marriage surprise you?"

Miss Tribbet flushed, then spoke with quiet dignity. "I am a lady, my lord. My father was a gentleman. So is Andrew. I believe he did what is called the honourable thing.''

Devlin examined the gloss of one highly polished Hessian, feeling properly chastised. "And your mama knew about it?"

"Oh, no, I told her later, after I returned home alone. Mama hasn't had a happy life," Miss Tribbet said with a sigh. "She is full of dreams of what might have been. After reading about Andrew's wedding to Miss Lowell she was put into a great flame and threatened to go to Miss Lowell's father. Fortunately, I prevailed on her not to. But she would insist on seeing Andrew and then his sister." She pressed her hands together. "Mama has undoubtedly told you that I'm pining away for Andrew. That isn't true."

"Why aren't you?"

"I hardly know him, sir," Miss Tribbet replied in her practical manner. "One can't pine away for a total stranger.''

"And yet you married him, a total stranger?"

"What else could I do? I was compromised. I'm grateful to Andrew, for some men wouldn't have offered me marriage and his good name. They might have had a far different response to finding me without a stitch of clothing on," she said with a shudder.

"I can't pretend to love him," Miss Tribbet went on, "I did hope that we could make a comfortable marriage together. Only now what do I do?"

"I don't know," Devlin said meditatively. This was the outside of enough. "Who else knows that you and Andrew are married?"

"Just Mama. And you. Oh, and of course his sister."

"Of course his sister." Devlin said, wondering just how he would ever break the news to Andrew's sister that her brother had wed not one lady of quality but two!

CHAPTER FIVE

THE FERRET-FACED MAN twisting his hat in his hands glanced up as Thalia Whorley swept into the room. In an unhurried fashion, she poured herself a glass of sherry, offering not a drop to her morning caller.

"Well, Kroll, what did you find out?" she asked, smoothing the lemon yellow folds of her morning dress with distracted fingers.

"His lordship is seeing a ladybird, just as you thought, ma'am," Kroll replied. "Her name is Tribbet. Miss Tribbet from Topping Green. That's a small village to the northwest. I followed Devlin there Friday last. He went into the cottage, walked in the gardens with Miss Tribbet and then returned to London."

Mrs. Whorley took a long swallow of sherry. "With Miss Tribbet?" she asked.

"No. She remains secluded in the village. From what I've been able to find out, she hasn't been seen much about. As though she don't want to go out in public." Kroll licked his lips and eyed the restoratives on the tray near at hand.

"How curious," Thalia said. "Describe this Miss Tribbet."

"She is nineteen, according to the villagers. Blond and blue-eyed."

"What are her circumstances?"

"Impoverished," Kroll replied. "Her mother married above herself. The father was a schoolmaster and died young."

Mrs. Whorley shook her head. There was nothing here that would interest Devlin.

"Is Miss Tribbet very beautiful?"

"Oh, yes!" Kroll said at once, and with such enthusiasm that the widow's frown deepened. The investigator realized his error a split second later and hastened to make amends. "Though not as beautiful as you," he added.

Mrs. Whorley inspected her fingernails. "He didn't spend the night with her," she said meditatively.

"She's far too innocent for that sort of thing. Not like you, ma'am. I mean—" Kroll bit his lip as Thalia's nostrils flared.

"Get out!" Mrs. Whorley said, white faced. She would not stand to be insulted by this East End ruffian.

Kroll clapped his hat on his head. "Shall I continue watch on Devlin?"

"No. Your job is done. I have the name of his ladybird. Miss Tribbet of Topping Green."

Despite these words, Kroll stood, not budging an inch.

"What are you waiting for?" she demanded. "I told you to get out."

"There's the small matter of my pay, ma'am."

Her eyes narrowed. "Fifteen pounds, wasn't it?" she asked.

"It was twenty-five and you know it."

Although inclined to squander the fortunes of her patrons, Mrs. Whorley had a profound dislike of spending her own.

"That's too dear," she said now. "Fifteen would be better."

Kroll crossed his arms on his chest. "Twenty-five pounds." The vehement look on his grizzled face convinced her to give up the sham. "Oh, very well." She crossed over to her escritoire in the corner and took out an envelope with the bank notes. "Here, now get out."

After the investigator departed, Mrs. Whorley poured herself a second glass of sherry. Her nails clicked against the cut crystal as she thought about Devlin and the innocent from the country who had usurped her place in his heart. Was that behind his sudden interest in landscapes the other day? A country miss? How had he met her? She wouldn't have thought it possible. But who really knew what knacky notions gentlemen took into their heads, particularly one as avidly pursued as Devlin?

Was Kroll's information reliable? She paused, with the sherry glass halfway to her lips. He came highly recommended as the best the East End had to offer at the price she wanted to pay. No, Kroll had done his job. Besides she didn't care to squander more money on another investigator.

Thalia stretched out a sandaled foot to the fire. The red tongues danced and crackled. She couldn't lose Devlin to a mere country chit. True, Hewitt and Long were already squabbling for her affections. Without question Oliver was the superior to both Long and Hewitt in looks and rank. And he was far more generous.

She swallowed the sherry. She needed to think more on this matter of Devlin's ladybird.

MR. BRIDGER, the proud new father of a six-day-old son, looked up from his hunched position in his billiard room. "Dev? What brings you by?" He waved his friend in. "I thought you were going to the races."

"Something's arisen, Roddy," Devlin said. "Do you perchance recall Andrew falling into a scrape a month ago?"

Roddy laughed as he sank a ball in the corner of the table. "Good Jupiter, you know that Andrew has always been in a scrape, outrunning his creditors, particularly McPherson and Kendril. But that's over now that the lovely Esmeraude and her fortune have come to the rescue. Why do you ask about Andrew?"

"A problem has presented itself which commands his immediate attention." Devlin said, leaning his elbows on the edge of the table and watching Roddy deftly work the balls. "I have to find him."

"You don't want to find him," Roddy expostulated. "That would mean a trip to the Lakes. Gone for days. And once you find him he'll be a regular bear jaw. You'll have interrupted their wedding trip."

"The Lakes, is it? You see, Roddy, you remember much more than I do about Andrew's whereabouts." The viscount snapped his fingers. "I have an idea. Why don't *you* find him and bring him back to London for me?"

Mr. Bridger quirked a speculative eyebrow. "What sort of game are you running, Dev? Another wager?"

"I can't say," Devlin said obliquely.

"I'll find it in the betting book at White's."

"It's not recorded there. In fact, there's no wager. I just need to speak to Andrew. He's probably told you more about his plans for the Lakes than he told me. Will you find him for me?"

"Dev, do be serious. I've just become a father. I can't go galloping about the kingdom."

Devlin plucked a piece of lint from Roddy's coat and eyed the new father carefully. "I have not forgotten the babe. I suppose you see a good deal of it? And what is it, a boy or a girl?"

"A boy," Roddy said proudly. "And no. I don't see a good deal of him. I've only had a few glimpses. Nurse keeps him to herself in the nursery."

"Nurses have a tendency to do that, so I hear. Is Emily very dependent on you, then?"

"Well, no," Roddy conceded again, scratching his head. "She had a difficult birth, you see, and is still recovering. When I talk to her, she's usually fatigued and snaps at me. Understandable in new mothers, or so I've been told by some of the other fathers at the club." He smiled ruefully. "I suppose under the circumstances no one should miss me if I were to take a trip to the Americas."

Devlin clapped him on the back. "Just the Lakes, Roddy. And don't worry. Absence makes the heart grow fonder. The babe won't utter his first words while you're gone, of that I do assure you, Roddy."

Mr. Bridger laughed. "Very well, Dev. I'll search for Andrew and Esmeraude at the Lakes, and I just pray that he doesn't run a sword point through me for disturbing their marital bliss!"

HIS CALL AT Cavendish Square completed, Devlin stepped out into the morning wind. The unpredictable spring weather had turned sunny, a rarity for London. This was his usual hour with Gentleman Jack, but he decided to skip the usual mill. Today was a Tuesday. Miss Atwood would undoubtedly be holding another of her Open Days.

He climbed into his phaeton, not relishing informing Miss Atwood about his tête-à-tête with Miss Tribbet. He'd be hard pressed to convince the beautiful bluestocking that a mother like Mrs. Tribbet could give birth to an angel such as Miss Tribbet. The viscount shook his reins, and his team of Welshbreds obediently moved forward.

Miss Atwood would probably think Miss Tribbet a dissembler. As one deemed a matrimonial prize by Lady Jersey herself, Devlin knew a good deal about the artifices of ladies. Miss Tribbet employed none. She was a veritable innocent.

He made his destination in record time, discovering Diantha's residence as crowded as the week previous. Fortunately this time no poet was reading.

He bowed to several of his acquaintances, recognising Sir Philip Forth deep in discussion with Fanshaw about the joys of matrimony. Forth had been happily married for a decade and had a nursery of five brats to prove it. The baronet lifted an enquiring brow in Devlin's direction, but the viscount merely bowed and did not accept the tacit invitation to join the conversation. Forth was a moralist who preached and wrote against drink and cards. The viscount had no intention of having his vices trumpeted in his own ear.

He caught sight of Sylvester holding a box under his arm. He immediately crossed the room to his friend's side, demanding to know its contents.

"What is that?" he asked, inspecting the curious device with his quizzing glass.

"A timing mechanism for fireworks. It's quite safe, really. I thought I'd bring it along to show Diantha. Have you seen her?" he asked eagerly.

"No, in point of fact, I haven't," Devlin replied. "I just got here myself," he told the inventor. "I missed the lecture. What was it on?"

"Moral implication of civilization. Courtesy of Sir Philip." Sylvester rolled his eyes.

"Ah. That explains the baronet's good spirits."

"Yes. I know he is supposed to be the most moral man in London, Dev, but he always strikes me the wrong way."

"No vices."

Sylvester screwed up his nose in puzzlement. "What do you mean?"

"It's hard to listen to someone who doesn't have any vices," Devlin explained. "Now if you'll excuse me, Sylvester, I believe I shall just help myself to some refreshments. You be careful with that fireworks thing."

Devlin joined the throng going into the refreshment room, waiting with patient forbearance in the crowd, not even resorting to fisticuffs when jostled in the ribs by a stocky gentleman with a bristling moustache.

"Excuse me," the other man apologized.

"Not at all," Dev said, feeling quite at home at this his second Open Day at Miss Atwood's. "Quite stimulating, isn't it?" he asked.

The moustachioed man scoffed. "I'd sooner be at Bedlam."

Whoever the fellow was, he didn't lack for sense. "I can vouch for the excellence of the lobster patties," Dev said, pointing to a tray.

But the newcomer did not appear interested in food. "I don't want any," he said dismissively.

"Then I envy you your cook," Devlin said, helping himself to two patties.

"The mincemeat pies are excellent," a voice said behind him. "As are the quails' eggs."

"Oh, are they?" he asked, putting two of the pies on his plate and one of the eggs before he turned to discover his hostess's amused eyes on him.

"I would have thought you'd have fired that incompetent chef of yours by now, my lord," Diantha said, looking quite exquisite in a pearl white morning dress. He was reminded of a tiny and delicate hummingbird.

"It's rather cowardly of me," he agreed with a sigh. "But I hate disagreeableness in anything, and firing him would be so disagreeable. Besides, the fellow tries so hard. Last night he presented me with a meal which he laboured over all day. I actually felt obliged to eat a few morsels." He shuddered.

Her irrepressible laugh bubbled up.

"Shouldn't eat food that's disagreeable," the stocky gentleman next to Devlin remarked. "Leads to indigestion and that can lead to gout, dyspepsia, a dozen odd ailments."

"How kind of you to let me know," Devlin said, wondering what ailments lay in store for him in his future.

The stocky gentleman turned away towards the door.

"Your friend has such distinguished manners, my lord," she murmured.

"He's not my friend," Devlin corrected this misguided notion at once. "I thought he was yours. This is your establishment."

"Yes, but I can't be expected to know everyone who comes to my Open Day," she replied. "I wonder who he is?"

"I haven't a clue. Seemed like a sensible chap until he began his tirade about gout and dyspepsia."

Diantha choked on a laugh. "Nevertheless, I shall find out who that gentleman is before he takes my mincemeat pies in an intense dislike."

Intrigued at the idea of Miss Atwood doing battle with a gentleman a foot taller and wider, Devlin followed her out of the refreshment room. But they were too late. The moustachioed man was already doing battle, and that with the peace-loving Susan Kirkpatrick.

Hearing the sound of raised voices emanating from her library, Diantha had no compunction whatever about bursting in to find Susan sitting on the crocodile-legged couch, all but mesmerised by the stocky gentleman railing at her.

Had she said something in praise of the lobster patties? the viscount wondered. Whatever the case, he felt duty-bound to intervene. No one should browbeat a lamb like Miss Kirkpatrick.

"Are you in need of assistance, Miss Kirkpatrick?" he drawled, his pleasant voice giving the lie to the dangerous slant of his brows.

"Oh, Lord Devlin," Susan said faintly. "And Diantha. Allow me to present Dr. Brewster."

"Dr. Brewster!" Diantha uttered a strangled sound. "Would that be Dr. Angus Brewster?"

"Yes," Susan said in faltering accents.

"How kind of you to call, Doctor," Diantha said now, holding out her hand. Susan's Dr. Brewster. How awkward that he should turn up now, looking so angry. In private they might have been able to explain but now with Devlin looking on...

Dr. Brewster ignored Diantha's hand. "It's not a social call, Miss Atwood."

"Are you ill?" Devlin asked Susan solicitously.

"No, she is not!" Dr. Brewster barked. "And it's no thanks to me."

"If it's no thanks to you, I fail to see why you are here at Miss Atwood's Open Day. You have made plain your dislike of lobster patties, so I know it cannot be on account of the refreshments."

Dr. Brewster stiffened, and although he gave up four inches in height to the viscount, for an agonizing moment Diantha thought that he was going to call Devlin out.

Briskly recalling herself to the problem at hand, she demanded to know of the good doctor why he was here at Portman Square.

"I am here," the doctor said finally, "because I have just received a letter from Miss Kirkpatrick's brother in Edinburgh, telling me how grateful he is that I treated his sister. He called my work nothing short of miraculous and intends to tell all his acquaintances so.

"It was a hoax," Dr. Brewster said, "a complete sham!" He pointed an accusing finger at Susan who seemed to shrink back even more against the couch. "I have never treated this woman in my life or hers, and I demand to know why she has told her brother such a Banbury tale?"

"Because if she didn't, she wouldn't be allowed to stay on here with me in London," Diantha replied calmly, speaking for the tongue-tied Susan. "She didn't mean to tell tales, but we didn't think that you would mind, since she had never met you. And it's not as though we were saying you were a bad physician—quite the reverse. And I for one don't see why you should be so furious. We haven't hurt your precious reputation."

"I did not earn my reputation catering to the whims of hysterical females," he said rigidly.

"Hysterical female?" Susan gasped. "I am no such thing, I assure you, Dr. Brewster."

"Indeed she is not!" Diantha exclaimed in quick defence of her friend. "It seems to me, Dr. Brewster, that you are making a Cheltenham tragedy out of this. You can see for yourself how fully recovered Susan is from her previous illnesses and is living comfortably with me. Her brother has mistakenly believed you to be responsible for this pleasant state of affairs. You have my solemn assurance that neither of us will utter any favourable word on your behalf ever again.''

The viscount's lips twitched, but the doctor was far from mollified.

''You find this amusing. I do not. I have my reputation to consider. I wish you good day, ma'am, my lord, Miss Kirkpatrick.''

''What an insufferable man,'' Diantha said after the doctor had departed the book room.

''Insufferably honourable, I would think,'' Devlin said. ''He and Sir Philip would make a good pair.''

''Are you feeling quite the thing, Susan?'' Diantha asked her friend.

Miss Kirkpatrick looked up with a bleak smile, signs of distress still visible in the blue eyes. ''Oh, yes. Though I admit I was bowled over when he descended on me that way without warning. I don't know why he should have taken such a dislike to me. It is most daunting. I must confess no one ever has before.''

''Well, he is gone and you may rest assured that I shall give Hughes strict instructions the good doctor is not to be allowed back on these premises. Don't fret, now,'' she said as Susan still appeared downcast. ''Perhaps you might play that new piece you composed the other day on the piano for Lord Devlin. I'm sure he would like to hear it,'' she said, directing an agonized look at the viscount who rose nobly to the occasion and allowed that he was a great lover of music.

The three of them adjourned to the music room where some of the other guests were happily grouped round the pianoforte. They gave way to Susan who soon became busily engaged at the keyboard. As the notes wafted over them in the music room, Devlin recalled that he had still not spoken to Diantha on the matter of Miss Tribbet. Nor was he inclined to. After the contretemps Dr. Brewster had created he hesitated to inflict more Sturm und Drang on Portman Square.

Watching out of the corner of her eye, Diantha saw the sober expression on the viscount's handsome face. Why was he so lost in thought? she wondered.

But of course she needed to look no further than to the pianoforte. Susan.

For just an instant Diantha felt a pang of envy. A most reprehensible feeling, which she quickly thrust aside. Susan was her dearest friend. If she had made a conquest of the viscount, Diantha should be happy for her. Diantha only hoped that Devlin was serious about fixing an interest in Susan and not merely amusing himself in a flirtation or entertaining thoughts of offering her carte blanche.

This notion made her stiffen in her chair and caused Devlin, sitting next to her, to enquire if anything were amiss.

"No," she said, staunchly determined to keep an eye on him throughout his courtship of Susan. He wouldn't dare trifle with Susan's affections under Diantha's roof.

"I've been meaning to have a word with you," Devlin said in a lowered tone. Like it or not he had to tell Diantha about Miss Tribbet.

"As you wish, my lord," Diantha said just as an explosion erupted from the hallway.

"What the deuce is that?" Devlin ejaculated.

"Goodness gracious!" Diantha exclaimed.

They ran from the music room to find Lord Sylvester standing amidst billowing clouds of smoke, explaining sheepishly to anyone who wasn't coughing and holding his breath that his latest invention of a new type of timing device for fireworks had gone off prematurely.

This by necessity brought the end of Open Day to a close since it demanded the evacuation of everyone in the household, much to the vexation of the hostess, the amusement of one viscount and the dismay of the apologetic inventor.

CHAPTER SIX

"SLOW DOWN, DIANTHA. I beg you, please slow down!"

Susan Kirkpatrick's heartfelt cry pierced the bubble of excitement surrounding Diantha as her Welshbreds galloped at near-breakneck speed in the Park. Her cheeks glowed from the thrill of the run this Wednesday morning, but now conscience-stricken she pulled up on the reins.

"Is that better?" she asked as the horses slowed to a walk near the Serpentine. She peeked at her companion from under a wide-brimmed burgundy riding hat.

The past twenty-four hours had found Miss Kirkpatrick in a lachrymal mood, hardly a surprise since the lingering odour of gunpowder continued to sting everyone's eyes. Susan's mood, however, seemed particularly downcast. She picked at her food, played plaintive melodies on the pianoforte and refused all amusements.

This type of behaviour reminded Diantha of Susan a year and a half ago, frail and teary eyed. And she knew exactly who was to blame. Odious Dr. Brewster.

"Poor thing. I shan't frighten you with my driving anymore," Diantha promised. "Let's turn our minds to something pleasant, like our appointment with Fanchon later this morning."

"What do you plan to buy, Diantha?" Susan asked, falling in willingly with this scheme. "A new walking dress, perhaps?"

A walking dress was just one of the dozen garments which Diantha required. A stringent inventory of her wardrobe revealed her most pressing needs to be a new riding habit to replace the dowdy rig she now wore, as well as a ball gown. Every gown she owned was hopelessly fusty and out of date.

If need be she could refurbish her old walking dresses and continue wearing her antiquated riding habit, but she simply had to have a new ball gown.

"Actually, I thought I'd buy a new ball gown," she said now in answer to Susan's question.

Susan's eyebrows lifted a fraction of an inch. Diantha knew what her friend was thinking. A gown by Fanchon would not be dagger cheap. But earlier in the morning Diantha had reviewed her accounts and felt that with some careful economies she might be able to afford the gown if Fanchon gave her a special price.

"If you are ordering a new ball gown, you must be planning to attend a ball," Susan said with infallible logic.

Diantha nodded. "Lady Jersey's soirée. The invitation arrived in yesterday's mail, and I have already accepted for the two of us."

"For the two of us! But I can't afford a ball gown."

"Fiddle-faddle. I have reserved some of the money you have been contributing to the household, and that should be enough!"

"Why are you so interested in balls?" Miss Kirkpatrick asked, toying with a ribbon at the neck of her apple green dress. "You never used to be."

Diantha coloured slightly, a hue that became even more pronounced when she recognized the solitary rider on the path now approaching them: Devlin on the back of a striking new Arabian.

"Where did you get that horse from?" she enquired after exchanging greetings with the viscount.

He smiled at her eagerness. "Do you mean Rex? He's a new purchase courtesy of the bankrupt Lord Mayerling."

"That Arabian looks like prime horseflesh."

"I can vouch for its excellence," Devlin concurred. "Do you ride, Miss Atwood? Miss Kirkpatrick? If so, you must permit me to mount you. I have several horses in need of exercise.''

"Diantha rides," Susan answered for them. "But I don't care overly much for horses."

Diantha wondered what Devlin—reputedly as horse mad as they came—would think of that. But the viscount seemed to take Miss Kirkpatrick's lack of interest in horses in stride.

"Quite understandable in ladies," he said, and promptly turned the topic. "I trust that all traces of Sylvester's invention have blown off with the wind by now?"

Diantha shook her head. "*Au contraire*. The odour of smoke clings like a pall. That is why Susan and I plan to spend most of the day out of doors to give the rooms a chance to air."

"Sylvester certainly knows how to clear a room. You should keep him in mind the next time Mr. Cumbert volunteers to read his poetry."

Diantha chuckled.

"I do hope Sylvester is not sunk too far beneath contempt," continued Devlin, his blue eyes gleaming as he gazed at her. "Perhaps you are not aware of it, Miss Atwood, but Sylvester thinks very highly of you. With a little encouragement, he might try and fix an interest in you."

"Don't be absurd," Diantha said, feeling embarrassed. Was he roasting her? And if not, why was he pushing Sylvester, of all people, at her as a suitor? Unless... She stole a quick look at Susan, responding to a pleasantry from Devlin in her usual shy manner. Perhaps he felt guilty at the possibility of taking her companion away.

Diantha became aware that Devlin was addressing a question to her. She leaned forward.

"I'm sorry, my lord. I didn't hear you."

"I asked if you had received any word from Andrew."

"No," she said, eyes widening at such a question. "Why, my lord?"

"Because of that problem you laid in front of me the other day," he said obliquely.

Was he alluding to Mrs. Tribbet's ridiculous accusation? She held her tongue for a moment since she had not acquainted Susan with the particulars of Mrs. Tribbet's visit. Back then she'd felt the fewer people who knew the story the better.

"Lord Devlin, I desire a closer look at your Arabian. Would you mind if I climbed down and inspected it?" she asked now.

"Not in the least," he said adroitly. "Would you care to inspect the animal as well, Miss Kirkpatrick?"

Susan declined the invitation with a shudder.

Diantha took the gloved hand Devlin extended. His other hand lightly circled her waist as he swung her easily down from the carriage.

She strolled towards the Arabian and stroked its foreleg.

"A prime specimen," she said.

"Yes," he agreed.

"Now, what is this about Andrew's problem?" she whispered. "I thought you said that it was naught but a hum."

"I might have been mistaken."

"Mistaken!" she exclaimed.

"Yes, I mistook the age of the animal," Devlin drawled for the benefit of Susan. "Not three years but two."

"A boon to you," Diantha said, playing along. "What was your mistake?" she murmured.

"I have met Miss Tribbet and find her as her mother described. A veritable angel."

"An angel!" Diantha exclaimed.

"An angel when it comes to speed would not be as quick as Rex," Devlin agreed heartily. "Do keep your voice down," he bade her.

"I'm trying to," she said, moving closer to the horse and reaching for its head in order to inspect its ears. Suppressing a smile, Devlin came to her assistance, holding the animal still so that standing on tiptoe she could continue her scrutiny.

"You spoke with Miss Tribbet yourself?" Diantha asked in a lowered voice.

"At length and I can assure you her manners were those of a lady. She is not like her mother at all. It's probably best if you spoke to her yourself. I have an idea. Since you plan to be out most of the day you could drive to Topping Green. Miss Kirkpatrick might enjoy an outing."

She threw a glance back over her shoulder at Susan. He was always thinking of her friend. A sure sign of a man struck by Cupid's arrow.

"I'll be happy to accompany you there," he said, in case she fought shy of facing Miss Tribbet.

Of course he would. Anything for a chance to be with Susan.

"We have an appointment with Fanchon in an hour," Diantha said.

"As soon as the modiste is finished with you, we will depart. By the by, I've sent Roddy to the Lakes to try and locate Andrew and bring him back."

"Does Roddy know why?"

The viscount shook his head. "He thinks it's because of a wager I want to bring Andrew back. I take it that Miss Kirkpatrick doesn't know about the situation, either?"

"No," Diantha admitted. "But I'll tell her on the way to Fanchon's."

After agreeing to meet later that morning, Devlin parted company with Diantha. She watched him ride off, admiring the newly purchased Arabian as it carried him out of sight. At least she told herself strictly that she was admiring the *animal* and not just the rider. Then she gave her head a shake, picked up the reins of her own cattle and as the carriage moved away from the Serpentine, revealed to Susan the depths of Andrew's problem.

Great was Miss Kirkpatrick's consternation at hearing the accusation levied upon the absent Andrew Atwood by Mrs. Tribbet.

"Andrew already married!" Miss Kirkpatrick's eyes nearly bulged from their sockets. "How can that be? You must be funning, Di."

"I wish I were. I pray it is a silly prank. The woman's mother descended on me last week. Now Devlin tells me he's seen the daughter, and she is of Quality."

"Good gracious. Whatever is to be done?"

"Devlin suggested a drive to Topping Green so I could see Miss Tribbet for myself. Are you too fagged for such a journey? We will depart after our appointment with Fanchon and will undoubtedly return by nightfall. Devlin will be accompanying us."

Susan was on the verge of crying off from the visit to Miss Tribbet, but upon hearing that Devlin would be accompanying Diantha to Hertfordshire she knew immediately that she had to accept. With Miss Bonaventure absent, the role of chaperone was thrust upon Susan's shoulders. Miss Kirkpatrick was no ninnyhammer and knew that she dared not let Diantha accompany the handsome viscount by herself to the country.

"Of course I will go," she said.

Of course, Diantha thought, her hand tightening on the reins. Apparently Susan was growing just as fond of Devlin as he of her.

"MON DIEU, YOU HAVE come to your senses and repented!" Fanchon exclaimed with Gallic fervor as she enveloped Diantha in an embrace. Di had a notion that the modiste's affection for her stemmed from the undeniable fact that Diantha was an inch shorter than Fanchon herself.

"Now, *madame*, there is no necessity to ring a peal over me," Diantha said when she and Susan were seated in the back room of the shop. "I know it has been some time since I last ordered anything from you."

"Four years," Fanchon asserted. "You ordered some new pieces because of Madame de Staël's visit to London."

"What an extraordinary memory you have, Fanchon," Diantha replied. "I'd forgot that myself."

The dressmaker received this compliment with easy grace. "So, what learned speaker is coming to London now?" she asked.

"Actually, no one. I just thought I would like to have a new gown made."

A sibylline smile crossed Fanchon's face. "A gown? *Bon.* I shall dress you in emerald green. I have some silks just in from China."

"Green?" Diantha hesitated. "But I thought blue would do."

"Blue for a bluestocking?" Fanchon shook her head decisively. "*Non.* Green is best with your colouring. A deep emerald green. So restful on the eyes."

"We will want Susan gowned as well," Diantha continued.

"*Bien sûr.*" Madame Fanchon's eyes took Miss Kirkpatrick's measure with approval. "Gold."

"Gold?" Susan was taken aback. "I thought something in lavender myself."

Fanchon threw her hands up towards the ceiling. "You two, with your heads buried in your books and music. Insipid blue and lavender. Those are the colours for old women. You are in your prime. You will be in gold which will match your hair, Mademoiselle Susan. And you in green, Mademoiselle Diantha. Now, let me get my sketches."

A half hour flew by with the three heads bent over Fanchon's sketchbook.

"Take off that old riding habit and let me measure you," Fanchon ordered when they had finally agreed on the style.

"In four years time your measurements may have changed."

"I haven't grown as much as a half an inch taller," Diantha lamented a few minutes later, as she and Susan submitted to Fanchon's tape. "I am still deplorably petite."

"I know the feeling," Fanchon sympathized. "*Eh bien*, just think tall. It is all in your mind. Remember Napoleon. He was short."

"I know," Diantha acknowledged. "That is why I never could disapprove of him as much as everyone else. Very well, Madame Fanchon, I shall think tall."

"When do you need the gowns?" was Fanchon's next question as she scribbled furiously on a sheet of paper.

"We need them by the fifth of May."

Fanchon frowned for the first time. "Seven days. That is not much time."

"No, only a genius like yourself would be able to pull it off."

This appeal to the modiste's vanity worked. Fanchon nodded. "Seven days. Very well. Is there anyone in particular who will be present that evening? A gentleman, perhaps?" she asked archly.

"You are so French, Fanchon!" Diantha laughed to mask her flustered emotions. "You think everything revolves around men, do you not?"

"Most things do," the modiste replied with a shrug. "Such is the order of the world. However, when it comes to love, women can for once even the score. Who is he?"

"Do stop teasing, Fanchon." Diantha skirted the question again. "I merely felt a wish for society. Now tell me how much the gowns will cost?"

Four years had brought a considerable increase in the cost of materials, Diantha realized with dismay after Fanchon added up all her expenses. Susan's eyes widened, too, at the sight of the amount for her gown.

"That is too dear," she said to Diantha when Fanchon left to consult with a customer in the front. "I don't see why I must have a gown myself. I needn't go to the ball. I confess I feel so awkward dancing. I'd as lief stay home."

"You must come with me, Susan," Diantha averred. "I can't go to Lady Jersey's ball by myself."

This display of missishness surprised Susan. Diantha was not usually one to worry about conventions.

"I don't know why not. You go everywhere else by yourself. Remember how Bonny used to scold you for driving alone or riding or calling on friends without a groom or maid?"

"That's different," Diantha said mulishly. "I cannot bring a groom or a maid to a ball. And I can't attend Lady Jersey's soirée unescorted."

"Why not? And just what, pray, is so important about Lady Jersey's ball?"

Diantha was saved from having to answer this question by Fanchon's return from the front rooms. "So, all is in order, *mademoiselle?*"

Diantha's brow knit. "Yes, Fanchon. Except..."

"Except?"

"I'm afraid that when I anticipated the cost of the gown I was using the figures from four years ago."

"Ah..." A knowing look came into the Frenchwoman's eyes. "You do not have enough funds?"

"Perhaps if we chose a less expensive silk."

Fanchon shook her head. "I only use the best, *mademoiselle*, as befits the best." She pressed her fingers together for a moment in thought. "Tell me, just whose ball are you attending in a week's time?"

"Lady Jersey's."

"Lady Jersey's? *Parfait.*" There would be many present at the Patroness's ball who would see Diantha and Susan gowned by Fanchon, and if the modiste were any judge of human nature, she would find her store flooded with even more customers.

"I will let you have the two gowns for the price of one, if you will tell those at the ball who ask that you purchased them from me."

Diantha and Susan eagerly accepted this solution and happily took their leave of Fanchon. As they moved towards the door, Diantha noticed a tall, gangly gentleman circulating in Fanchon's store arm in arm with a tall, statuesque brunette.

"That's Sir Arthur Long," Fanchon said under her breath. "With Mrs. Thalia Whorley. The one they call the merry widow. I daresay she will want to order several new gowns now that she has the baronet in tow."

"Good news for you," Diantha said.

The Frenchwoman shrugged. "*Peut-être.* I preferred her old patron. Devlin. He was always prompt about the bills. Sir Arthur takes his time with his creditors."

So that was Devlin's old chère amie, Diantha thought, darting a quick look at Susan to see how her friend would absorb such information. To her credit, Miss Kirkpatrick received the news with composure.

"He's not half as handsome as Devlin," Diantha could not help observing.

"You are acquainted with his lordship?" Fanchon enquired.

"Slightly. Why in heaven would Mrs. Whorley replace Devlin with Sir Arthur?"

"Maybe it is not a case of her replacing Devlin but he replacing her," Fanchon said with impenetrable logic.

But whom had he replaced Mrs. Whorley with? Diantha wondered as she finally left the shop. Unless. She glanced over her shoulder at Susan, who stopped to finger a bolt of cloth.

Was Devlin's feeling for Susan strong enough that he was severing ties with Mrs. Whorley? If so, his interest was keen indeed.

WHILE DIANTHA and Susan had been discussing gowns with Fanchon, Devlin had ridden to Gaston's and ordered a picnic hamper to be filled. He couldn't predict what refreshments Topping Green offered and thought it best to be prepared.

By the time he reached Di's Portman Square residence, their rendezvous site, he was ten minutes late and apologised profusely to the two ladies waiting in the curricle.

"You need not be sorry. We've just arrived a minute ago," Diantha confessed. "Fanchon kept us longer than we expected. What's that in the basket?"

"Our luncheon. Do put it up in the carriage," he said, handing it to her.

She eyed it with acute suspicion. "Did that food come from your estimable chef, my lord?"

He grinned. "Rest easy, Miss Atwood. It comes from Gaston."

"Ah, then you are enjoying his restaurant."

"Since you introduced me to him, I have taken dinner there daily. I am in your debt. Now, shall we go on to Topping Green?"

"Lead the way, my lord," Diantha said, picking up the ribbons once again.

It was an easy drive to the country, so easy that Susan Kirkpatrick soon fell asleep, lulled by the rhythmic sway of the carriage on the road. Diantha inhaled the fresh air of the country, a welcome change from the city soot.

Riding Rex, Devlin dropped back to point out the sites of interest to Diantha, a cathedral here, a haunted abbey there.

"Is it really haunted?" Diantha asked sceptically, shielding her eyes and gazing at it from the distance.

"Certainly! No fewer than a dozen people one Christmas Eve can attest to hearing a vigorous rattling of chains. And on certain nights a distinct moaning can be heard from the field."

"Fustian!" she hooted. "Next you'll be telling me of a milky white spectre seen on the lawn."

"Actually, there were two spectres," he said with crushing pretension.

The laughter in his eyes mirrored her own. "You can't really believe in spectres and the supernatural, my lord."

"I don't disbelieve in them," he said promptly.

"Next you will be telling me that you believe in love at first sight or something similar."

"By no means. If anything I am a firm believer in love at second sight."

"Do be serious."

"I am. Love at second sight is infinitely more agreeable. At first sight one never knows what is happening. At second or third sight, we can tell a few things about the other."

"Such as?" she asked, curious to hear his thoughts on love.

"Well, take us for instance. Strictly speaking hypothetically. I daresay at our first meeting you must've thought that I was an insufferable man, luring your brother to various gambling hells. By the second meeting you saw that I was actually a gentleman used to sleeping on library couches, and a victim of his inadequate chef."

She laughed. "And upon third meeting, sir? What did I think then?"

"That I was as susceptible to smoke as any normal person could be. Shall I tell you what I thought of you at our meetings?" he asked softly.

She looked away from those penetrating blue eyes. "I don't think so."

"It's all to the good, I promise," he said. "I thought you a tiny hummingbird."

Her head shot up. "Tiny! I loathe that word."

"Petite?" he asked. "Dainty?"

"Worse and worse," she said. "And upon our second meeting, what did you think then?"

"That you were not so tiny! I'd just received you on my chest, if you recall."

"I remember," she said, flushing at the memory.

"Now you tell me what you thought of me? At the church?"

"I thought you quite the handsomest man I'd ever seen," she said truthfully.

He pretended to doff his hat. "Thank you."

"I shouldn't have said that."

"I don't see why not. Gentlemen are always giving compliments. It's nice to receive one. Do go on. What about your second meeting?"

"I thought you were very hungry, my lord. And," she lifted her gaze to his, "I quite liked you."

CHAPTER SEVEN

NOW WHY DID I SAY THAT? Diantha thought, turning away from Devlin's startled eyes. Her team of Welshbreds sensed her inner confusion and shied at an approaching vehicle. She was obliged to pull the ribbons hard to the left. The curricle swerved, tottering on two left wheels.

Devlin dropped a hand on Diantha's, helping her to hold the team steady. Finally the carriage righted itself, and she brought it to a halt.

"Easy, easy now." Devlin spoke as much to himself as to the horses.

As one deemed a matrimonial prize by the ton, he was quite accustomed to jaded beauties flinging themselves at his head or missish females casting out lures. He was not accustomed to directness such as Miss Atwood possessed. Directness, intelligence and innocence.

The combination boded ill for him. Blast it, she was a bluestocking and Andrew's sister. It would be akin to playing with fire, he warned himself. As though she were a mindreader she took off her wide-brimmed hat and fanned herself.

For a moment neither of them spoke, then Miss Kirkpatrick, no longer lulled by the rhythm of the swaying carriage, opened her eyes.

"What is the matter?" she asked, blinking owlishly at the rolling fields. "Why have you stopped?"

"Just to catch our breath," Diantha replied, putting her hat back on her head. "I came within an ames-ace of ditching us all."

Miss Kirkpatrick sat up straighter. "My word! Where are we?"

"Quite close to Lord Mayerling's bankrupt estates." Devlin furnished an answer to her question. "That stream borders his property. I recognise it from my last visit, as does Rex, I daresay."

"Since we've stopped," he continued, "shall we picnic now? The stream meanders close to the fields. We can water the horses and eat our lunch under the shade of an oak tree."

Diantha fell in willingly with this suggestion, and several minutes later the viscount was spreading a blanket out under a tall oak tree. He rubbed his palms together as he opened the hamper, soon unearthing chicken legs, two different kinds of cheeses, a peach pie and a flask of lemonade, as well as apples for the horses.

Diantha chewed meditatively on a chicken leg, feeling uncharacteristically shy. When would she learn not to blurt out things to Devlin? She wiped her fingers with a napkin and watched him out of the corner of her eye.

He was lounging on the blanket, chatting amicably with Susan about Scotland. One question from Devlin concerned the salmon season in Scotland.

"Ian could answer you better than I," Susan protested. "He's a great sportsman. You should meet him. I know you would deal famously together."

"I look forward to making his acquaintance," Devlin said.

Thoughts of likely familial scenes between Devlin and Susan's brother floated into Diantha's mind. To distract herself, she poured lemonade from the flask into a glass. But it was no remedy. To witness Devlin dangling after Susan grated on her nerves, coming as it did on the heels of her own stupid declaration of affection for him.

She sipped the lemonade.

"I quite liked you." Her cheeks burned with mortification. A malicious sprite must've possessed her tongue for

that fleeting moment; otherwise, it made not a particle of sense. She didn't usually go about blurting out that she liked any gentleman, particularly one who showed such a keen interest in her friend.

Di plucked at a loose blade of grass by the blanket's edge. She had no wish to indulge in a jealous pulling of caps with Susan. The relationship between Susan and Devlin seemed to be progressing at a sedate pace. She must not throw a spanner in the works.

But she felt unable to sit calmly by and witness the wooing in front of her. She picked up a few apples and walked down to the stream where the horses were drinking. They lifted their heads and their ears flattened as she called their names and fed the fruit to them.

Devlin's horse, Rex, drinking a few feet away, stared at her, too well bred to beg. She held the last apple in the palm of her hand. Sniffing, he approached and ate it off her hand. She stroked his mane. He really was a magnificent creature.

"He likes you."

She jumped, one hand to her throat. Unnoticed, Devlin had walked down to the stream. "I think he just likes the apple," she said, regaining her composure.

The viscount smiled and shook his head. "You don't know Rex the way I do. He is a temperamental animal. He doesn't take food from just anyone, unlike his new master," he said with a grin. "Did I tell you I have been trying to lure Gaston away from his restaurant? I've offered him any salary he could name. He still refuses."

"The restaurant is his dream. He's had positions before in many high-ranking residences," Diantha said. "His last employer was a Royal duke. Clarence, I believe."

"No wonder Gaston turned me down. A mere viscount would be quite a comedown for him."

She led the horses back towards the carriage and Devlin hitched them. Her Welshbreds seemed to understand he was their friend.

"How much farther are we to Mrs. Tribbet's?" Susan asked.

"Another twenty to thirty minutes," Devlin replied, turning to answer Susan's query. "I can tie Rex to the back of the carriage and drive if you are too fatigued, Miss Atwood."

Diantha was not in the least fatigued but heard in the question that the viscount was silently requesting more time alone with Susan.

"Actually, I'd like to ride Rex, with your permission."

Devlin paused, her request not what he'd expected.

"I promise to keep him close to the carriage. This will permit you to drive Susan the way you want to."

The viscount was looking puzzled by this oblique reference to Susan when the lady herself entered the discussion.

"You can't ride Devlin's horse, Diantha. You don't have a side saddle."

Diantha was momentarily nonplussed by the scandalised look in Susan's eyes.

"Rex would look deuced odd with a side saddle on his back," Devlin said with a grin.

Diantha was forced to agree. "So he would. He was not meant to be a lady's mount. Perhaps I should just drive to Mrs. Tribbet's, my lord."

"I will ride ahead and show you the way," he said, swinging himself into the saddle, a thoughtful expression growing in his blue eyes.

Miss Tribbet was in her garden, tending a rosebush when the clatter of horses alerted her to the presence of visitors. She looked up, her fair complexion protected from the scorching sun by a large straw bonnet.

"Why, Lord Devlin," she said with surprise and laid down her pruning shears.

The viscount dismounted swiftly and lifted his arms to help first Diantha and then Susan down from the carriage.

"Good afternoon, Miss Tribbet," he said, turning to her. "I hope we have not called at an awkward moment. May I present Miss Diantha Atwood, and her friend Miss Susan Kirkpatrick? I thought it best if you and Miss Atwood met."

"To be sure." Miss Tribbet said, offering her hand.

Devlin had warned her, but still Diantha was jolted. Close up, Miss Tribbet seemed like a perfect lady with smiling intelligence in her eyes, and her blond curls did give her the look of an angel. Nothing at all like Mrs. Tribbet.

"So you're Andrew's sister," Miss Tribbet said. "I am pleased to make your acquaintance. He spoke to me at great length about you. How you were a bluestocking and so intelligent. You don't have the look of him."

"No, I am said to have favoured my mother. Andrew takes after my father."

"Do come in," Miss Tribbet invited as she unlatched the gate and began leading them towards the small house. "Your visit couldn't be more timely. My mother is visiting friends and won't disturb us."

"Thank heaven for that," Diantha murmured then bit her tongue. "I'm sorry..." she said quickly.

"Don't be. Mama has her eccentricities. I don't blame you for thinking that I might be a hurly-burly female who trapped your brother into marriage."

Miss Tribbet led her guests into a small but spotlessly clean parlour and in due course brought out a tea tray.

"I still don't quite understand your claim to be married to Andrew," Diantha said as she accepted a cup of tea from Miss Tribbet.

"Didn't Mama tell you how that came to be?"

"She said something about your bathing in a stream?" Diantha said, stirring sugar into her tea.

Miss Tribbet nodded and leaned back in her Windsor chair. "I didn't know anyone was about. Andrew happened upon me, and since I was compromised, he did the honourable thing. He married me."

"Was it his idea?" Diantha asked.

Miss Tribbet paused a moment in thought. "I don't remember. We were both very confused. He was possibly more mortified than I. Kept talking about his reputation and plans. I could see he was a gentleman. Then he swiftly said he must do his duty by me and we must be married. So we arranged to meet at a church the next day. I thought he might not appear, but he arrived with a special licence and so we were married."

"And this took place when?" Diantha asked.

"March the twelfth."

Weeks before Andrew had married Esmeraude. Diantha sipped her fragrant tea, thinking hard. Andrew *was* a gentleman and might have felt duty bound to marry Miss Tribbet. But surely he would have told someone—if not his sister, then his cronies, Roddy and Devlin.

"Where is Andrew?" Miss Tribbet enquired. "Is he still off on his wedding trip with Miss Lowell?"

"So you know about his wedding!" Diantha exclaimed.

Their hostess dimpled. "Mama has a great weakness for the gossip pages of the *Morning Post* and the *Gazette*. When she saw the wedding announced, she was put into a great flame."

"Why didn't you stop the wedding before it took place?"

Miss Tribbet nibbled on a biscuit. "We only get the London papers that others in the village discard. I had no notion that Andrew was going to marry Miss Lowell until we saw the announcement in an old issue of the *Gazette*. By that time the wedding had already taken place. Mama wanted to descend on Mr. Lowell and tell him everything. I prevailed on her to wait before informing the Lowells. But she couldn't resist seeing you, Miss Atwood."

Diantha stared into her teacup. Her brother secretly married?

"I still can't believe Andrew would do such a havy-cavy thing," Diantha said. "To marry you and then Esmeraude. It's most unlike him. He would not marry you and just forget you. He must've suffered a blow to his head.''

"Loss of memory?" Devlin asked, throwing her a sceptical look.

"It is known to happen," she said defensively.

"Oh, certainly it happens. I recollect my own cousin once falling off a horse and not even knowing his own name. We had great fun persuading him that he was Prinny. He went about barking orders to everyone before his father boxed his ears, which immediately restored his memory."

"Oh, Devlin, don't be idiotish. No one besides your family cares a jot about your cousin," Diantha said.

"If Andrew did lose his memory," Susan put in gently from the corner where she had been sitting unobtrusively, "he would have forgotten considerably more than Miss Tribbet. He'd be unable to remember his own name, his sister and his friends. And he showed no such difficulty in remembering the rest of us."

"Susan's right," Diantha acknowledged, giving up this idea reluctantly.

Miss Tribbet put her teacup down on the table. "All I want is for Andrew to put in process the necessary papers for a quiet bill of divorcement."

"A divorce may be unnecessary," Devlin pointed out. "You could probably get the marriage annulled. I take it you didn't—" He paused delicately while Miss Tribbet flushed.

"Devlin, really!" Diantha said with some exasperation. "There is no call for such questions."

"I was merely trying to determine the facts," he said, much stung. "I ain't a Nosy Parker."

"Unfortunately the facts are Andrew has married and abandoned me," Miss Tribbet said.

"I have dispatched Roddy to the Lakes to locate Andrew and bring him back," Devlin said. "Once he returns we can resolve this coil. Until then—"

"I shall stay here in Topping Green," Miss Tribbet said, anticipating his next words. "I have no wish to make trouble for anyone, and I promise I won't go about spreading the tale of what happened between Andrew and me."

Diantha rose and held out her hand. "Goodbye, Miss Tribbet. I wish I could do more for you."

"There is nothing for you to do. I have my mother—"

Who would undoubtedly be returning anytime soon. All four were of one mind when it came to avoiding Mrs. Tribbet, and the three visitors hastily made their adieux.

Diantha was silent during the return trip to London.

"Not quite what we expected, is she?" Devlin asked finally, as they neared the outskirts of London.

Diantha lifted her head slightly. "Good heavens, Devlin, she's as respectable as you or me."

"More. She doesn't have fireworks going off in her halls."

She laughed. "What a pity I can't dismiss her as a vile creature out to trick us."

"But I still can't believe Andrew would play such a cruel hoax on anyone," Susan put in. "Why would he marry Esmeraude after marrying Miss Tribbet, who seems ever so nice and sweet?"

"Miss Tribbet doesn't have a fortune, does she?" Diantha asked.

"Not a groat, as far as I could see," Devlin replied.

"Andrew would need a fortune to pay off his debts," Diantha said softly and glanced at the dark-haired man riding next to her curricle. Debts which Devlin was in large measure responsible for.

THE DAYS PASSED with no word from Andrew or Roddy. On Monday Diantha returned to Bruton Street with Susan for a fitting with Fanchon. Despite some trouble with the sleeves, the emerald green gown was taking shape nicely.

"If you wear your hair up like so—" Fanchon lifted the curls in one hand to demonstrate. "*Voilà*. Very dramatic. Bewitching. You shall captivate your gentleman."

"I have no gentleman, Fanchon."

"*Eh bien*. Dress your hair like so and you will get one, *n'est-ce pas?*"

Diantha laughed. She would never win the war of words with the modiste. Very carefully, she stepped out of her gown and back into her walking dress, while Susan waited to be prodded and pinched and pinned by Fanchon.

A half hour later, the two ladies stepped out of the shop directly into the path of the last man in Christendom Diantha wished to see. Esmeraude's father.

Sir Philip Forth was walking with Mr. Lowell, and any hope Diantha nursed that the two gentlemen might pass her by without a bow went by the board.

"Good day, Miss Atwood," Sir Philip said, tipping his hat. "And Miss Kirkpatrick."

"Good day, Sir Philip, Mr. Lowell," they replied.

"Buying a new dress?" the baronet enquired.

"Er, yes," Diantha admitted. Undoubtedly Sir Philip would think fashion frivolous.

"Esmeraude was fond of Fanchon's designs," Lowell said with an indulgent smile. "The bills nearly put me into a poor house. But I could never say no to her. She always was my favourite. So pretty and obedient."

"Excellent traits in a wife," Sir Philip agreed.

"What are?" A voice enquired.

They turned to find Devlin favouring the baronet with one of his enigmatic smiles.

"Eavesdropping, Devlin? Bad ton, that," Lowell said with a laugh.

"I confess it was inadvertent," Devlin said, after greeting Diantha and Susan. "My ears pricked up when I heard Sir Philip speak on excellent traits in a wife. Those would be—?"

"Prettiness and obedience. Possibly traits which you are unfamiliar with when it comes to your dealings with the gentler sex," the baronet said disapprovingly.

"You are too harsh on me, Sir Philip. I could be turning over a new leaf."

"Impossible."

Mr. Lowell smothered another laugh. "A new leaf is doing it too brown, Devlin. What prompts such a change of heart?"

"Perhaps I was persuaded by one of Sir Philip's lectures on morality. You spoke last week at Portman Square, did you not on the dangerous vices of women, drinking and gambling?"

"Just so." The baronet puffed his cheeks up self-importantly and turned to Diantha. "I've been meaning to ask, Miss Atwood, if I might give the second part of my lecture tomorrow."

"Are there more vices to enumerate?" the viscount asked. "Surely you covered the main ones."

"There are many, my lord. But I thought to speak on gluttony and sloth."

"A potent combination, to be sure."

"Tomorrow then, Miss Atwood?" Sir Philip turned his head towards Diantha.

"Well, I don't know," Diantha said, casting about wildly for some way to fob the baronet off.

"Come, come, Miss Atwood, we can't just have the first part and not the second," the viscount said, dipping two fingers into his snuff box and giving her a teasing look under lazy lids.

Her eyes shot daggers at him. This was his fault for provoking Sir Philip. She had no wish for Forth to bore her guests tomorrow or anytime soon. "In truth, Sir Philip, Susan is planning a recital for tomorrow."

"I am?" Miss Kirkpatrick asked with a furrowed brow.

"Yes, dear, you do remember my saying that you must play again for us sometime soon? And next week we start rehearsal for Mr. Fanshaw's epic."

"A pity we shall have to wait for the second half of your talk on morality," Devlin said, inhaling a pinch of snuff. "I am on tenterhooks to hear the end of it. But never fear, anticipation is its own reward. I'm sure Miss Atwood will let you deliver it sometime in the future."

"I hope so," Sir Philip fretted. "It is one of my favourite lectures. I have given it three times already this year."

"Three times. Excellent. All in London?"

"No. Once in Cheltenham, the second time in Bath and just a month ago in Hertfordshire."

"Splendid. Practice makes perfect," the viscount said.

In which case Diantha thought dourly a good deal of practice would be necessary. She climbed into her curricle with Susan, ruminating on what Sir Philip would have to say on the moral implications of bigamy.

CHAPTER EIGHT

WORD THAT Susan Kirkpatrick would be performing at Miss Atwood's Open Day spread throughout London, and a much larger crowd than usual flowed through Diantha's proud Palladian residence Tuesday morning.

"After we have listened to Cumbert and Forth on successive weeks, Susan's music will be a balm to our ears," Lady Daphne, one of the regulars, declared with some alacrity, her view seconded by others trailing in.

"Miss Atwood, I say, Miss Atwood!"

Sylvester pressed forward, carrying a parcel in his hands. Not another bomb, please God, Diantha implored.

"Good day, Sylvester," she said with composure as he unwrapped the parcel. "What do you have there? Not more fireworks, I hope."

The inventor flushed nearly as red as his hair. "No. It's a gift to apologize for what happened last week." He opened the box. "See. It's a specimen of a butterfly which comes from the Americas."

Her mind boggling at being a recipient of such a gift, Diantha gazed down at the dead butterfly, its lovely, delicate wings mounted against two solid blocks of wood.

"Do you like it?" he asked eagerly. "I wracked my brains to think of a present most like you."

A dead butterfly was most like her? Diantha thought ruefully as she struggled to find words to thank Sylvester for his gift.

"I shall always think of you when I look at it," she said finally and went off to find Hughes and direct him to take the specimen to the library.

Devlin, standing to one side in the foyer, had witnessed the presentation of Sylvester's gift, and he moved across the black and white lozenges towards the inventor after Diantha glided away.

"A moth as a gift for a lady," he drawled. "What a knacky notion."

"It's not a moth," Sylvester said stiffly. "It's a prize butterfly, a specimen from the Americas. Sydney Danvers went on an expedition there last year and showed it to me. I begged leave to buy it from him because I knew Miss Atwood would appreciate its beauty. She has a most superior mind and a keen intellect."

"Also the most dazzling eyes," Devlin observed, giving him a sidelong glance. Sylvester had all the look of a man about to put his fate to the touch.

"What's that?"

"I said doubtless you are wise," the viscount replied adroitly.

"Of course I am," the inventor declared. "I have known Diantha longer than you."

"It's not how long you are in the race, Sylvester, but who finishes first."

"Race? Why are you talking about sport?" Sylvester asked, an expression of complete befuddlement on his freckled face.

"Nothing. Just my stupid babbling. Shall we go into the music room and hear Miss Kirkpatrick play?"

Twenty-four hours was not much notice, but Miss Kirkpatrick rose to the occasion, playing several new compositions at the pianoforte, including her latest one about Scotland, which so moved Mrs. Purdy, seated in the front row, that the woman burst into tears at its completion.

"It reminded me of home. I must write to my mother today," she said, dabbing her eyes with a handkerchief.

Alarmed at the transformation of a member of her audience into a watering pot, Susan prevailed on several other friends to join her for a round of country songs, and while these were being enthusiastically sung Diantha stole away to the refreshment room.

Devlin saw her leave and was on the verge of following her when he noticed Sylvester in a very purposeful fashion set foot after her. He'd wager a pony that the inventor was going to pop the question. And what would Miss Atwood say to that? Devlin wondered, as he settled back in his chair. He felt uncharacteristically jolted at the notion of her actually accepting an offer of matrimony from Sylvester.

When the inventor entered the refreshment room, Diantha was busy counting the number of cakes on the table.

"Unfair, Sylvester!" she chided, turning a stern countenance his way. "You are too early for the cakes."

"Oh, bother the cakes. I don't want any. I want a word with you."

"If it's about your butterfly, Hughes is at this very moment attempting to find a suitable place for it in my library," she said, now holding a silver fork up to the chandelier.

"That's not it, either." Sylvester crossed to her side. "Miss Atwood. Diantha. I know you must think me a coxcomb after the way the fireworks went off last week."

"Do stop plaguing yourself about that. I know you didn't mean to do it on purpose. All I ask is that you be a trifle more careful in the future. I am not as comfortable as you are with these newfangled inventions." She picked up a plate of lemon cake and a fork and held it towards him with a smile. It wouldn't hurt for Sylvester to try a piece before the others.

"That's not what I want to talk to you about." Sylvester ran a finger between his collar points. "Oh, dash it all, Diantha. I am trying to make you an offer."

The fork in Diantha's hand clattered to the floor.

Having got the declaration out, Sylvester perceived that the second step in making his offer entailed planting a chaste salute on a suitable spot on the female's body and stepped forward to take Diantha into his arms.

To her utter astonishment, Diantha found herself being hugged exuberantly to the inventor's bosom. Unfortunately the plate with the lemon cake was being hugged, too, its contents squashed between Sylvester's waistcoat and her cornflower blue day dress.

Only the thought of an irreparable stain recalled Sylvester to his senses. Hastily, he released Diantha before more damage could be inflicted on his best Weston.

"Oh, I beg your pardon!"

"Think nothing of it, Sylvester," she replied, dabbing her bodice with a napkin. "This is an old dress, but your waistcoat looks new."

"It is new," he said mournfully, patting the stain with his handkerchief. "I just hope it isn't ruined. Weston worked for a month on it." He frowned, becoming aware that only a gapeseed fretted about fashion in the midst of making a declaration to a lady. "But what about us, Diantha? You haven't accepted my offer yet."

"Yes, I know," Diantha said hastily. "And it was so good of you to offer for me. Truly, I'm honoured. But I can't marry you," she said gently. "I don't think it at all the thing. We wouldn't suit. You deserve a woman more attuned to your, er, inventive qualities. I confess that I am thoroughly at a loss when it comes to electricity. Even when Mr. Watt, who invented the steam engine, came here himself to explain its workings, I still could not make head nor tail of it."

"It's dead easy, really. Take boiling water—"

"I'd as lief not," she interjected. "Truly, Sylvester, no more nonsense, please. The whole idea of my marrying you is absurd."

Sylvester's usually genial smile faded. "Absurd, is it?" he asked stiffly. "Nonsense, is it? I have made you an offer of marriage, and you laugh at me."

"Oh, Sylvester! Pray, don't go away angry," she pleaded, but it was too late. Sylvester turned on his heel and stalked out the door just as the others in the crowd came surging through.

Diantha fought her way through the horde, but by the time she reached the entryway Sylvester had already stormed out the door. As she sank into a nearby chair, Devlin walked over to her.

"Problem, Miss Atwood?" Devlin enquired, trying to contain his intense curiosity. Sylvester had quit the refreshment room as though chased by a tiger. What the devil had happened between these two?

"If you must know, it's Sylvester."

"Not another smoke bomb, I hope?"

She laughed, then sobered quickly. "An entirely different kind of explosion, my lord."

"How intriguing. Do tell me more."

It was on the tip of her tongue to do just that, but luckily she realized that it would be de trop to discuss one man's offer of marriage with another.

"I shall attend to my own problem, my lord. Thank you just the same."

WONDERING JUST WHAT HAD happened between Sylvester and Diantha, the viscount set out in systematic fashion to find the inventor. A search of Cribb's Parlour and Manton's Gallery proved futile, but in the reading rooms of White's, Devlin discovered Sylvester feeding crumpled sheets of paper into the fire.

"Sylvester, Good God! What are you doing?"

"Burning all the plans for my inventions," Sylvester answered gloomily.

"Here now. What do you want to do that for? You have copies of them at home, I hope."

"Yes," came the reluctant admission.

Devlin took off his beaver felt. "That's a relief."

Sylvester glared at him. "You don't need to dissemble, Dev. I know your low opinion of my inventions."

"How can you say that?" the viscount asked mildly. "I've never seen one—properly that is. Perhaps I shall sometime when you speak at Miss Atwood's Open Day."

Sylvester scowled. "Miss Atwood, bah, humbug."

"Are you in her black books?" Devlin probed delicately as more flames leapt in the fireplace.

"No," came the cold rejoinder. "She is in mine."

"Ah. That makes a world of difference, to be sure. What has she done to make you as cross as crabs?"

Sylvester walked away from the fire to his chair where a tray and a half-empty bottle of claret rested.

"She refused my offer of marriage. Said the whole idea was absurd nonsense."

"That is the risk which one takes," Devlin said gently. "You can make the lady an offer, but it's her decision whether to accept or refuse."

"She thinks me a coxcomb," Sylvester said moodily, picking up the bottle of claret.

"Did she say so?"

"She didn't need to." Sylvester gestured with the bottle. "Have a glass with me, Devlin?"

Since he would drink it all up by himself, Devlin consented to a glassful.

"Have you ever offered for a lady, Devlin?" Sylvester asked after the bottle was emptied.

Devlin suppressed a shudder and shook his head.

"You're very wise. The Bachelors, that's what they called you and your set, right?"

"Yes. Though it has been reduced to one bachelor at the moment, namely myself."

Sylvester brightened. "I'd like to join you. I'm bound and determined never to marry."

"My dear fellow, just because you have suffered a disappointment with Miss Atwood is no reason for you to say such a thing."

"It's not a disappointment. In fact, I'm quite relieved. I wish to celebrate. Let me stand you another bottle of claret. Bachelors two, we are. Agreed?"

"Yes, of course, if it means that much to you."

Obviously it did mean a good deal to Sylvester, for by the time the viscount left White's he had learned that Sylvester would never darken the door of Portman Square again, that in fact he would never speak to any of the female sex again. To this list of woulds Devlin added one other. Sylvester would have a devil of a head the next morning.

ON FRIDAY EVENING Diantha, garbed in Fanchon's emerald green gown, with Susan wearing the modiste's gold masterpiece, climbed the huge marble stairway of the Jersey residence. True to Fanchon's instructions, Diantha wore her hair up that evening and attracted her share of attention from the exquisitely dressed gentlemen.

"My dear Miss Atwood," Lady Jersey, a vision in seablue satin this evening, greeted her graciously. "And Miss Kirkpatrick. How delightful to see you both. I am all agog at having snared two such noted recluses."

"Hardly recluses," Diantha replied. "Our Portman Square residence is open to everyone."

"So I understand." Lady Jersey chuckled. "But if I were you I'd ban Lord Sylvester from the premises. I warn you he is in attendance this evening."

"Really?" Diantha said hopefully.

"He is refusing to speak to any female," Lady Jersey said in accents of despair.

"Good heavens!"

"I know. I was obliged to insist that my husband tell him that everyone will think him queer in the attic if he persists. But that is enough about Sylvester. You are both prettily attired tonight. Monique's work?"

"No, Fanchon's."

"Ah, yes, Fanchon of Oxford Street, isn't it?"

"Bruton Street," Diantha replied.

"I must stop in and see her new gowns."

A thousand candles shimmered in the chandeliers swaying above the ballroom when Diantha and Susan entered. Diantha's reputation as a bluestocking had preceded her, but few, except for those frequenting her Open Days, had realized that she was a bonafide Beauty, too. The gentlemen soon confirmed this in the best way possible, stepping over each other in their haste to beg for one of her dances. Susan found herself similarly besieged.

Perhaps she had been wrong not to attend more balls, Diantha thought giddily as she danced from one end of the room to the other. It was certainly enjoyable to have the attentions of the gentlemen, even though some of them were foolish.

"Miss Atwood." Mr. Lowell smiled a greeting as he passed her chair. "How splendid to see you here. Andrew told me that you rarely attended balls."

Diantha swallowed the lump in her throat which the sight of Esmeraude's father occasioned. "Good evening, Mr. Lowell."

"You are the belle of the ball. If Esmeraude weren't married and enjoying her nuptial trip, I would be hard put to say a civil word to you, knowing the inevitable tantrum that she would throw!"

"You malign poor Esmeraude."

"I miss her," he confided. "I confess that your brother was not the choice I would have made for her, but he's proved the test well enough." Lowell wagged a playful finger. "He had just better not treat her badly. I shan't stand for that."

"No, of course he won't," Diantha promised, wondering if bigamy would constitute ill treatment of the fair Esmeraude. Fortunately she was saved from further discourse with Lowell by the arrival of Major Cathcart whom she greeted with such enthusiasm that the good major was emboldened to ask if he could take her in for supper and she had no recourse except to say yes.

As she danced with Cathcart and attempted to listen to his tales of military derring-do during Wellington's last campaign, she could not help wondering if Devlin were going to make an appearance.

The viscount had indeed already made an appearance, thinking only to stay an hour at the most, but thanks to the determined efforts of Lady Jersey who would make him known to all the marriage-minded mamas in the room, he was still in attendance two hours after his arrival. He caught fleeting glimpses of Diantha and Susan and toyed with the idea of asking them each for a dance. But first he was obliged to fight his way free from all of the Season's new debutantes.

As he approached Diantha, he smiled, utterly enchanted by the riot of curls swept up high this night, teasing him with the image of what it might be like to let down that hair. Her figure, always trim, was shown off to perfection in a gown of emerald green that brought out the pale beauty of her skin.

"Good evening, Miss Atwood," he said, bowing before her.

"Oh, Devlin, you're here." She had thought him good-looking before, but now, seeing him for the first time in a black swallow-tailed coat, she thought he looked like a top-of-the-trees Corinthian.

He smiled down at her. "I hope your dance card is not too filled."

"You may see for yourself," she said, holding the dance card out to him.

"Bluestocking turned belle," he said, as he hastily scribbled his name down on two of the dances. Both waltzes. But she had no further opportunity to speak to him because Mr. Cunningham appeared for the quadrille now under way.

Devlin's waltz followed the quadrille, and Diantha's heart was in her throat as he gathered her into his arms for the dance. Waltzing was certainly nothing like the other dances, and she could see why many in the ton frowned upon it. Happily, Lady Jersey was not among that number.

"Are you enjoying the ball?" Devlin asked, spinning her dizzily from one end of the ballroom to the other.

"Oh, yes," she said breathlessly. "Aren't you?"

"Balls aren't my usual sport."

"Mine either," she admitted, her head still reeling from the last dizzying set of turns.

"Then why are you here?" he asked. Was it her imagination or had his blue eyes always been so penetrating?

"I could well ask you the same question, my lord," she said, still trying to catch her breath.

A smile lifted the corners of his mouth. "Touché..."

"I hear that you have accepted Sylvester as another Bachelor," she mentioned casually.

"It is not so formal a thing as an acceptance," he replied.

"Will you tell me why he won't talk to me?" she asked, a slight frown wrinkling her brow. "He wouldn't exchange a greeting with me or Susan the other day. It's most peculiar."

"I believe that is his method of recovering from a broken heart. The one you inflicted on him."

"Did he say that?" She asked, nearly missing a step.

His arm tightened about her. "No. He said he wouldn't speak to any female ever again. And since you are female and so is Miss Kirkpatrick..."

She stared at him incredulously. "My stars, Devlin. How can he be such a nodcock? He never intends to speak another word to any female as long as he lives?"

"You could always accept his offer," he pointed out.

"So he told you about that!"

Devlin nodded. "Do you miss Sylvester?" he asked, conscious of more than a modicum of interest in her reply.

Diantha considered the question for a moment. "I suppose I do. You see, he's always been underfoot at Portman Square, rather like a pup that lies in the exact spot that causes you to trip. And after he finally moves, well, you miss tripping over him. Does that make any sense?"

"Certainly. And yet you don't want to marry the pup, I mean Sylvester."

"Precisely. It's just that his offer came as such a shock and I've had little experience in refusing an offer."

"Sylvester's was the very first offer you received?" he asked. "I wouldn't credit that. Don't tell me the gentlemen frequenting your establishment, helping themselves to your refreshments, were blind to your charms?"

Diantha laughed. "Blind to my charms, indeed, Devlin. And as for their devouring my refreshments, you have eaten your fill at my table, and I don't see you making me an offer, do I?" she asked.

Now why did I say that? Diantha scolded herself as soon as the words left her tongue.

"Very true," he murmured, looking momentarily disconcerted at her words, as well he might.

To her intense relief the waltz ended and Major Cathcart arrived to claim the supper dance. Devlin watched her go with a frown. Could she be interested in that military buffoon? Cathcart did cut a dashing figure in his regimentals, but Diantha was too intelligent to fall for such trappings, wasn't she?

Casting his mind about to which lady he might escort in to the supper room, he noticed Susan Kirkpatrick. As she was Diantha's bosom bow, the two ladies would naturally gravitate towards each other. Swiftly he made his way to her side.

"May I have the honour of this dance, Miss Kirkpatrick?" he asked.

"Oh, my lord, I don't know. I did tell Mr. Ludlow he might have this dance. But I don't see him anywhere."

"Then his loss is my gain," the viscount said, crooking his arm to her. "Shall we?"

"Certainly. So kind of you."

By the time Devlin and Susan entered the supper room, it was crowded with tables and guests and servants arranging fresh platters of food on the huge buffet. Diantha and Cathcart were seated at a table in the corner with two vacant chairs.

"Where shall we sit?" Devlin asked Susan.

"Some place quiet," she begged. "I fear I have the beginning of a headache."

He made a pretence of scanning the room. "I see Miss Atwood's table."

"Oh, yes. That would be splendid."

With meticulous courtesy, Devlin escorted Susan over to Diantha's table.

"You don't mind if we join you?" Susan asked Diantha.

"Not in the least," Diantha replied. "The major has just left to bring us back a plate."

"You will allow me to get you one, Miss Kirkpatrick," Devlin said with a bow and strolled off.

"So you have attached Devlin. My felicitations, Susan," Diantha said with what she hoped was cheerful good humour. In truth the sight of Devlin with Susan on his arm had caused the most appalling sensations within her. She was no better than a jealous cat.

"Don't be absurd, Diantha," Susan said, massaging her temples. "I haven't attached him. Just because he brought me in to the supper room..."

"Most females here would give their eye teeth to be singled out in such a fashion."

"Then they are silly widgeons," Susan replied. "Devlin is very amiable but hardly the type of man I am interested in."

Among the females who *would* have given their eye teeth at some sign of interest from Devlin was Thalia Whorley, who sat at the opposite end of the supper room with Sir Arthur Long. The widow had not failed to notice the viscount's entry with Miss Kirkpatrick. A brief enquiry as to the name of Devlin's partner in the supper room elicited not Miss Tribbet as expected but a Miss Kirkpatrick.

The arch look in the widow's eyes grew more pronounced. Devlin was already playing fast and loose with Miss Tribbet? Good. That was a sign of dwindling interest in the country chit. If so, that meant his heart was not taken yet. Mrs. Whorley smiled and licked her lips. With luck she could regain her hold on him.

Mrs. Whorley's first opportunity to speak to Devlin came late that evening in the ballroom when the viscount stood in a corner watching the others dancing. Pleading fatigue, she asked Sir Arthur to fetch her a glass of champagne, and when the baronet had left her side she made a circuitous path for the viscount.

"Well, Ollie, we meet again."

Only one female of his acquaintance had ever called him Ollie. The viscount turned, a frigid smile on his face.

"Thalia, you are looking lovely this evening."

"Thank you." She tapped him playfully with her Chinese fan. "You haven't asked me to dance."

He looked over his shoulder. "Where is your baronet?"

"Arthur is off fetching me a glass of champagne. Just one dance, Ollie. Just to assure me we are still old friends."

Although Devlin had no real wish to dance with her, he deemed it best to do so in the interests of harmony. A gleam of satisfaction glittered in the widow's eyes as she held her hands out to the viscount, but when she pressed her body closer to his than convention allowed for the waltz he pulled back.

"Do try for a little conduct, my dear," he said dampeningly. "Your baronet will run me through with his sword point."

"You're better at swords than he. Better at pistols. Better at everything," she said huskily. Her hand caressed the back of his neck.

He jerked his head away. "What sort of game are you playing at, Thalia?" he asked, becoming aware that Lady Jersey was observing his partner's machinations with a keen eye. How the tongues would wag tomorrow.

"I've missed you."

"Have you, now?" he asked ironically. "I daresay you missed my purse more."

Mrs. Whorley's lips tightened. "Don't be cruel, Devlin. I am trying to apologize."

"Is that what this is? Well, I accept your apology, Thalia. And I wish you happy with your baronet."

"He's not my baronet. He's not half as obliging as you. Oh, Oliver, let's go back to how things were between us."

Devlin felt a distaste for the scene about to unfold.

"Sorry, my dear," he said as gently as he could. "That's impossible."

"Is it because of that Miss Tribbet?" she snapped.

Devlin's grip on her hand tightened, and Mrs. Whorley cried out, "You're hurting me."

"What do you know about Miss Tribbet?" he demanded, a thundercloud look on his face.

"I know enough," she said, rejoicing at scoring this hit. "That she is a country miss that you are grooming to be my replacement. I won't stand for it, do you hear?"

"And I tell you, madam, that I won't be threatened," he said, giving up all pretence of dancing and leaving her in the middle of the ballroom floor all alone.

Twirling the perimeter of the room with Mr. Crabbe, Diantha was an avid witness to Devlin's encounter with Mrs. Whorley. Had Susan seen it as well? she wondered. Within minutes Susan, looking rather wan and tired, approached Diantha, asking if they might leave the ball, all the confirmation Diantha needed that her friend had seen the stormy exchange between Devlin and his former chère amie.

CHAPTER NINE

"WHAT A GOOD TIME we've had!" Diantha declared, leaning back against the velvet squabs as the carriage rolled over the darkened streets. "I vow you had so many admirers. Lord Eustace kept pestering me with questions about you." She turned to her friend, who had not responded to any of her prattle.

"Susan, did you hear me?"

Miss Kirkpatrick roused herself to answer. "Oh, yes, Di. It's just that I feel a trifle hagged."

"We'd best get you to bed," Diantha said. "A night's rest will set you to rights."

But in the morning when Diantha looked in on her friend, alarums went off in her head. Susan looked quite pale and drawn. Knowing her friend's precarious health and fearing a relapse into the invalidism they both thought ended, Diantha dispatched a footman to fetch her physician.

Unfortunately, Dr. Caldwell, who usually attended her, was out of town and his replacement was none other than Dr. Angus Brewster. Diantha was taken aback by the sight of the stocky, moustachioed physician, who looked just as disconcerted as she to be back at Portman Square. After their previous meeting, Diantha was not sure whether to admit him to the sickroom, but Susan was ill, and he was a doctor. Miss Kirkpatrick, however, held an entirely different opinion and refused point blank to submit to any examination by Dr. Brewster.

"That horrid man called me an hysterical female," she insisted.

"That was earlier when you weren't sick. I don't think he will ring a peal over you now. He seems to prefer sick patients to healthy ones. Won't you relent?"

"No, never!" Susan said.

Fearing that further speech would exhaust Susan completely, Diantha abandoned the argument.

"Susan does not wish to be examined by you," she explained moments later to the doctor who paced in the hallway. "You did overset her last week."

"Yes, but she's ill!" Dr. Brewster exclaimed. "I can help her now."

"Yes, I know, but your previous display of temper unsettled her."

Dr. Brewster's moustache quivered. "Rubbish! I'm not an ill-tempered ogre," he protested.

"You needn't try to convince me," Diantha retorted. "I am not your patient. Nor is Susan."

"Very well, but since I did not see Miss Kirkpatrick, you must describe her symptoms to me."

Willingly, Diantha described Susan's fatigue and listlessness.

"Any temperature?" Dr. Brewster stroked his chin.

Diantha shook her head.

"Any unusual activities?"

"We went to a ball last evening. We don't usually go to balls."

"A ball." His brow beetled. "Did you drink champagne?"

"A few glasses," Diantha admitted.

"That may explain the fatigue. I still think it may be a touch of the grippe or influenza. If she does develop a fever, send without delay for another physician."

Dr. Brewster departed, and Di returned to Susan's bedside, feeling helpless as she gazed into the wan face of her friend. During Susan's previous illnesses, Bonny had been present to offer her support and advice. Diantha missed her now more than ever. She drew the coverlet over Susan's shoulders and held on to her hand, which felt dry and hot.

An hour later, a knock sounded on the door. Answering it, she found Hughes with a Dr. Hardy waiting to examine Susan.

"Dr. Hardy? I don't believe I called you." Diantha gazed from her butler to the bald man next to him.

"Lord Devlin instructed me to tell you that Dr. Hardy was his personal physician, Miss Atwood," Hughes said.

Devlin? What did he have to do with this? And how did he know of Susan's condition?

"Where is my patient?" asked Dr. Hardy impatiently.

Diantha indicated her friend lying on the bed.

"His lordship is in the blue drawing room, Miss Atwood," Hughes volunteered.

Quickly Diantha descended the Adam staircase. Devlin stood by the fireplace in the blue drawing room. He turned immediately when he heard her step.

"How is Miss Kirkpatrick?" he asked at once.

"The doctor is with her," Diantha reassured him. "But how comes it that you knew she felt poorly and required a physician?"

"Dr. Brewster descended on me an hour ago, informing me of Miss Kirkpatrick's refusal to be examined by him. He demanded that I prevail on her to change her mind. I took the liberty of calling my own physician, Hardy. He is an excellent man and will diagnose the trouble in a trice."

"Thank you. I admit I was worried about Susan."

As Devlin must have been to bring Hardy himself. Diantha entertained no further doubts about the viscount's feelings for her friend. They ran deep.

Twenty minutes later, Dr. Hardy came down the stairs.

"Brewster was on the mark when he said it sounded like the grippe or possibly the influenza. Watch for fever, that's the thing. And a teaspoonful of this medicine three times a day. If fever arises, send for me."

"Of course." Diantha took the bottle. "Thank you, Dr. Hardy."

He grunted a reply and left.

Diantha waited for Devlin to go, but he seemed unwilling to depart. After only a second's thought, she realized why. No doubt Devlin was chafing to visit Susan.

"Would you like to see Susan?" she asked.

The question floored the viscount, who didn't have the temperament to enjoy sickrooms. But under the circumstances he thought it impossible to refuse.

"Her room is just to the left," Diantha said as they mounted the stairway.

When Diantha opened the door to Susan's bedchamber, Miss Kirkpatrick lay on the four-poster with her eyes closed. Sensitive to Devlin's wishes, Diantha hung back in the doorway, motioning him to approach the bed.

A bit surprised at this—he could see perfectly well from the distance—Devlin took a few tentative steps forward.

He cleared his throat. Susan's eyes fluttered open.

"Who's there?"

"It's Devlin, Miss Kirkpatrick. Miss Atwood tells me you're feeling poorly." He smiled down at her, hoping that this constituted proper conduct in a sickroom.

"Fatigue only," she murmured.

"You must rest," he said, then fell silent at a loss to know what to do next. Further speech would only tire her. What did visitors to sickrooms do? He pressed her hand in a comforting way.

At this exchange of affection Diantha blinked hard.

Susan turned her head and gestured for Diantha to draw closer.

"What did the doctor say?" Susan asked.

"That you may have a touch of the grippe and must rest," Diantha reassured her quickly. She laid a hand on her friend's brow, glad to find that there was still no fever. After a few moments, Susan closed her eyes. Diantha stole away, with Devlin at her side.

"Thank you for taking so keen an interest in Susan's health," she said as she saw him to the front door.

The viscount accepted this compliment uneasily. He'd had no choice. Dr. Brewster had ranted and raved so, and he knew Diantha would be worried about her friend.

"It is the merest trifle."

"Indeed it is not." Diantha held out her hand. "Thank you, my lord. I shall tell Susan when she is better all you have done for her. She will be grateful."

"It's not her gratitude I want," he said, holding Diantha's hand in his much larger one.

A knowing look came into her eyes. "I know, but sometimes gratitude is a start, my lord."

Devlin left Portman Square, mulling over these cryptic words.

He was still puzzling over the matter of Miss Atwood and her effect on him when Roderick Bridger sought him out at Manton's that afternoon.

Mr. Bridger had returned from his trip to the Lakes without a clue to the whereabouts of the missing Andrew Atwood.

"I've combed the area and found not a sign of him or Esmeraude," Roddy reported, watching Devlin take aim at a target.

"Odd."

The viscount squeezed the trigger. A near miss at the bull's-eye.

"Perhaps they went to another region. That would throw anyone out for a lark off their scent," Roddy pointed out.

"Doesn't sound like Andrew." Devlin loaded his pistol again.

"Are you going to tell me what the wager is about?" Roddy quizzed.

Devlin looked blank. "What wager?"

"You dispatched me to bring Andrew back because of a wager, gudgeon!"

"Oh, that," Devlin said, now recalling the ruse which had persuaded Roddy to make the trip to the Lakes. "Now that I think about it, I can't remember whom the wager was with."

"Devlin!" Roddy exploded with laughter. "Oh, you are the most complete hand. Never mind. I am off to be reunited with my wife and babe."

Devlin returned to his shooting, still brooding over Roddy's report, more evidence in the growing tide against Andrew. Thinking about Andrew brought his sister to mind.

"Devlin, you've missed the target!" shouted one of the onlookers.

"Did I?"

"Never did that before."

Never been bewitched by a beautiful bluestocking before, he muttered inaudibly as he put down the pistol and left Manton's.

As THE AFTERNOON SHADOWS lengthened across the floor of her bedchamber, Susan turned in her sleep. Diantha was sitting at the corner table, writing a letter to Miss Bonaventure and looked up at once, but Susan burrowed back into her pillow. Soon her breathing became rhythmic once again.

Reassured that Susan was resting comfortably, Diantha reapplied herself to her letter. In between the account of Lady Jersey's ball and her hope that Bonny had benefitted by the sea air in Brighton, she added that both she and Susan longed for her return.

She didn't want to alarm Bonny by telling her about Susan's current illness. Satisfied with the letter, Di blotted it and took it downstairs to be sent off.

"Will you be taking tea, Miss?" Hughes asked, accepting the letter from her.

"Tea? It can't be teatime, already," she said and realized as the grandfather clock in the hall bonged the hour that indeed it was.

How quickly time had passed. She went into her library and nibbled a biscuit off the tray which Hughes brought in to her. It had been such a surprise that Devlin had brought Dr. Hardy by. She had thought perhaps she might be mistaken about the viscount's interest in Susan, but had rather a more difficult time convincing herself of that now.

Devlin and Susan. She sipped the fragrant Bohea and felt her stomach churn. She must find something else to do besides fret. She would read something. Yes, that was what she would do.

Rising to her feet, she crossed to the library stairs and began the tricky manoeuvring required to get from one end of the room to the other. The stairs reminded her of Sylvester and his silly quarrel with her. How she disliked being on the outs with him. She never anticipated that he would develop a tendre for her, even though Devlin had warned her about it.

Devlin, again. Why was she thinking so much about that man? She glanced down from her position on the stairs, noticing the sofa on which the viscount had been sleeping a fortnight ago. Her hand jerked convulsively at the memory, and once again she lurched off the side of the bookshelf, dislodging several volumes.

"Botheration!" she exclaimed, quitting the stairs at once. She gave the contraption a kick and then recoiled as it seemed about to attack her.

And she couldn't even ask Sylvester to look at it. He cut up so stiff whenever they met. Wearily, she stooped to pick up the books. It had not been the best of her days. Susan sick, Sylvester in the mopes with her. At least she hadn't come to cuffs with Devlin.

Devlin. For pity's sake, was there no escaping him in her thoughts? And why wasn't he there to help her shelve these stupid books!

"WHERE DID DR. HARDY come from, Diantha?" Susan asked the next day, as Diantha ran a silver brush through her hair. Miss Kirkpatrick was much improved and seemed in need of conversation.

"My dear, haven't I told you?" Diantha asked as she divided Susan's golden strands into thirds. "Devlin brought him. You do remember refusing to let Dr. Brewster examine you?"

Susan flushed slightly. "Yes, I remember that."

"Well, he marched off to Mount Street and demanded that Lord Devlin prevail on you to allow an examination. Devlin summoned his own physician, Hardy, and brought him here. And very glad I was to see him, let me tell you."

"He did all that for me?" Susan asked, her blue eyes bright with wonder.

"Indeed he did," Diantha said. She began plaiting Susan's hair.

"So good of him," Susan murmured.

"Yes."

"I wouldn't have thought he would be concerned."

"I know," Diantha said, wondering just when Devlin would make Susan a definite offer.

Although the influenza raged in other quarters, Susan was spared and quickly recovered from the grippe, none the worse for the experience. Within a week she was back to her pianoforte.

With Susan recovered, Diantha realized that they had not yet visited Emily or the babe, and they set out one Monday morning to rectify this mistake.

Emily exclaimed over the quilt and the sweater which Diantha had knitted for the babe, and both ladies were treated to the sight of the new heir sleeping in his cradle. In Diantha's opinion, young Harry was a perfect copy of Roddy.

"He reminds me of Prinny. All he does is sleep and eat!" Emily laughed, the indulgent mother.

"And he has the chins to prove it!" Diantha said, chucking a finger under the babe's chin. "Just like Prinny!"

"He's adorable," Susan agreed.

"Yes," Emily said proudly, leading the way back to her sitting room. "Of course he cries a good deal, but I must admit that I think he will grow up very nicely. Now how have you been? And what, pray, has been happening outside? I haven't been out of the house since Andrew's wedding."

The mention of Andrew's wedding startled Diantha, but there was no trace of guile on Emily's face. The three friends fell into a long and hearty cose on everything which had been happening in Town since Emily's confinement.

How long the chat might have lasted was left up in the air by the arrival of Emily's doctor, who, to both Diantha and Susan's astonishment, turned out to be Dr. Brewster.

The sight of Susan sipping tea with Emily brought Dr. Brewster up short.

"I didn't know you had company, Mrs. Bridger."

"We were just leaving," Diantha said, gathering her fan and gloves. She pecked Emily on the cheek. "Do take care of yourself, my dear. And tell Roddy that his son is as handsome as he is!"

She turned, observing that Susan was involved in conversation with Dr. Brewster.

"How do you go on, Miss Kirkpatrick?" the doctor asked.

"Fully recovered from the grippe," she assured him shyly.

"I'm relieved to hear that it was nothing serious," responded the doctor politely.

Susan smiled. "Odd, sir. At one time you distinctly tasked me for not being ill so you could cure me as your reputation warranted."

The doctor flushed. "I didn't mean any such thing, truly. I was just surprised at getting that letter from your brother. I thought that you were making sport of me." He broke off as Diantha approached, her goodbyes to Emily at an end.

"Your patient is yours, Dr. Brewster," she announced.

"Thank you, Miss Atwood," he murmured.

"What on earth was he saying to you?" Diantha asked Susan later in the carriage.

"Nothing of importance," Susan said, an odd smile on her lips.

Feeling in fine fettle, they returned to Portman Square where their mood suffered a change for the worse. Mr. Lowell, his face a choleric red, was stomping down the front steps to their residence.

"Mr. Lowell, what a pleasant surprise," Diantha greeted Esmeraude's father.

"Surprise it may be. Pleasant, I think not," he barked.

Susan retreated at once to her bedchamber, which left Diantha alone to face Esmeraude's father in the blue salon.

"I'm here because of a visitor I received an hour ago," Lowell began, sinking into a sturdy Hepplewhite and waving off any suggestion of refreshments. "One I shall be happy never to lay eyes on again. Painted, rouged and rude. She carried such a tale of infamy that I could scarcely credit it," he said forcefully.

"If you found the tale preposterous, my lord, I wonder that you did not show her the door immediately," Diantha said in her coolest manner. "You must know that many unscrupulous females seek to take advantage of gentlemen as kindly disposed as yourself."

She darted a quick look at him, hoping she hadn't done it too brown.

"Frightful creature. Bold as brass. That woman claims her daughter and mine are both married to Andrew."

"Mr. Lowell, are you telling me that you and this woman have enjoyed a past dalliance?" she asked in dulcet tones.

A look of utter stupefaction passed over Lowell's face. "I do not mean any such thing!" he roared. "The mere notion of myself and that woman! Your brother is guilty of bigamy. That is what I mean! He married Esmeraude when he was still married to that woman's daughter."

"Bigamy? That's absurd. You can't believe such a tawdry tale."

"She is bringing the proof to me in the form of Andrew's wife, and I don't mean my daughter, Esmeraude. If this story is true..." He left the threat unvoiced.

"Mr. Lowell, please. Andrew would never have married Esmeraude if he were already wed."

Lowell shook his craggy head. "I don't share your confidence. Andrew's been wild. Gambled away his inheritance, didn't he? Even you were showing marked concern about it, weren't you?"

"In dun territory," Lowell went on as Diantha nodded, her eyes focused on his angry face. "I didn't want Esmeraude to marry him and I said so. But that didn't stop him from wooing her. And if I ever get my hands on him!" Lowell's complexion turned pale. "Poor Esmeraude. What will happen to her now? What gentleman would marry her now?"

His eyes filled with tears, and Diantha felt a wave of pity sweep through her. The future he had painted for Esmeraude was not a pleasant one.

"But I'm so certain the greedy woman in question is just out to cause mischief," she said now, hoping with all her heart that this was true.

Blinking hard, Lowell regained his composure. "I have sent men to find Andrew and Esmeraude at the Lakes. When he comes back to London, I will have their marriage annulled and put him in prison where he belongs."

"Prison!" Diantha exclaimed.

"Aye, prison!" Lowell said, looking grim.

CHAPTER TEN

IN VAIN DID DIANTHA TRY to persuade Lowell that there was not a shred of proof to Mrs. Tribbet's wretched tale. But Esmeraude's father remained adamant. Lowell had already spoken to his banker, and Andrew would not receive a single farthing of Esmeraude's fortune.

"And those creditors of his will soon be dunning him again. Not that he'll mind, since he'll be in gaol!" On that Parthian shot, Lowell stomped off.

With every bone in her body trembling, Diantha collapsed into her Trafalgar chair, then sat bolt upright again. Where was Andrew? She would gladly strangle him for landing her in this bumblebroth. And, pray, what could she do?

When she had needed advice in the past, she had sought out her father, but he was gone now. Her other counsellor in the past had been Andrew, who despite his mad-as-a-lark ways, did not lack for sense, but Andrew this time constituted the problem!

And even Miss Bonaventure so full of sensibility was absent. Diantha felt curiously bereft. What could she do? As she sat mulling over the poor choices available, Hughes entered, announcing Devlin and Mr. Fanshaw.

The playwright entered on the heels of the butler, while the viscount languidly brought up the rear. Diantha's brow puckered in surprise at seeing him again, so soon after their meeting in the street. But no doubt he wanted to see more of Susan. Unfortunately, Susan needed her rest after the racketing about they had done this morning.

"I am sorry, but Susan is resting abovestairs," she told the viscount as she shook hands.

Devlin frowned, increasingly puzzled by these continued references to Miss Kirkpatrick. On his visits to Portman Square during this past week, he had twice found himself next to Miss Kirkpatrick. Oddly enough, the only one in a position to arrange that was Diantha.

Before he could respond to her greeting, Fanshaw took his fences in a rush.

"Miss Atwood, I must beg your help on a matter of great urgency."

"Hugo, if you are talking about your epic, I wish you would not," Diantha said. "I told you that I would let you hold the theatrical under my roof. But I am not going to entangle myself in the whos, whats and wherefores of the production."

"But only you can speak sense to Lady Hogarth," Mr. Fanshaw protested, one hand to his vermillion neckcloth. "You know how top lofty she can be. She insists on playing the part of Helen of Troy. And you know very well that Helen is not even mentioned in my play. Troy is a myth. And my play is based on fact, not speculation."

"Perhaps if you told her this," Devlin drawled.

"I have, repeatedly. She will not listen." Mr. Fanshaw clutched a fistful of his hair and appeared on the verge of yanking it out. "And do you want to know what Lady Menloe plans to do?"

"I suppose you must tell us?" Devlin asked in the voice of one inured to misfortune.

"She's playing the part of Sparta and wants to hide a fox in her shirt and have him nibble away."

"I've heard that particular story," the viscount said, his mind boggling at what the broad-bosomed Lady Menloe was prepared to endure for the sake of the theatre. One look at Diantha and he knew by her quaking shoulders that the same thought had waylaid her.

"I won't stand for it! I won't have them turn my play into a spectacle!" Mr. Fanshaw railed, oblivious to the amusement between Diantha and Devlin. "Miss Atwood, I beg you. What shall I do about Lady Hogarth and Lady Menloe?" Fanshaw entreated.

"Let me see if I can persuade Lady Menloe not to hide a fox under her blouse," she suggested. "Perhaps if I tell her that Sir Philip Forth would be greatly shocked, she will acquiesce. You know what particular friends she is with Mrs. Forth."

"And Lady Hogarth?"

"Tell her you will write another play about Troy and she may have the part of Helen then," Devlin suggested.

"Now, I should have thought of that," the playwright said with a chuckle. "Very good. Thank you. I shall go off straightaway and tell her that."

"What a good idea you had," Diantha said after the playwright had left them alone in the blue drawing room. "Another play for Lady Hogarth."

"I just hope that you will not be called upon to host that theatrical here."

"As do I," she said from the bottom of her heart. She gazed across at him, his lanky figure settled comfortably in the chair next to the fire. "I am sorry that Susan is resting, my lord."

"I'm not," he said promptly before realizing that his words might be considered uncivil. "Miss Kirkpatrick must take every precaution against a relapse."

"So you do understand." She felt relieved and heartened to know that he understood Susan's sometimes ticklish state of health. "I am glad you came by, my lord."

"You are?" he asked, conscious of the glow of pleasure her words sparked within him.

Diantha nodded and leaned forward in her chair. "It's about Andrew that I must speak to you."

"I confess I was vexed when Roddy could find no trace of either Andrew or Esmeraude in the Lakes," Devlin replied, disappointed that her interest had more to do with her brother than himself. "I vow, I am thoroughly stumped. When your brother returns I shall give him a trimming, I promise."

"You'll have to stand in line, my lord. Mr. Lowell will do the throttling first. He just left me minutes ago. He's heard the whole wretched story."

Devlin frowned. "But how?" He fixed his blue eyes intently on her brown ones.

"Mrs. Tribbet," Diantha pronounced the name dolefully.

"Blast it."

Diantha nodded. "He has threatened Andrew with gaol upon his return and has taken measures to cut off the funds which were supposed to repay Andrew's debts."

"Serious measures," Devlin said, recalling the prodigious sums Andrew owed to several prominent gentlemen in London.

"It's horrid," Diantha said, unable to sit still another minute. She paced back and forth, nearly crashing into her Chinese screen. "I can't bear to think of Andrew in a dungeon."

Devlin followed her and laid his hand on her shoulder. "Courage, Miss Atwood."

The touch of his hand caused an unfamiliar sensation to flicker in Diantha's breast. She turned and forced a smile onto her lips. "I'm sorry, my lord. I'm turning into such a sad creature."

"Sad? You are no such thing. I've never known a more spirited lady than you. If you like I shall pay a call on Lowell and attempt to dissuade him from prattling on about Mrs. Tribbet to whomever he chances to meet."

"How will you do that?" Diantha asked, hope and scepticism warring within her.

"By reminding him of his daughter's reputation. Telling everyone about this alleged trick of Andrew's will make

Esmeraude fuel for the prattle boxes. No father will want that. I shall speak to him at once."

A wave of gratitude suffused Diantha. "You are so kind to do that," she said.

"Nonsense. Just glad to help."

She felt embarrassed. "After all I've said to you about Andrew's debts. I know now that they were probably all his doing and not yours."

"I did introduce him to one of the greeking establishments," Devlin admitted in strict conscience. "But just once and never again."

"Thank you, my lord, in advance for your talk with Lowell." She held out her hand.

Devlin took it and after the briefest of hesitations brought it to his lips. Astonished, Diantha drew it away quickly as though scorched.

"I shall let you know about my chat with Lowell tomorrow," he said to cover the confusion he felt, as well. "You are still having your Open Day, are you not? I confess I arrange my week round your Tuesdays."

She laughed, recovering her poise. "I should warn you that Fanshaw will be in the throes of his rehearsal tomorrow, but you are always welcome."

Devlin drove his team away from Portman Square in a pensive mood. His thoughts were not on his impending talk with Mr. Lowell but on the lady he'd just left behind. Kissing Miss Atwood's hand. What in thunderation had got into him? She wasn't the type of female a gentleman offered carte blanche to. Miss Atwood definitely was the marrying kind.

Marriage. For several moments he waited for his throat to tighten and his stomach to lurch alarmingly as it always had in the past when he contemplated stepping into parson's mousetrap. But today nothing of the sort occurred. All the attendant difficulties of marriage seemed to pale next to the possibility of a future with Miss Atwood at his side.

Was this love? Devlin felt on uncertain ground. Love was the province of poets. Not his thing at all. And yet ever since he'd met Diantha he felt a need to protect her, offer his assistance, in a way that had never been true with any other lady of his acquaintance. Was it possible?

She would be a wife to make him proud. Intelligent, beautiful and he had a suspicion he'd never get bored with her. But did she want him? For someone used to women casting out lures it was humiliating to admit that Miss Atwood did not seem to search for his attentions. He knew she liked him—she'd said so during the carriage ride to Topping Green—but of late she seemed to fob him off on her companion, Susan.

"Well, no longer," the viscount murmured as his highsteppers turned a corner. He would mount a campaign for Diantha's hand in earnest.

Still absorbed in the details of this campaign, Devlin pulled his carriage in front of Lowell's residence on Hill Street. He was ushered into Lowell's book room by a dourlooking butler. Mr. Lowell sat, nursing a bottle of Madeira. The viscount's expression did not change as he greeted the older man but privately he was alarmed. Lowell did not have the habit of drink.

"Ah, Devlin. What brings you by?"

"I see no point in peeling eggs, Lowell," replied Devlin. "I'm here because I believe you have heard an outrageous tale from a Mrs. Tribbet."

Lowell's hand tightened on his glass. "So you know of it, do you?"

"Miss Atwood confided in me earlier when she also received a visit from Mrs. Tribbet."

"My poor Esmeraude. My poor child!" Lowell dashed the remaining Madeira in his glass onto the fire. The logs hissed. "Atwood'll pay for this, Devlin, I vow."

"Indeed, he will, if he's guilty." Devlin kept his voice calm. "Yet despite his faults, I don't believe Andrew married Esmeraude unlawfully."

"I'd be the happiest man alive if you could prove that."

"When Andrew appears, all will be set to rights."

"And, pray, when will that be?" the older man scoffed. "I warned his sister I'd clap him into a prison as soon as look at him."

"May I suggest we keep this story quiet until his return?"

"I'll do nothing to save that scoundrel's reputation."

Devlin lifted an ironic brow. "What will you do to save Esmeraude's reputation? It will scarcely do her credit if everyone believes Andrew is a bigamist. Do you wish to have your daughter the target of idle speculation?"

Lowell's lips tightened. "Never thought of that. What you've said makes sense, I admit. I don't want Esmeraude's name bandied about. The only one I've seen so far is the Atwood chit."

"Have you told Mrs. Lowell?"

Lowell snorted. "Are you daft, man? She'd have one of her spasms and be in bed a week."

The viscount's lips lifted in a smile. "Very sensible."

"I'll keep silent till Atwood returns," Lowell said grudgingly, "but if this story proves true, I'll loose thunder and lightning bolts on him!"

And he wouldn't be the only one, Devlin thought.

THE FOLLOWING MORNING as Devlin applied the last of a series of dextrous turns to the linen cloth about his neck, he heard a tap on his dressing room door.

It was Lindell, his butler, with the message that a female had called and had been waiting belowstairs for the past thirty minutes.

"She refuses to budge, my lord."

"Did she? Her name?"

"Tribbet, my lord."

Devlin's eyes narrowed. Unconscionable that Mrs. Tribbet would invade his household for mischief making. He would take great pleasure in telling her precisely what he thought of her.

Shrugging into his coat, he stalked down the stairs and into the green drawing room, where he was stunned to discover not Mrs. Tribbet but her daughter waiting for him.

"Miss Tribbet?"

"Oh, Lord Devlin, you are here," she said, rising quickly. "I was beginning to think that you weren't. I know that I shouldn't be here. But I hope you don't mind. I needed to warn you. Mama and I have had a frightful row. She intends to visit Mr. Lowell and tell him about Andrew's scrape."

"Yes, so I have heard from Lowell himself. Her visit had the desired effect."

Miss Tribbet's face paled. "Then I am too late?"

"The damage has been done," he agreed. "But pray, be seated and tell me why you quarrelled with your mother?"

Miss Tribbet sank back in a Chippendale chair, her hands clasped in her lap.

"My mother is not wise. She has not been in wealthy circumstances for years, and she saw this whole episode as an opportunity to better her lot."

"You don't share that feeling?"

She smiled bravely at him. "I just wish the whole thing were over and done with. Even if Andrew were to return and despite him being a gentleman, I should try for an annulment."

"Where is your mother now?"

"At home. I cannot return there."

"Have you no other people to turn to?"

Miss Tribbet shook her head. "I had an aunt who died. She was very kind to me and left the funds for my education. Mama was amazed how well turned out I became. She hoped that some wealthy gentleman might marry me. Or failing that, that I might become some wealthy noble's mistress."

"Outrageous!" he said, appalled at the very idea.

"But she doesn't mean any of it," Miss Tribbet said. "It is only her peculiarities. She suffered numerous disappointments in her youth, and she has a problem with drink."

"Nonetheless, living under the same roof with her cannot induce much assurances of your safety," Devlin said with a frown.

"I shan't be living there with her any longer," Miss Tribbet said. "After our last quarrel, and learning she went to Mr. Lowell after promising me she would not! I have decided that I can't live with her any longer. I shall stay at a hotel here in London while I try to find employment."

The viscount eyed his guest uneasily.

"Employed in what capacity?"

"As a governess."

"I see, well, a hotel is out of the question," Devlin said. "It is no place for a gently nurtured female like yourself."

She blushed.

"And you can't put up here with me, the proprieties being what they are. I could put you up in a house I hold the lease on except that will give rise to speculation that you are, er, *my* mistress."

"Oh, dear," Miss Tribbet said, and blushed again.

"Have you no acquaintances in London?"

Miss Tribbet shook her head sadly. "Just you, my lord, and Miss Atwood."

"Miss Atwood. Yes, you have a tie to her through Andrew."

"But I don't think I should impose on her."

"No," Devlin agreed. It was bound to get sticky if perhaps Lowell called on Diantha and came across Miss Tribbet with her. He thought hard for several minutes, then snapped his fingers.

"You've thought of something, my lord?" Miss Tribbet asked, a hopeful look on her angelic countenance.

"You say you wish a position as a governess?" The viscount stroked his chin, mulling over the sudden inspiration which had struck him a moment ago.

"Yes. Do you know of someone?"

"I know of someone with a son who has no governess at the moment," Devlin said, and began to chuckle to himself. "Come along with me and we'll get you acquainted with them!"

Much to her amazement, Miss Tribbet found herself minutes later sitting next to Devlin in his high-perched phaeton, a position which had never occurred to her in her wildest dreams. She held her breath as they took one turn after another, and when they finally stopped on the flagway at Cavendish Square she let out her breath in a whoosh.

"Too fast for you?" he asked solicitously.

"No, well, perhaps, just a trifle."

"Come. I hope Roddy and Emily are in." He frowned. "Do you think it would be possible for you to adopt another name temporarily? Just in the event your mother reappears in London and calls on people."

"That is a splendid suggestion," Miss Tribbet agreed. "I've always disliked Tribbet, anyway. My aunt's name was Marsh."

"Good. I shall introduce you to Roddy and Emily as Miss Marsh."

Roddy and Emily were at home, and Devlin soon left Miss Tribbet in Emily's capable hands. A brief enquiry into the presence of a babe soon found them exiting to the nursery where the two ladies could view the young master in his kingdom. That afforded Devlin the opportunity to stand Roddy a game of billiards and to sound him out on hiring Miss Tribbet as young Harry's governess.

"Devlin, are you queer in the attic?" Roddy asked, taking a cue stick from his case. "Of all the addled notions. What does young Harry need with a governess now!"

"There is an excellent saying that the earlier one starts, the more one learns."

"Truth to that, I suppose," Roddy agreed, chalking his stick. "But Harry is two weeks old! He can't even hold up his head!"

"He won't need to. But imagine if he were read to in Greek or Latin. He'd be speaking them like a native by the time he is two."

"He'd be a queer nab, is what he'd be," answered young Harry's father. "And you'll be to blame!"

Devlin laughed. "It would be a favour for me, Roddy. Miss Marsh is a friend. She has no people here in London and no position. I can't put her up with me. You know how the quizzes will talk. But you and Emily and the babe are the height of respectability, and no one will question Miss Marsh's position with you. It will just be temporary I assure you."

Roddy shook his head. "I don't know, Dev. It seems I am doing you more favours of late than you have ever done for me!"

"You forget that hell I bailed you out of when you were foxed!"

"No, I haven't," Roddy said cordially. "But who was it who told me about it in the first place?"

"Tell is one thing. It weren't an invitation for you to go there," the viscount said derisively. "And have I told anyone about it?"

"No," Roddy acknowledged. "I don't begrudge hiring the Marsh woman, Dev. But what will Emily think? She might take the notion that I had a tendre for this female!"

"Emily is not a shatterbrain," Devlin said. "And if you have no objection I think I can rely on Miss Marsh to win her over."

In this respect Devlin was correct, for upon the ladies' emerging from the nursery, Emily immediately made for her husband, drawing him aside for a private word.

"Roddy, Miss Marsh is in need of a position."

"Oh?" asked Mr. Bridger.

Emily clasped her hands together. "And I have a splendid idea. I think we should hire her as a governess for Harry. Now, before you say no, do think about what Dr. Watson said at Diantha's Open Day."

"Which Open Day was that?" Roddy asked in a fog. He usually avoided Diantha's Open Days if he could help it.

"He spoke on education, and the importance of young minds to be stimulated."

"Can't get any younger than Harry's," Roddy agreed.

"Then you don't object if Miss Marsh becomes his governess?"

"If she wants the position."

Emily threw her arms about her husband. She had the best husband in the world. She knew as well as he did that Harry didn't need a governess now. But Miss Marsh was so sweet and friendly. Nothing at all like Nurse who was alarmingly competent when it came to Baby. Miss Marsh was gentle and full of praise whenever Emily handled little Harry. Nothing, Emily decided, would give her greater pleasure than to have Miss Marsh join their household.

CHAPTER ELEVEN

"NO, NO, NOT LIKE THAT!" Mr. Fanshaw yanked at his hair as the rehearsal Tuesday morning spluttered to a stop. By the time the actual play was staged seven days hence, he'd be bald, Diantha predicted, standing just outside the doorway of her Long Gallery.

The playwright resembled a Bedlamite suffering all the ill effects of a profound case of the jitters.

"And if medicine could cure Fanshaw of that I would be grateful," she said to Dr. Brewster later as he stopped to speak to her after a brief call on Susan.

"I'm afraid I have no such magic potion in here," Dr. Brewster said, holding up his bag. "But I could mix something up for him."

Diantha laughed. She had to admit that Dr. Brewster was not half as odious as she'd thought before. Indeed, he had visited Susan twice in the past week to check on her progress, and these visits certainly appeared to hasten Susan's recovery.

After the doctor left, she peered into the Long Gallery, where the rehearsal was once again under way. Thank goodness both Lady Menloe and Lady Hogarth had acquiesced to the suggestions offered by Diantha and Fanshaw. No Helen of Troy and no nibbling fox. As she backed out of the doorway lest Fanshaw see her, she collided bodily with Devlin, who was just on his way in.

The viscount sustained the blow manfully, holding on to her shoulders and turning her round to face him.

She was wearing a peach-coloured frock with lace-trimmed sleeves. Old-fashioned perhaps, but he thought it very alluring.

"Good morning, Miss Atwood," he said.

She hushed him with a wave of her hand and pulled him away from the Long Gallery.

"Not so loud, I beg you. I don't want Fanshaw to see me."

"Do you intend to hole up in your book room?" he hazarded a guess.

"You have found me out, sir," Diantha confessed.

"And Miss Kirkpatrick?"

"Is in bed until the rehearsal is ended," she said.

"I have a notion. Take a ride with me in my carriage," he suggested. "You need diversion."

The thought of riding with him was tempting. "But it is my Open Day," she lamented. "Deserting my guests in their hour of need would be the outside of enough even for me!"

"Your guests are all involved in the theatrical," he pointed out. "No one will notice. Indeed, you don't want them to notice. Besides, I have something I must tell you in private."

Her curiosity piqued by these words, Diantha summoned her butler and informed him that she would be stepping out for a brief drive with Devlin.

"And I hope that doesn't ruin my reputation," she murmured when she was comfortably settled in the high-perched phaeton. She felt a trifle dizzy as she gazed down at the street below.

"You are safe with me," he assured her, setting his horses off at a brisk trot.

Her brows flew up. "Heavens, I know that. Anyway, I am past the age to worry about chaperons."

"Do I perceive you at your last prayers, ma'am?"

She chuckled and nodded, holding on as he took the corner without pausing. "Both Susan and I joke about it in private." She inhaled a deep breath. "How nice this is."

"Far too nice a day to be cooped up," Devlin agreed as he turned into the Park.

It was not the fashionable hour, so she didn't have to worry that the pinks or quizzes would laugh at her fusty old walking dress which had been refurbished only the day before.

"What is it you wish to tell me which you don't want anyone to overhear?" she asked, turning towards him.

The heart-shaped face she lifted to him was so delectable that Devlin very nearly reined in his team and kissed her. He restrained himself. Not only was it de trop to make love to a lady in public view, but only remember how she had treated Sylvester when the inventor had made his offer. Miss Atwood did not like declarations catching her by surprise. Nice and slow, that was the thing. He reminded himself of this strategy to woo her. First a drive in the Park. Then perhaps a trip to the Opera. Maybe a discreet invitation from his mother to visit their family estate.

"Devlin, did you hear me?" she asked, wondering why he was staring at her in that blockish fashion. Did she have a smudge on her nose?

"Indeed, yes." He gave his head a shake and brought his eyes back to the road in front of him. "I've spoken to Lowell and received his vow of silence at least until Andrew returns."

"Thank you, my lord. That is good news."

"Delay your jobations a moment. There is an added complication. Miss Tribbet quarreled with her mother and has left Topping Green and come to London."

"Oh, Devlin, no!" Diantha shrank back against the carriage seat. This muddle grew worse with each passing day.

"Don't agitate yourself," he said, laying a gloved hand on one of hers. "She was seeking employment, and I persuaded Roddy and Emily to hire her as a governess for young Harry. Yes, I know he doesn't need a governess yet, but at least she will be safe under their roof.''

"Do they know the truth about her?'' Diantha asked, absorbing this news as the carriage rolled near the Serpentine.

"Only that she is a friend of mine. But if you chance to meet her there, you must pretend not to know her. Her name is Miss Marsh. We thought it best not to use Tribbet. One doesn't know how large a swath her mother has cut through London.''

"How clever of you. I'm sure Andrew will appreciate the pains you have taken to help him with his problem.''

It wasn't Andrew's appreciation he wanted but hers. And not appreciation but love. She really ought not to look up at him in that delectable way or he would not be responsible for his actions. He tore his gaze free from hers and stared down at his team of Welshbreds.

"Would you like to take the reins?'' he asked suddenly.

Her eyes lit up. Was he roasting her?

"Here ...'' He handed the ribbons to her gently. "This stretch of the road is straight and clear.''

Diantha had never driven such prime cattle before. Devlin kept one hand on hers and coaxed his team into following her lead.

"You have a gentle touch. The team responds well to it,'' he said, inhaling the sweet scent of her hair.

"Thank you, my lord,'' she said. "But compared to you I am the merest whipster.''

"I think you can let them go a little faster,'' he said.

Diantha quickly obeyed, tapping the reins lightly against the back of the horses. Immediately they darted forward.

"Steady ...'' he murmured.

A few minutes later, they rounded a bend, and he saw Sylvester standing in a grass field, throwing a stick up in the air.

"Slow down,'' he murmured.

Dutifully Diantha obeyed.

"Sylvester!" Devlin called out.

Recognizing Devlin's carriage, Sylvester ran forward with a smile which faded when he recognized the lady in the seat next to the viscount.

"Good day, Devlin," he said shortly.

"Good day, Sylvester," Diantha called down. "I'm pleased to see the cat no longer has your tongue."

"Hmmph!" Too late, Sylvester realized that he had broken his solemn oath not to speak to a female, particularly the one in front of him.

"Now, Sylvester, don't be a gapeseed. You can't keep giving every female in London the cut," Devlin said.

"Why not? William Fortescue does."

"Fortescue has seventy years in his dish. He's entitled to a crotchety old age. You are not."

"I have nothing to say to Miss Atwood." Sylvester crossed his arms on his chest.

"But I have much to say to you, Sylvester," Diantha replied. "I am so sorry that I refused your offer in that hen-witted way. I've never had an offer before, so I didn't know the proper way to do such a thing. Can't we be friends? I have missed you. Portman Square is not the same."

"You have? It isn't?" Sylvester asked, his indifference melting in the face of her sincerity.

"So has Susan. What kind of stick is that you have there?"

"It's a throwing stick," he said eagerly. "The design is supposed to bring it back to the thrower, but I confess it hasn't worked yet for me."

"Is it your invention?" Devlin asked. Sylvester quickly answered that he'd heard about it from one of his cousins who'd gone on expedition to Oceania.

"Native tribes in Australia are said to use it. It's called a boomerang."

"When you have it perfected, I hope you will demonstrate it to us at an Open Day," Diantha said.

"Indeed I shall." The inventor frowned. "But today is your Open Day. Why are you not there?"

"We are hiding from Fanshaw," Devlin confessed.

Sylvester grinned. "No interest in theatricals, either of you?" he teased and Diantha knew their quarrel had come to a successful conclusion. Thanks to Devlin.

Later, back in her sitting room as she tried to refurbish yet another old dress, she realized that she had much to thank the viscount for. All his help with Andrew's troubles, finding employment for Miss Tribbet and now helping to mend her quarrel with Sylvester.

She owed him much. But what could she offer him in return? Frowning, she pinned a ribbon on the sleeve of the dress. Then the answer flew into her brain. Susan, of course. Devlin was dangling after Susan. Diantha could repay him for his many kindnesses by persuading her friend to look at him in a favourable light. Of course such a payment would extract its own considerable toll on Diantha's heart.

AT LADY HOGARTH'S musicale Wednesday evening, Diantha learned that Lowell had made good his threat to withhold the money due Andrew's creditors.

As she sat with Susan attempting to keep a smile on her face during the abominable harp playing of Lady Hogarth's simpering niece, she noticed Mr. Jonathon Baillie seated a few rows away, attempting to catch her attention.

After the harp playing, Mr. Baillie manoeuvred his way to her side, asking for a moment of her time.

Mr. Baillie, a stoop-shouldered gentleman with a prominent Adam's apple, rubbed his hands nervously together as Diantha stepped to one side with him.

"I've had a talk with my banker, Miss Atwood. It seems that the money your brother promised me is not in my account."

Diantha flicked open her Chinese fan. "Really?" she enquired. "Most unusual."

"It's more than that," Baillie protested. "I haven't seen a single groat. Andrew promised me before the wedding that I would have payment in full." He cleared his throat. "I had made arrangements of my own to buy some new cattle at Tattersall's and to make some purchases for my estate."

"I think you shall just have to wait on Andrew's return," Diantha returned civilly.

"I can't," Mr. Baillie raised his voice and glowered darkly. "Truth is, Miss Atwood, I've debts of my own. Gaming debts," he muttered. "And my creditors have been pressing me."

"How unfortunate," Diantha said, closing her fan. Above all, she wished to avoid a distasteful scene. "How much does my brother owe you?"

"Ten thousand pounds."

"What!" she ejaculated. She could no sooner lay her hands on ten thousand pounds than on the moon. "I can't pay you such a sum. But," she said quickly as he looked ready to speak, "what if I advanced you two thousand pounds?"

A wary expression came over Baillie's lean face. "Five."

"Three."

A light of respect kindled in his eyes. He nodded. "If you can advance me the three thousand pounds by Monday, I can stave off my creditors until your brother returns."

"Done!" she agreed, and he went off to join the throng at the refreshment table.

Diantha made no attempt to follow. She had more pressing matters on her mind than the contemplation of delectables from the Hogarth kitchen. Namely, how to lay her hands on the three thousand pounds she'd just promised Baillie?

Her income was ample for her needs. She had inherited a tidy competence from her mother, but she was no heiress like Esmeraude.

Her establishment, while comfortable enough, entailed a good many expenses with the servants and continual guests. So where would she find the money?

Across the hall, enjoying a plate of lobster patties, Lord Devlin noticed Miss Atwood's solitary contemplation. He had seen her deep in conversation with Baillie minutes earlier and wondered how on earth the two were acquainted? Manoeuvreing his way through the thick of the crowd, he stopped a few yards away from Roddy and Sylvester.

His two friends were standing with Sir Philip Forth, who was droning on about the dangers of gluttony. Judging by the glazed expression of their eyes, the two men were in need of rescue, but Devlin was not interested in a lecture from the moralist. A tray of sweetmeats temporarily diverted him. And it was poised over it that Roddy and Sylvester found him when they had finally extricated themselves from Forth's grip.

"Devlin, how could you just leave us to that long-winded bag pudding?" Roddy declared.

"Yes," Sylvester agreed. "Very bad form, Devlin."

"You seemed thoroughly entranced by his stories. Which was it—the one about his drunkard of an uncle who came to grief and was found with a broken neck at the bottom of a staircase? Or the one about his fourth cousin who gambled away the family fortune and went about in sackcloth and ashes?"

"It was about the drunkard uncle," Roddy said, much struck, "though he said nothing about a staircase. What are we doing at this musicale, anyway?" Roddy demanded. "Come home with me and let's play some billiards."

Sylvester seconded this motion, and they looked towards Devlin to make it unanimous.

"Sorry, lads. I am still eating, and I have plans for later this evening."

"Looking for a ladybird to replace Mrs. Whorley?" Roddy enquired with a knowing wink.

"No!" Devlin said sharply.

"Just a jest. No need to get your back up," Roddy said hastily, observing the viscount's thundercloud face. "You must know that the quizzes are laying bets as to which lady will be Mrs. Whorley's successor."

"Are they?" Devlin felt a flicker of distaste. How could he conduct a proper courtship of Miss Atwood when any sign of partiality would give rise to speculation and rumour?

"I think I see Forth coming this way, Roddy," Sylvester interrupted.

"Oh, devil. Good night to you, Devlin," Roddy said and took Sylvester off for a round of billiards.

Sir Philip approached the viscount with a vacuous smile. "Where are your two young cronies off to, my lord?"

"A game of billiards, I believe," Devlin replied.

"Billiards," Forth sniffed. He cast a baleful eye at the glass in Devlin's hand. "And is that champagne you are drinking?"

"No, Forth," Devlin said patiently. "Not champagne. Claret, your great-uncle's favourite drink!"

The moralist reddened, then, obviously believing that Devlin was beyond hope, went off to preach to someone else.

A choke of laughter alerted the viscount to someone behind him. He turned to find Diantha nearby.

"Good evening, Miss Atwood."

"What an outrageous fellow you are, my lord," she said, amusement dancing in her dark eyes.

"Yes," he agreed, "an ugly customer. Has no one warned you about me?"

She laughed at his self-description, and he felt an irresistible urge to cup her chin and kiss her mouth. He fought the impulse. To show any sign of affection for her would make her a target for the quizzes.

"Miss Kirkpatrick is not with you?" he asked, searching for a neutral topic.

"Yes, she is," Diantha said, jolted by this reminder again of his interest in Susan. "She only stopped to talk to some friends. I'm sure I can persuade her to join us, if you wish."

"No, that shan't be necessary." He had no wish to single out Miss Kirkpatrick and make her the target for speculation. What a coil this was to court a respectable female. No wonder gentlemen remained bachelors.

"I don't see Fanshaw here tonight."

"Probably because he is rewriting the play. I vow, every time he holds a rehearsal, there is a new script. The actors are quite up in arms."

Devlin smiled. "Undoubtedly he will get a fever of the brain from all the activity. What time is the performance?"

"Eight on Monday night. Do you mean to attend?"

"Such was my intention, unless you'd rather I didn't," he said.

"No, of course not. You are always welcome. Although I didn't think amateur theatricals were much in your line."

"They aren't," he agreed. "But I sometimes make an exception in special cases. What is Fanshaw's wretched play about?" Devlin asked.

She nearly choked on her champagne. "Government."

"Government? I see..." He patted her on the back, a move that sparked an attack of the hiccoughs. Sir Philip, passing them and observing Miss Atwood's afflicted state, rolled his eyes heavenward.

"Now, hic, he will think I'm foxed," she said, laughing and hiccoughing at the same time.

Devlin brought her a glass of water and bade her drink it down while holding her nose.

"What?"

"It's an old trick. It's supposed to work. Would you like me to hold your nose for you?"

"No, that's ridiculous. Hic...oh, I shall try it." She pinched her nostrils tight and swallowed the water in a huge gulp.

"Bravo, Miss Atwood." He took the empty glass away from her. "Any hiccoughs left?"

"No, not one. You've done the thing. Now what were we talking about?"

"Fanshaw's wretched play. On government, you did say?"

"His play covers government through the ages, from the ancient Greeks to the modern empire, I think it is. And having observed some of the rehearsals, I must acknowledge that I pity the poor Greeks and the Gauls. Fanshaw has taken considerable liberties with their past."

"Have you made a prodigious study of the Gauls?" he asked, astonished.

"I have been reading Caesar's account—a jaundiced view, I grant you, but still quite educational."

"Have you ever been across the Channel?"

"Once, as a child. But I don't remember much about it. I should like to see it again, and Italy, too. I suppose you took the grand tour years ago?"

"Yes," he admitted.

"Was it as beautiful as they say?"

Not half as beautiful as you, my dear. He almost spoke aloud the thought in his mind.

"They are beautiful," he said now. "The Alps are particularly impressive. And the sunshine in Italy is not to be imagined."

"I should like to see it some day."

And he would love to show it to her, perhaps on their wedding trip. But how the devil was he to wed her when he couldn't even court her properly?

"Perhaps you shall, someday," he said softly. "I noticed Mr. Baillie speaking with you. Is he an old acquaintance?"

"No," she said quickly, wondering if she ought to confide this new worry in Devlin. But she decided against it.

She must learn to solve her problems by herself lest she grow too accustomed to seeking counsel from Susan's future husband.

CHAPTER TWELVE

MRS. WHORLEY LOOPED the belt of her dressing gown about her waist, ignoring the baronet crossing the threshold into her private room.

"I am sorry, my dear," Sir Arthur Long said in his indolent way. "I tried to get here sooner but the oddest-looking creature accosted me. Perhaps this will put things right between us."

The present in his hand squelched the sharp words of dismissal the widow was about to utter.

"Oh, Arthur!" She threw her arms round him, abandoning all signs of temper. Could this be the ruby necklace, finally? Heaven knew she'd dropped enough hints. She snatched up the gift, tore off the wrapping and unearthed a strand of topaz beads.

"Topaz!" she said, crestfallen, resisting the urge to hurl the beads in the vacuous face next to her. The very idea. When he knew full well she had her heart set on the rubies. Men! Their stupidity exceeded all bounds!

"Do you like them, my dear?" Sir Arthur asked. "You know I told you before that you are the only female of my acquaintance who can wear the colour yellow."

With difficulty Thalia controlled her disappointment.

"Yes, of course I like them. But so many men have told me that rubies bring out my colouring more than topaz. Did I mention Rundell has a stunning ruby necklace?"

"No, I don't believe so."

Mrs. Whorley expelled an angry breath. She had had many beaux in her day, but Sir Arthur had to be the stupidest of them all. She tossed the beads carelessly back in the box.

"What's this about some creature accosting you?" she asked.

"A dreary connexion several times removed," Sir Arthur divulged, surveying a tray of restoratives.

Mrs. Whorley's eyes narrowed, wondering if the baronet could be inventing the tale. "I daresay she is a beauty?"

Sir Arthur nearly pitched the sherry he was pouring down his shirt front. "By Jove, Thalia, what an idea. She's not even passably good-looking. The wretched woman only wanted to know if I'd seen her daughter. Seems the chit ran off to London from Topping Green and can't be found—"

"Topping Green?" Mrs. Whorley interrupted Sir Arthur's tedious recital. "What is the name of your connexion?"

"Oh, let me think." The baronet tapped his forehead as though to jog his memory. "What is the female's name? Tipton? Tripton? Something of the sort."

Mrs. Whorley fought the urge to box his ears. "Could it have been Tribbet?" she asked.

"Perhaps. Yes. It may well have been. Why? Do you know the woman?" he asked, looking at her over the rim of his sherry glass.

"I have heard the name before," she said obliquely, running a fingertip over the arm of her chair. "You say the daughter ran off. Why?"

"Mrs. Tribbet would only say because of a broken heart. Seemed to think that a gentleman had ruined her daughter."

Mrs. Whorley's pulse quickened. By heavens, this was an on-dit she could use to considerable advantage against a certain viscount. "Ruined," she said now, "a most serious charge."

"Mind you, I've never laid eyes on the daughter. She might be a hurly-burly sort of female."

"Who was the gentleman who ruined her?"

"Mrs. Tribbet wouldn't say. Claimed she and her daughter fell into a terrible quarrel because of her saying too much about the situation."

"And what assistance do you propose to offer her?" enquired Mrs. Whorley.

Sir Arthur looked even more befuddled than usual.

"No help at all. Dash it all, Thalia, I don't know this woman or her daughter. A fellow can't be too careful."

"You turned her out, then?"

"I suggested she go back to Topping Green where her daughter might be in communication with her. Now really," he said, placing his glass down on a dressing table, "that is enough of those tiresome people. Have I told you how fetching you look tonight, my dear?"

"Thank you, Arthur," she said, letting the dressing gown fall from her shoulders, all the while thinking ahead to the morrow when she would summon Kroll, her East End investigator, back with orders to find just where Miss Tribbet of Topping Green had disappeared to when she arrived in London.

KROLL, HOWEVER, PROVED resistant to her demands that he pick up the threads of his investigation.

"You didn't want to pay me my full pay last time," he pointed out the next day at Grosvenor Square.

"That was only a temporary necessity," Mrs. Whorley said, pouring him a glass of claret. "I was making some dire economies, you see."

"Still less reason for me to take your case," he murmured with a sidelong glance at her.

Mrs. Whorley cursed her own slip of the tongue. Maybe it was seeing so much of Sir Arthur. His stupidity was contagious.

"You are the very best man for this job," she said, handing him the claret. "I don't know if anyone can find the trail."

Mr. Kroll puffed out his cheeks. "I can find any trail."

"Yes, I know. You told me that Devlin went to Topping Green to see a Miss Tribbet. Now you must find out where she went in London. You must check the Mail Coach stations, visit the posting houses."

"I must do a lot of work, and for what appears to be very little money," Kroll said, in no hurry to accept the case. The widow was a demanding client, but her claret was excellent.

"What about this, then?" she said, holding out the box of topaz beads. "Will these persuade you?"

The ferret-faced investigator laced the beads round his fingers. He didn't trust Mrs. Whorley, but he did have a favourite woman friend who enjoyed pretty jewellery.

"Very well. I'll see what I can find."

THE SCOWLING MAN holding a magnifying glass to one eye craned his neck as he surveyed the paintings on the wall before him. Step by careful step he moved, dislodging dust and cobwebs.

"I've never seen a collection like this before, ma'am," he said finally putting his magnifying glass away.

Diantha beamed. "Good. How much do you think the paintings will fetch me?"

"I'd say five hundred pounds."

Diantha clapped her hands in delight. After two days' wondering where she could find the money to pay Andrew's creditor, salvation was now at hand.

"Five hundred pounds each. That's a good price, indeed."

"Oh, no, Miss Atwood," Mr. Hathaway looked shocked. "Five hundred pounds total."

"How can that be, Mr. Hathaway?" Diantha asked, stricken to the core. "My parents spent considerable sums amassing this collection."

The appraiser wiped a cobweb from his forehead with a handkerchief. "It's a rather ramshackle collection, if you excuse my language. I see they favoured young painters whose works are the most lacking in value. You might be able to find a collector who will take a chance at acquiring one painting or two, but hardly the whole thing and not at five hundred pounds a painting.''

"Oh, dear." Now how would she be able to pay Mr. Baillie?

"I wish I could have brought you more cheerful news," Mr. Hathaway said.

"It's not your fault that Mother and Father would wish to collect what they did. It's just that I had hoped the collection would bring me three thousand pounds."

Mr. Hathaway stared at her incredulously. "Three thousand!"

"Yes, an air dream, I know..." She flicked off the lingering dust about her skirt. "Shall we go down, sir? It's dreadfully dusty."

"One moment, Miss Atwood," Mr. Hathaway said. His scowl was replaced by a thoughtful look. "I believe I caught a glimpse on my way in of a vase which you have in your hallway. It's a striking piece."

"A Ming vase," Diantha said. "And I have a twin to it in a bedchamber. But they're not for sale."

"A pity," the appraiser said with feeling. "The two would undoubtedly fetch more than three thousand pounds."

"They would?" she asked, considering this judiciously.

"I will need a closer look at them, but I think a buyer could be found who would be willing to pay four thousand pounds."

"I only need three thousand."

"You must realize that I take a commission from the sale," he said with a deprecating smile.

"Yes, of course. But the vases were not for sale." Indeed they were her most prized possessions. Just thinking of how much her father loved the vases brought tears to her eyes.

"Then I suppose you will have to find the three thousand pounds you need from some other source. You could, of course, borrow the money."

Diantha pulled off a loose strand of cobweb from her hair. Sighing, she glanced round the crowded attic. So many things, but so few of worth. Perhaps she should just sell the Ming vases. How could she think of enjoying them with Andrew locked away in a debtors' prison?

"Do you know someone who might purchase the vases?" she asked.

"Indeed, I do, Miss Atwood," Mr. Hathaway assured her. "I have several prospects in mind."

"I will not accept a penny less than three thousand pounds as my share."

"You won't be disappointed," Mr. Hathaway said, beaming. "I shall just go belowstairs and have a closer look at the vase. If you would be so kind as to bring the twin down at your earliest convenience." With a smile replacing his scowl, he climbed down the attic stairs.

"Who was that man, Di?" Susan asked an hour later after Mr. Hathaway had completed his inspection and left. "I vow, he had cobwebs on his coat."

"I wouldn't be at all surprised," Diantha murmured, still reeling from the enormity of having sold the vases.

"And you have some on your hem," Susan pointed out.

Diantha quickly dusted off her skirt. "Oh, dear, I suppose I shall have to change. Fanshaw is due to arrive any moment for more rehearsals. Will you see that he doesn't destroy my Long Gallery?"

"Yes, of course," Susan said, not realizing until she was in the Long Gallery with Mr. Fanshaw that Diantha had not explained just who the dusty man was. Her friend was growing quite secretive of late.

MISS KIRKPATRICK was not the only person in London to find a friend becoming increasingly introspective. Devlin's friends, Roddy and Sylvester, found him more peevish of late.

"I think he's in love," Sylvester speculated to Mr. Bridger during one of their billiard matches at Cavendish Square.

"Don't be a nodcock," Roddy hooted. "Devlin's been in love a score of times. It's never made him act so queerly."

"Perhaps that's because it wasn't real love, merely a light-hearted dalliance."

"If so, who do you think he's fallen in love with?" Mr. Bridger asked, making a particularly tricky shot in the corner pocket.

"Haven't the foggiest. Perhaps it's a schoolroom miss he's met in the country. You know what they say about hardened bachelors. They inevitably give their hand to females who haven't even been to London."

Roddy rejected this with a frown. "Devlin's never cared for milk-and-water misses. Actually, the only female I can recall that has interested him of late has been Andrew's sister, Diantha."

"Miss Atwood? The bluestocking?" Sylvester suffered a profound shock. He had offered for Diantha only a few weeks earlier himself. And yet, he was obliged to admit that an alliance between them would not augur well. While one between Devlin and Diantha might have all the makings of a suitable match.

"He has been attending her Open Day."

"I thought that was owing to his inadequate kitchen," Sylvester said.

"Maybe that is just a ruse for a deeper interest. And if so, that may be why he nearly bit my head off when I asked about his current amour."

"He's being protective of her reputation."

"Poor Dev, he has got it bad," Roddy said with a laugh, completing the entire run of the table. He and Sylvester were just laying aside their sticks when Emily and Miss Tribbet came in from an excursion to a linen drapers.

"Come and see what I have bought, Roddy," Emily coaxed. "You too, Sylvester."

"Lud, I know nothing about draperies," Sylvester protested, noticing that Emily's companion was a comely young woman with a beguiling smile.

"A famous inventor such as yourself must certainly have an opinion about draperies. Perhaps you will invent one that will not burn in the event of fire!" Roddy said, leading the way out of the billiard room and into the drawing room where the draperies were displayed.

"Are you an inventor, then?" Miss Tribbet asked, looking quite riveted by such a statement.

"Sylvester has invented any number of things," offered Roddy. "What about the library stairs at Miss Atwood's residence? You invented that, didn't you? And that stick you've been fiddling with?"

"Stick? A new walking stick?" Emily asked, still absorbed in the rich assortment of brocades she'd brought home.

"No, it's not a walking stick. It's a throwing stick," Sylvester explained, falling into step next to Miss Tribbet.

"A throwing stick? Is it a play thing for a dog? You throw it and he fetches it?" she enquired.

"No. Well, in a way, except he wouldn't have to fetch it. You see, it returns on its own."

"Really? How extraordinary. And you invented it?"

"Oh, no. Tribesmen in Australia have used something similar. I can't take credit for inventing it. Fact of the matter, I'm still trying to perfect it. Doesn't seem to want to return to me the way it's supposed to," he confessed gloomily.

"Perhaps the problem lies in the angle of the toss," Miss Tribbet said.

Sylvester brightened. "You could very well be right," he agreed. "Would you like to try it sometime? When I have it perfected, I mean."

"Yes, very much, if Mrs. Bridger doesn't mind."

"Now Margaret, I told you to call me Emily," said her employer. "And of course I won't mind if Sylvester shows you his throwing stick. Now turn your mind to the brocades, please. All of you," Emily commanded, and after a vigorous discussion, they settled on the pale green for the baby's room.

"The colour is so restful for a child's room," Miss Tribbet concluded. "Almost like being in the country."

"Are you from the country, Miss—" Sylvester asked, seated quietly with her in a corner of the room.

"Trib—I mean, Marsh," Miss Tribbet said. "I'm from Hertfordshire. I confess I miss it."

"But surely the city has so much diversion."

"Oh, yes. London is ever so grand," she acknowledged. "But it's rather noisy, isn't it? And there are so many people. Not to mention the crush of traffic. One coachman nearly ran me down in the street today."

"You are seeing the worst of London. What about the good? The Zoo. The Gardens? Have you been to the Museums? And what about the Opera or Drury Lane?"

Miss Tribbet flushed. "You mistake my position, sir. I'm here as a governess to young Harry and as a companion to Emily. I'm not free to see the sights, as it were."

"Surely Emily wouldn't object if you spent one evening out," Sylvester said and promptly went off to discuss the matter with Emily and Roddy.

Mrs. Bridger, far from begrudging her employee the night off, bade her take two.

"You are very good, but I mustn't," Miss Tribbet said, when the inventor returned. "Really, my lord, you are kind to invite me, but I have no wish to go to the amusements that you sketched."

"Oh?" Sylvester's face fell. He'd been indulging in the air dream of showing Miss Marsh the Opera and Drury Lane. What manner of man was he that every female paid him hardly a second look?

Miss Tribbet felt a guilty pang at the disappointment on Sylvester's face. She thought him quite civil and charming, and he certainly was intelligent.

"It's not that I wouldn't want to," Miss Tribbet said. "But I lack the proper wardrobe, and the cost of refurbishing it would be prohibitive. But I should like to see your throwing stick sometime."

Sylvester felt immediately uplifted. It wasn't him she found wanting, but the lack of the appropriate wardrobe, something he could fully understand. Perhaps it were best if he just took Miss Marsh out sometime to the Park to toss the throwing stick.

"ARE THEY NOT THE MOST exquisite vases you have ever seen?" Mr. Hathaway demanded in his office. The afternoon light filtering through the bay window fell on the glazed porcelain and accentuated the beautiful blue and white colours.

Viscount Devlin examined the glaze through his quizzing glass. "Very pretty."

Mr. Hathaway snapped his head back up in rigid shock. "Pretty? My lord, the vases are a triumph." As befitted one who served collectors in their every wish he did not expect raptures from someone of Devlin's rank, but certainly he could manage more enthusiasm.

Mr. Hathaway frowned. He had thought Devlin the best buyer for the Ming pair, but if the viscount didn't want them, he could always advise Petersham about the pieces. Petersham, of course, was subject to freakish whims and harder to deal with. Hathaway much prefered Devlin's forthright ways. Either he liked a piece or he didn't.

And he didn't seem to like these.

Wondering if he had been foolhardy to advance Miss Atwood the sum of three thousand pounds, Hathaway picked up his magnifying glass. Knowing the viscount's unerring eye, the appraiser went over the vases meticulously, yet no flaw in the porcelain or the glaze or the composition could he detect.

"I'm sorry, my lord. I thought that you would be cast in alt at such an opportunity. My apologies."

Devlin looked up from the window. "What? Oh, the vases. They will do, Hathaway."

The appraiser relaxed. "You'll take them?"

"What is the price being asked?"

"Four thousand pounds."

"Rather dear."

"A matched pair," Hathaway pointed out.

Devlin nodded. "Very well. I'll take them both."

"Excellent, my lord." Mr. Hathaway began sharpening a quill.

The viscount crossed to the desk and pulled out his cashbook. "How comes it that the owner is selling such a pair? Bankruptcy, perhaps?"

"I don't know, my lord," Hathaway said, dipping the quill in ink.

"You did obtain the vases legally, Hathaway?"

The appraiser rose from his chair. "My lord, I am no thief."

"Take a damper. I know you're not. But one can't be too careful." Devlin picked up the quill and wrote out the cheque. "Why was the owner selling?"

"She seemed rather desperate for cash."

"Poor creature. Does she have anything else worth selling?"

Hathaway shook his head. "Just odd bits of paintings. I wouldn't recommend any of them, my lord."

Devlin blotted the banknote with sand and blew on it before handing it to the other man. "Who was the previous owner?"

"Miss Diantha Atwood of Portman Square," the appraiser said.

Devlin paused. "Diantha Atwood, you say? Desperate for money?"

"Very desperate, my lord."

CHAPTER THIRTEEN

"SUSAN, HAVE YOU SEEN—oh, I beg your pardon!" Diantha halted in the doorway of the music room as she beheld Miss Kirkpatrick at the pianoforte with her blond head nestled comfortably against the broad shoulder of Dr. Brewster.

The two drew apart at once.

"Oh, Diantha. Do come in, pray. I was just playing my new composition for Angus—I mean Dr. Brewster."

"You needn't explain to me," Diantha said, though in truth she was beset with the liveliest curiosity.

"But I feel I must," the physician said, rubbing his moustache. He rose with Susan's hand clasped in his. "Miss Atwood, you will be the first to know I have made Miss Kirkpatrick an offer, and she has done me the great honour of saying yes."

For a brief moment Diantha could do naught but stare at her friend in rigid shock. Emotions tumbled within her breast. Chief among these were happiness and astonishment for her friend, and a wild relief for herself. Devlin would not after all become Susan's husband. At the same time, she knew how bitterly disappointed Devlin would be.

"You're not displeased, are you, Diantha?" Susan asked, searching her face with concern.

"Not if this is what you want, my dear."

"It is my most cherished wish," Susan replied with such feeling that there could be no doubt where her heart lay.

Dr. Brewster smiled warmly across at Susan. "And mine, as well. I shall have to get acquainted with your brother

soon. Bad form to marry his sister without communicat-
ing my intentions to him. Now, I must be off. Good day,
Miss Atwood."

"I shall see you to the door, Angus," Susan said, following him quickly.

In the now-deserted music room, Diantha gathered the
folds of her blue dimity and sat down on the piano bench.
Susan to marry Dr. Brewster, not Devlin.

"Not Devlin," she murmured, feeling an irrepressible
hope beginning to dawn within her. Yet she couldn't help
recalling Devlin's steadfast interest in Susan.

"Diantha, you do like Angus, don't you?" Susan was
back, and her question summoned Diantha from her rev-
erie.

"Certainly I like Angus," she replied. "But I didn't
know that you did."

Susan bit her lip. "I don't suppose I knew my own feelings until today when he offered for me. He'd been visiting
about twice a week and was always so kind and full of interesting stories about his patients. I found myself waiting
for his visits."

"But marriage is an entirely different situation," Diantha pointed out. "Have you considered what life will be as
a physician's wife?"

"Oh, yes, Diantha. And that is the good thing. You
know how invalidish I used to be. I can really sympathize
with his patients and help him."

"But think what you will be giving up if you marry
Brewster."

To Diantha's astonishment Susan's eyes filled with tears,
and she threw herself on Diantha's chest. "My dear friend,
I have. You mustn't think that I am deserting you."

"Oh, Susan, I am not worried about myself!" Diantha
said, warmly embracing her friend. "I shall miss you
dreadfully, but I shall endeavor to carry on. It's just that
you have other suitors who could offer you a different sort
of life than Dr. Brewster, not that I mean to say anything

against him," she said hastily. "Just do consider the total picture."

"What other suitors do you mean?" Susan asked, looking puzzled.

"Well, Devlin, for example."

"Devlin!" Miss Kirkpatrick choked. "I vow, you must have windmills in your head to think such a thing, Diantha."

"He comes to Portman Square almost every day. He's always so solicitous of your well-being. And he was the one who fetched Dr. Hardy for you."

"He only fetched Dr. Hardy because Angus went to see him and demanded he do so," Susan pointed out. "And I hope you are just funning. I should not like to think Devlin may have a tendre for me. He never spoke a word of such feelings to me," she fretted.

"He's a gentleman, Susan. Besides would it make a difference now? Would you take him over Dr. Brewster?" Diantha asked, conscious of a real anxiety. Would Susan knowing now of Devlin's interest throw over the good doctor?

But Susan shook her head so vigorously that one of her braids dislodged itself from the top of her head. "No. It's plain as five pins that Devlin is much richer and has rank far exceeding Angus, but he'll never win my heart. I hope he doesn't make me an offer. How disagreeable it would be to turn him down." She looked at Diantha anxiously.

"Do you think he will offer for me, Diantha?" she asked.

"I don't see how you can prevent him from doing so," Diantha responded as she tried to peck out a tune on the pianoforte.

This comment caused Susan to pace wildly about the music room.

"Oh, Diantha, you must help me prevent such an embarrassing turn of events."

"I don't think I can be of much assistance," Diantha said, still fingering the keys. "Only think what mice feet I made of Sylvester's offer. I'm not a very good person to seek advice from."

"If I decline the viscount's offer, he might fly into a rage." Miss Kirkpatrick gnawed on her lip. "His consequence is enormous, and it might cause trouble for Angus's career."

This was something which Diantha had not foreseen.

"I shall take pains not to speak with Devlin hereafter," Susan went on. "You must be my intermediary and tell him that I should only look upon such an offer with disfavour."

"A pretty hoydenish thing for me to say!" Diantha protested.

Susan threw herself down on the piano bench next to her friend. "But you must," she beseeched. "Please, Diantha. Can't you just tell him that my heart is given to another?"

Susan's agitation so alarmed Diantha that she gave in. If an offer should come from Devlin, she would decline it on Susan's behalf.

ON THURSDAY MORNING, emotions ran high at the rehearsal of Mr. Fanshaw's play. Diantha thought it best to absent herself from the playwright's temper tantrums. She persuaded Susan to accompany her on a shopping expedition. Ordinarily, Susan avoided the tedium of comparing shoes, reticules, gloves and dresses, but today they both enjoyed the shops on New Bond Street and Bruton, excitedly discussing all the items necessary for Susan's trousseau.

After an hour at Miss Starke's, the noted milliner, they emerged, carrying two hat boxes. As they threaded their way towards the tilbury, Diantha heard her name called and, turning, found Mr. Baillie lifting his hat to her.

"Good day, Miss Atwood." Andrew's creditor appeared a great deal more cheerful than when they had last met.

"Mr. Baillie," Diantha replied with a civil nod.

"Would you allow me a word with you in private, Miss Atwood?"

Diantha handed Susan her hat box. "I shan't be a minute," she promised and walked with Mr. Baillie to the corner.

"I just wanted to say that I received your cheque from your banker an hour ago," Mr. Baillie said, shaking her hand. "It came not a second too soon. I'm grateful to you."

"You are quite welcome. I hope that will give you the time you said you needed, until Andrew returns."

"I think it will," Baillie agreed. "I have learned my lesson and shan't sit down at the green baize tables for considerable time."

"Good. You can come to ruin from gaming, Mr. Baillie."

He chuckled. "I know that well enough. As did your father and brother, I'm sure."

Diantha's smile faltered. "My brother and father? Pray, what do you mean? My father never gambled. Perhaps just a game of whist in the privacy of his home, but nothing more than that," she assured him. "Indeed, he was quite opposed to gambling, calling it a dangerous vice which brought more than one man and family to ruin."

"I daresay he would know," Mr. Baillie tittered. His Adam's apple moved in his bony throat.

Diantha's brows rose high in astonishment. "Mr. Baillie! I beg you to speak plainly. Are you implying that my father made a habit of frequenting gambling dens?"

"Nothing so bad in that, Miss Atwood," Andrew's creditor hurried to calm her. "All gentlemen must try their luck at the tables. His luck was bad, more's the pity."

Diantha swayed but recovered her balance after a moment. "Well, yes, a bit. A trifle, no more than that," she said.

Mr. Baillie said nothing but his expression spoke volumes.

"I see," Diantha said coldly. "Papa's gaming was not just a trifle."

Mr. Baillie hastened to apologize. "Miss Atwood, it was not my wish to bring you distress by carrying old tales about your father. Thaddeus Atwood was an honourable man. Everyone knows that."

With a gloved hand, Diantha waved off these apologies. The Pandora's box had been opened, and she had to have the truth once and for all.

"The money my brother owes to you—are those his debts or ones he inherited from my father?" she asked quietly.

Mr. Baillie's eyes met hers slowly. "The bulk of it came from your father," he confessed.

Diantha digested this news as she would have a mound of cold gruel.

"Was my father similarly indebted to Andrew's other creditors?"

Mr. Baillie nodded his grizzled head.

"And Messieurs Smith and King, the moneylenders?"

"I do believe so. But Esmeraude's father will take care of the debts, Miss Atwood."

Esmeraude's father? Diantha's heart sank as she recalled Mr. Lowell's threats. And now to find her own father was in large measure a gamester?

Woodenly, Diantha returned to her tilbury.

"What did he say to you?" Susan asked as Diantha settled back in the driver's seat.

Diantha inhaled a breath. "Nothing," she said, her mind still at sixes and sevens.

It had to be a mistake. And yet she knew in her heart it was not.

She had always idolized her father. The greatest pleasure of her life was to sit with him as he read aloud in his library, or to share the reins as they drove his carriage. It was her father to whom she turned for advice, and who comforted her in times of distress.

And to think he was nothing but a sham.

Her cheeks burned now as she remembered the tongue-lashing she had given Andrew for falling into debt so quickly after he had reached his majority. Poor Andrew had never said a word about their father's debts. He had shouldered the blame willingly.

And how quick she had been to lay the blame for Andrew's debts at Devlin's door. She reddened at the memory. The words she'd spoken to him at St. George's on Andrew's wedding day came back to haunt her. How could she ever face him again, knowing what a cake she'd made of herself?

Diantha was destined to come face-to-face with Devlin sooner than she wished, for as she picked up her reins again and started to drive, her team nearly stepped in the path of another.

With an oath, the driver of the second vehicle pulled alongside and pushed back his high-crown beaver felt. Devlin, of all people.

"Miss Atwood, if you're in the habit of driving like a greenhorn you'll never drive my Welshbreds again," he said. "You shall drive Miss Kirkpatrick into another decline!"

"What? Oh, heavens! I am so sorry," she said, her words coming in a rush.

He peered at her more closely. She looked ashen faced and not just from their near accident. Something obviously was troubling her. Was it more of Andrew's tiresome problems?

"What's amiss?" he asked at once.

"Nothing whatever," she said, wishing she could just drive off, but his carriage blocked her entry into the lane of traffic.

She became aware that Susan was nudging her with an elbow.

"You must allow me to accompany you back to Portman Square, just to be sure that if you fall faint your team does not carry you away," the viscount said.

Susan's elbow beat a frantic rhythm against Diantha's ribs.

"No, that won't be necessary," Diantha said.

"I insist. You don't look well. The grippe is raging through the ton." He pulled his team aside and motioned her to precede him.

"Now that's done it," Susan fretted. "We shall have to invite him in. I shall plead a headache and if he presses you about me, you can warn him off making me an offer."

"I do believe I have the makings for a headache myself," Diantha murmured, pressing the fingers of one hand to her temples.

"Di! You mustn't leave me with him. You promised. You must be my intermediary."

"Oh, very well," Diantha said, giving in.

True to his word, Devlin followed Diantha's tilbury to Portman Square. He did not like the wan expression of her usually lively face. Had Mrs. Tribbet returned to vex her?

He thought about the Ming vases he'd bought and wondered if she had sold them in order to pay Mrs. Tribbet off. Foolish chit. She should have come to him at once with her problem.

When he reached Portman Square, Diantha invited him in to share some tea. Judging by the level of noise, she concluded that Fanshaw's rehearsal was still under way in the Long Gallery, but Diantha did not look in and merely led the viscount to the blue drawing room.

Just after Hughes placed the tea and assorted cakes in front of them, Susan pleaded fatigue and bolted from the room. Diantha shot a quick glance at Devlin who looked surprised at Miss Kirkpatrick's errant behaviour.

The viscount *was* surprised and secretly pleased to get a few moments alone with Diantha. As a rule they were surrounded with people, and he felt sure that any moment Fanshaw's rehearsal would end and hordes of hungry players would descend upon them. Before that happened he wanted to eat his cake and delve deeper into Diantha's problem.

"You didn't have to follow me in your carriage," Diantha said, as she took a cup of tea for herself. What she really wanted was to lie abed with a cloth over her forehead and contemplate the hoax her father had perpetrated. Instead she must entertain Susan's suitor.

"I wanted to," Devlin said now.

Probably because it gave him a reason to see Susan.

"You were driving erratically, and the streets are dangerous enough. You still look exceedingly pale. Tell me, won't you, what is wrong?"

The gentle tone in his voice was a further rebuke to her. She could scarcely look him in the eye. "Nothing at all," she said, putting down her teacup before she spilled it all over herself.

He leaned back in his chair, his face thoughtful. "Tell me the truth. Is it Mrs. Tribbet?"

"Good heavens, no!" Diantha exclaimed, surprised by his query. Mrs. Tribbet was the last thing on her mind.

"Lowell hasn't been around to hound you about Andrew, has he?"

"No. Really, there is no problem, my lord. I was just distracted during my driving. A serious offence, I acknowledge."

He'd go bail she was lying. But he couldn't shake the truth out of her or force her to confide in him. Devlin finished the lemon cake. It was delicious. He wondered if it would be bad ton to ask for a second piece. As though she'd anticipated such a request, she handed him another slice.

"I see you like the cake."

"First rate, like everything in your household, Miss Atwood."

"Prettily said, my lord."

"I meant it."

"Well, I have ordered some special treats for Fanshaw's play on Monday night."

"I look forward to it. You will be glad to have the playwright out from underfoot?"

She laughed and nodded. "I'm surprised Hugo isn't here in the room, telling me about yet another hitch in his plans. That's one reason Susan and I went on our errands today."

"How has Miss Kirkpatrick been feeling these past few days?" he asked politely.

Diantha straightened her back. Here they came. The inevitable questions about Susan. "She is fine. I do believe she just had a touch of the headache."

"Is she prone to them?"

"Unfortunately, yes. However, since Dr. Brewster took over her care she is much improved."

"They go on famously together these days, don't they?" he observed.

"Yes."

Devlin laid his fork and empty plate down on the ormolu table.

"More, my lord?" she offered.

"No, thank you." He blotted his mouth with a napkin.

She waited for him to leave, but he merely sat in the Trafalgar chair, looking at her with a bemused expression on his handsome face.

Why wasn't she confiding in him? His one wish in the world was to ease her way, take all her burdens on his own shoulders.

"I am afraid that I must join Susan abovestairs, my lord," she said, hoping this would nudge him towards the door.

"Miss Atwood, there is something I must say to you!" Devlin said, prepared to cross his Rubicon. He had had his fill of trying to outwit the rumour mill. Let the prattle boxes say what they would.

Diantha held up a slim hand. "Don't, my lord. It will merely distress the two of us, I assure you."

"But you can't know what I am about to say!" he exclaimed, fighting the urge to take her in his arms.

"I'm not blind, my lord. I have been blessed with two sound eyes, and your actions these past few weeks have aroused interest. I know full well what you've been feeling. Otherwise why would you be so faithful every Tuesday?"

He chuckled. "I suppose it was obvious. But you must give me a chance to make my offer properly."

She looked away from his eager face. How she hated to inflict pain on him. "Please don't utter another syllable, my lord."

He chose to utter two. "Why not?"

"Because what you wish is impossible to fulfill."

For a moment he was taken aback. Then he realized that his reputation as one vehemently opposed to marriage may have preceded him.

"I'm not offering carte blanche, Miss Atwood, but marriage with all that it entails," he said hastily. "My rank, my name."

"I realize that, my lord, but the answer will still be no."

If Gentleman Jackson himself had suddenly landed a facer over his guard, Devlin could not have been more stunned. In all his dreams about making Diantha the offer, he'd thought only of the right way to do it. He'd certainly not anticipated being turned down.

But he loved her!

"I may have behaved badly beforehand," he said now, determined to open his budget completely, "and made remarks I shouldn't have about marriage being akin to gaol. But I assure you, Miss Atwood, I would be a devoted husband. No wife of mine would ever have to worry about my straying. I would shower love on her every day."

"I'm sure you would make an excellent husband," Diantha said, almost choking over the lump in her throat. "But the answer will still be no."

"Why?" he demanded. "You will be civil enough to answer that. You must. I had no idea my attentions were so unwelcome. Why is my offer being declined?" he thundered.

Diantha lifted her chin. "There is another man, my lord."

CHAPTER FOURTEEN

THE DARK-HAIRED WOMAN striding impatiently into the office held a lace handkerchief drenched with lavender perfume to her nose to cover the noxious odours emanating from the hallway.

"What a hovel this place is, Kroll," she said.

The investigator stared over the clutter of his desk, in no way disturbed by his client's churlish greeting.

"Well, what have you discovered?" Mrs. Whorley demanded.

"I shall be having my payment first, as we agreed, ma'am," he said, holding out his hand.

Mrs. Whorley took a roll of notes from her reticule and tossed it at the investigator. "Now what about Miss Tribbet?"

"Oh, she's come to London, right enough." Kroll gathered the money and whisked it away in his desk drawer. "I found the driver of the Mail Coach who distinctly remembers putting her down in the Piccadilly area. From there it was harder, but fortunately I have my sources."

"Enough boasting and tell me all!" Mrs. Whorley commanded.

"A flower seller in the area remembers a lady from the country asking the way to Berkeley Square. The flower seller thought the lady too pretty to go wandering the streets of London by herself, so she sent a street urchin off to show her the way."

"And did you find the urchin?"

"After considerable difficulty, I did. And he led me to number fourteen Mount Street."

Mrs. Whorley dropped the handkerchief from her nose and let out a small shriek. "Number fourteen? You are sure of that, you awful creature?"

Kroll's smile displayed stained teeth. "I am.

"The urchin showed her to number fourteen Mount Street. She gave him a few coins, and he ran off to buy some bread to eat. That's the last anyone could find of her."

"There must be more."

The investigator shrugged. "I even tried to bribe an underfootman in the house. Fellow threw me into the street," Kroll said, rubbing the small of his back.

Devlin's servants had always been appallingly loyal to their employer, Mrs. Whorley thought. But at least the path of Miss Tribbet had led to Mount Street. She wasn't really interested in the whereabouts of the stupid chit from the country as much as what her knowledge could extract from a certain viscount.

AT NUMBER FOURTEEN Mount Street, a certain Viscount Devlin stamped into his library, yanked off his York tan gloves and threw them into the fire, an action which would have wounded his valet to the core.

Females were nothing but trouble. He'd known that from the start, but he'd allowed a certain dark-eyed, dark-haired slip of a beauty to cause him to forget the cardinal rule of bachelorhood. Well, no longer. The blinders had come off.

Another man in her heart! Devlin sank into a chair. He'd never dreamed of a rival for her affections. And who the devil was it? He'd been too stunned by the news to question her or do much of anything but bow out of the room.

Blast it! Cupid had extracted a cruel revenge by making him fall top over tail in love with this bluestocking.

Quite plainly she did not wish his advances. Very well. He would not inflict them on her again. He gazed into the fire, unable to help speculating on his rival.

Who could it be? Sylvester, perhaps? He had proposed to her, but she had turned him down. Laughed off his proposal. Had she changed her mind? And if not the inventor, then who?

As he sat brooding over the possible identity of Miss Atwood's lover, he heard the sound of voices in the corridor. One of them sounded like a female.

Was it Diantha? Ignoring his just made vow never to have anything further to do with her, he crossed to the door and opened it. In the hallway his butler stood impassively, at sword points with a would-be caller.

"His lordship will see me," Mrs. Whorley was saying to Lindell.

The combatants looked up from their war of the wills as Devlin emerged.

"What is going on?" he asked in a voice of dangerous calm.

"Mrs. Whorley insists on seeing you, my lord," replied his butler. "I told her you were indisposed."

The widow turned her back on the butler. "Fiddlefaddle. It's quite important, Oliver. I wouldn't call on you, if it weren't."

Devlin eyed her speculatively for a moment. "That will be all, thank you, Lindell. Mrs. Whorley?" Devlin said, holding the door open for her to pass through.

"How good it is to see you again, Oliver," Mrs. Whorley said, as she settled onto his Etruscan armed couch. A sibylline look came into her dark eyes. "And I daresay I know the cause of your indisposition."

"Do you?" he enquired politely, shutting the door.

"A woman."

His lordship's smile was cool as he produced an enamel snuff box from his coat pocket. "Those of your sex are responsible for much of the indisposition of those of mine," he agreed. He dipped two fingers into the mixture, a new blend which Mr. George Berry had recommended. "Come now, I have had an exhausting morning. What is the important matter you must discuss with me?"

"I possess information which might prove embarrassing to you, Oliver, possibly even incriminating," Mrs. Whorley said, deciding to lay her cards on the table.

The viscount's expression of affability did not change a bit.

"Incriminating? Thalia, you are speaking like a heroine in a lending-library romance."

"I am speaking of the disappearance of Miss Tribbet of Topping Green," she said, and had the satisfaction of seeing the tiniest frown pucker the viscount's distinguished brow.

"A Miss Trenton, you did say?" he asked, putting the snuff box down.

"Miss Tribbet of Topping Green," Mrs. Whorley repeated. "And you needn't bother to dissemble, Oliver. I hired an investigator who saw you with her within the fortnight. A man of impeccable reputation," she said, perjuring her soul and hoping she wouldn't have to produce the far-from-impeccable Kroll anytime soon. "You entered her residence at Topping Green. Now she's disappeared."

"What an imagination you possess, Thalia," the viscount said cordially.

"Mrs. Tribbet, her mother, was quite distraught," Mrs. Whorley continued, riding over this interruption. "She came to London to seek help from Sir Arthur Long."

Devlin's eyes narrowed a fraction at the mention of the baronet. "What is Sir Arthur's part in this Banbury tale of yours?"

"The Tribbets are a connexion to his family. When Arthur mentioned the name to me, I immediately remembered your link to her. That same investigator has discovered that she came to London and was escorted by a street urchin to this address."

"And you have duly reported all this to Sir Arthur?" he asked.

Mrs. Whorley reddened, for the first time looking out of countenance. "Sir Arthur doesn't know anything about this. He told Mrs. Tribbet he couldn't help her and advised her to return to Topping Green."

"And instead you took on the onerous task yourself of finding Miss Tribbet for her mother," the viscount clucked. "Such a charitable impulse, Thalia."

"Don't fence with me, Devlin," she snapped. "I could have told Sir Arthur what I knew. Instead I am telling you. Be grateful that I value old friends."

The viscount stretched a champagne-buffed Hessian out to the fire.

"Friends? Hiring investigators, Thalia? That's not how friends play the game."

"It's your fault," she shot back, batting her long lashes at him. "You replaced me with another. And now no trace of her can be found. Bow Street might call it foul play."

"Then you would be a foolish widgeon to be chatting with a would-be murderer," he said calmly meeting her gaze.

Her lips parted in a smile. "You are no more a killer than I. But you undoubtedly had a hand in the chit's disappearance. Do you know what I think happened to her? You dispatched her to a nunnery."

Devlin stared at her. "I did what?" he ejaculated.

"Dispatched her to a nunnery," Mrs. Whorley repeated. "You should really not toy with country misses, Ollie. They are not prepared for the inevitable problem of children resulting from such a liaison. Naturally, when she came to you with the problem you sent her somewhere to have the babe."

"Is that your reading of my character?" he asked, taken aback by such an imaginative scenario.

"What other reading could there be?" she replied.

Served with his own sauce, Devlin thought ironically as he surveyed this sticky situation. He had thought Miss Tribbet safe at Roddy's, but if Mrs. Whorley had learned of her trip to London, perhaps others would, too. He had to buy the widow's silence temporarily. Fortunately, he knew just what to do.

"It was good of you to come to me before you went to the quizzes," he said.

Mrs. Whorley rose and crossed over towards him. Her hand trailed up the sleeve of his coat.

"My dear Oliver, you know that I have been desolate since you and I parted. Sir Arthur is a hopeless bore, something no one has ever accused you of being."

"And a purse squeeze."

"Yes, that too," she acknowledged. "Indeed, I hope that I might induce you to rekindle our romance."

"You are too obliging. I daresay I should show you my thanks in an appropriate way."

She closed her eyes and waited for his kiss. But when none ensued, she opened one eye.

Devlin was gazing at her with a most peculiar expression on his face.

"I wonder if Rundell still has that ruby necklace you wanted."

"Oh, he has, Oliver. He has."

A wintry smile crossed the viscount's face. "Checked on his merchandise before you came to me, did you? Never mind. It seems that we are birds of a feather, my dear Thalia. And we must fly together once more."

The trip across the Strand and over Ludgate Hill was accomplished in record time. Mrs. Whorley at last received her heart's desire and lost not a second in displaying it and the viscount for all to see, and by the end of the day her reattachment of Devlin was the talk of the Town.

THE NEWS MADE ITS WAY in a more desultory fashion to Portman Square Monday morning where the dress rehearsal of Mr. Fanshaw's play was taking place. The performance was slated for that evening at eight, and the playwright was in the throes of last-minute changes to his masterpiece, thus infuriating all the players forced to learn new lines.

As she attempted to memorize her new dialogue, Lady Menloe let fall to Lady Hogarth that she had seen Devlin acting the indulgent benefactor to his old chère amie.

Diantha was helping to block out the positions for the play, and her face grew pale at this news.

"But why would he go back to her?" Lady Hogarth asked, scratching her neck. The collar of her lavender costume itched. "Thalia's a grasping harpy. I thought it high time he saw through her ruse."

Lady Menloe snorted. "You know what fools men can be," she said in her forthright way.

"Devlin never struck me as one wanting for sense. There's more to this than meets the eye. I wonder why he returned to that Whorley creature?"

Standing frozen a few feet away, Diantha could have enlightened both ladies. Quite obviously the viscount had fled to Mrs. Whorley's arms because his interest in Susan had been discouraged. Discouraged by Diantha.

She had seen the pain in his eyes before he'd left Portman Square and had hoped that in time he might come to realize *she* cared deeply for him. But instead he had turned to Mrs. Whorley. She had not anticipated he might seek comfort from the widow after his disappointment with Susan.

"Such licentiousness is not to be tolerated." Sir Philip Forth interjected his opinion into the story circulating the Long Gallery.

Lady Hogarth looked down her aquiline nose at the moralist. "It's not licentiousness, sir. Devlin has always been faithful, in his own fashion, to whichever lady he has been involved with at the time. Not like some of the younger set who hop from bed to bed."

"Perhaps he just needs the love of the right woman," Diantha murmured.

A round of laughter greeted her words.

"You are a romantic, my dear," Lady Hogarth said.

"What about Sir Arthur Long?" Lady Menloe asked. "Does he know?"

"Of course he knows," Lady Hogarth replied. "It's public knowledge. She rode with Devlin in the Park, flaunting that ruby necklace."

"Was Sir Arthur furious?" Diantha asked.

Lady Hogarth tugged at her collar. "Don't know if he's got the temperament to be furious. I daresay he's not pleased at having his place usurped, but there's little he can do other than call Devlin out. Which he won't."

"Duelling over a lady of such questionable character wouldn't be at all the thing," Lady Menloe pointed out.

"Character ain't the point. Devlin being a crack shot is," Lady Hogarth said succinctly before the group turned to another page of Fanshaw's new copy.

THE GENTLEMAN STANDING in the middle of Hyde Park wore a frown of furious concentration as he threw a curved stick up into the air.

"Blast!" he swore moments later as the stick fell to the earth with a thud. "Oh, I do beg your pardon, Miss Marsh."

"Not at all, Lord Sylvester," replied Miss Tribbet, holding a parasol over her head. "It's so vexatious, I know. Your patience during this past hour passes all belief."

"Well, I do want the thing to work," Sylvester said. "Though I suppose it is very boring for you to just watch it go up and down. What a wasted morning."

"Not at all," she protested. "I enjoyed myself immensely."

"Did you really?" Sylvester asked, his face nearly the colour of his red hair. He was a trifle hot from his exertions.

She smiled. "Yes, my lord, I did. Why don't you sit for a moment and tell me more about your other inventions?"

Willingly, Sylvester fell in with this scheme, detailing his attempts at various devices, including one which might render candles unnecessary.

Miss Tribbet looked at him questioningly. "But we must have light, sir," she said.

"Oh, yes, I know." Sylvester nodded his agreement. "But I have a notion that light could be produced mechanically, without the wax and candles. Just think of the convenience of being able to use a mechanical device to light an entire room."

She looked startled, then thoughtful. "It sounds quite terrifying to me," Miss Tribbet said frankly. "Have you invented this?"

"Not yet. It's just a notion. I have dozens of ideas. What do you think of a carriage without horses?"

Miss Tribbet's angelic countenance looked startled. "A carriage without horses? But what would propel the carriage, sir?"

"That's what I'm still working on," Sylvester admitted. "I have a good many ideas, but unfortunately none of them has worked as yet."

"But you are making good progress with the throwing stick," Miss Tribbet said encouragingly. "I'm sure you will succeed."

So encouraged was Sylvester that after his rest he made another attempt with the stick and found that it did return. This he could only put down to Miss Marsh's influence. Remarkable woman.

He actually found himself reluctant to return her to Cavendish Square but knew he couldn't keep her out much later than mid-morning.

When they returned to Roddy's, he found Mr. Bridger and Devlin enjoying a game of billiards. It had been the viscount's intention to secure a private word with Miss Tribbet, suggesting that she return to Topping Green or at the very least warn her that Mrs. Tribbet had been trying to find her. Upon discovering Miss Tribbet's absence, he had lingered in the billiard room with Roddy.

"Ah, Sylvester," Devlin said now. "Good day, Miss Marsh, back from your outing?"

"Yes," Miss Tribbet said breathlessly. "Lord Sylvester was kind enough to demonstrate his throwing stick to me."

Roddy picked it up gingerly with two fingers. "Just what is it supposed to do?" he demanded.

"It flies in the air and returns to the sender," Sylvester said eagerly.

"Dangerous sort of invention. Risk of decapitation," Roddy observed, putting it down.

"Natives in Australia use it for hunting."

Devlin's eye glinted appreciatively. "Good, if we ever go to Australia we shall bring one along. Better yet, we'll bring you."

Sylvester laughed. "I thought it might be amusing for Harry."

"Harry!" Roddy gulped.

"Sylvester, you'll brain the child with that thing if you let it loose in the nursery," Devlin said strictly.

Still laughing, Sylvester held up his hands. "No, I meant for others to throw to amuse him."

"I think I'd sooner shake a rattle than throw this," the viscount said good-naturedly. "Do take my place here in this game with Roddy. I would like to ask Miss Marsh her opinion on something."

Sylvester in a fog stared at the cuestick thrust into his hand.

"I have a cousin whose young daughter is acting quite peculiarly in the schoolroom," Devlin said, turning to Miss Tribbet. "May I solicit your advice on the matter?" he asked, smiling and taking her over to a corner chair.

"Certainly, my lord, but I know really very little about schoolrooms."

He couldn't help smiling. "You should not spread that about, Miss Tribbet. After all, you are supposed to be a governess. In any case, I thought you should know your mother has been searching for you here in London."

"Mama!" Miss Tribbet exclaimed, then looked over at the two other men in the room with them. Neither seemed to have overheard. "Has she been to see you again?"

"No, but she's seen others. Sir Arthur Long is related to your family?"

"Distantly," Miss Tribbet said. She considered the question, her face troubled. "You mean she has gone to Sir Arthur? She used to say he was the slowest wit in the world. She didn't tell him about Andrew, did she?"

Devlin thought back to Mrs. Whorley's communication. Apparently Mrs. Tribbet had not related the matter of Andrew to Sir Arthur.

"She asked his help in finding you."

"Oh, no." Miss Tribbet's eyes were riveted on the viscount. "And did he agree?"

Devlin shook his head. "He told her to return to Topping Green, and she has done so. I'd advise you to do the same."

Miss Tribbet clasped her hands in her lap and looked uncomfortable. "I can't."

"I'm sure that your mother will gladly mend the quarrel," he prodded gently.

"No, you don't understand. This has nothing to do with Mama. I just can't leave London now."

The viscount felt at point non plus. "We still do not know where Andrew is," he explained.

"This has nothing to do with Andrew, either," Miss Tribbet said, looking mulish. "I have personal reasons for staying in London. But I assure you I shall stay indoors. I promise I won't leave the house. I just can't go back to Hertfordshire."

Devlin was puzzled by these signs of intractability. Miss Tribbet had always been willing before to heed his advice. Then he glanced up and intercepted a passing look between her and Sylvester. Good God, he thought. Not Sylvester and Miss Tribbet.

CHAPTER FIFTEEN

"DO YOU NOT THINK Miss Marsh the most pleasant lady in all London?" Sylvester asked as he and Devlin strolled towards St. James's Street and White's.

The viscount jabbed his ivory-handled cane at a loose cobblestone as he repeated part of Sylvester's question aloud.

"The most pleasant lady in all London? I couldn't rightly say, Sylvester. I haven't spoken to every female in the city."

"She is the most beautiful creature, so soft-spoken, with the face of an angel." The inventor paid not a jot of attention to Devlin's off-hand remark.

"How long have you been acquainted with Miss Marsh?" Devlin asked, glancing at his friend and not liking the thoroughly besotted look on the inventor's face.

"Just a few days," Sylvester acknowledged, "but time doesn't signify. I feel as if I've known her all my life. She's the lady of my dreams."

Devlin cast an imploring look to the heavens. He had to find a way to bring Sylvester down from the altitudes.

"Didn't you think that about Miss Atwood?" Devlin asked.

His question brought Sylvester to a dead halt in the middle of the street. "Miss Atwood," the inventor expostulated, standing like a stock until Devlin yanked him out of the path of a carriage. "Oh, no, Dev, that's wasn't the same thing at all," Sylvester protested. "That was a mere schoolboy crush."

"You did offer for her," the viscount pointed out.

"I know. Fortunately she had the foresight to refuse. Only think how awful it would be had she accepted. I might be facing Miss Marsh now as a married man."

Which would probably be quite in keeping with the present marital status of Miss Tribbet, Devlin thought.

He'd presumed Miss Tribbet would be safe at Roddy's, never for a moment imagining she would meet and captivate Sylvester.

"How is Eugenia Price?" he asked, determined to play Cupid's adversary.

Sylvester cocked his head as they mounted the steps towards the club. "Eugenia Price? Who is she?"

"The female you were top over tail in love with back in February," came the acid rejoinder.

The inventor's face cleared. "Oh, Genie. I understand she is on her wedding trip. She never really noticed any of us dangling after her. The Marquis of Durville cast us all in the shade."

"And Lady Alice?"

"Lady Alice?" Sylvester frowned as they entered White's.

"The flaxen-haired lady with the consumptive air about her." Devlin furnished this clue as he took off his beaver felt. "You spent all last Season fetching her potions and tonics."

"Oh, that wasn't Alice, but Agnes. She's taking the cure at Bath, I believe. Why do you bring up Lady Agnes and Miss Price?"

"Merely to remind you that you have thought yourself thoroughly in love in the past. So you'd do well not to do anything rash with Roddy's governess. You can't take your fences in a rush with such a female. She's bound to think you're freakish or making sport of her." This last comment hit its mark.

"Making sport? 'Pon rep, Dev, that's not so," Sylvester insisted. "I am in earnest."

"I know it." Devlin seized his advantage. "But does she? Slow and easy—that's the ticket, I think, Sylvester."

"Well, I shouldn't like to scare her," Sylvester agreed. He paused at the Reading Room, where Devlin announced his intention to peruse the journals. "Shall I see you this evening?"

The viscount turned an apologetic eye on his friend. "This evening? You know my abominable memory, Sylvester. Did we have an engagement?"

"Fanshaw's play. You are going to it, aren't you?"

"Actually, I've changed my mind about attending." He had no wish to dangle after Diantha now that she had made her wishes known. "It's bound to be a bore. Besides, Thalia said something about a soirée I must attend with her."

To show him off like a fatted calf.

"That's a pity. I think Miss Atwood will be relying on having her friends in the audience." Sylvester left, but his innocent remark continued to reverberate in Devlin's brain. Friends in the audience. Was it possible that the gentleman Diantha had lost her heart to would be in attendance at Portman Square this evening?

The viscount's face grew grim. Part of him longed to see her, and another part didn't want anything to do with her. He felt thoroughly battered by the storm of emotion in his breast. But if he did attend the theatrical tonight he might be able to learn just which gentleman had succeeded in cutting him out.

OVER AT PORTMAN SQUARE Diantha was attempting to dissuade Mr. Fanshaw from any more changes in his masterpiece. The sooner the theatrical was over the better. Her household was in disarray, with an underfootman and a maid giving notice.

By the time the seven o'clock hour sounded on the grandfather clock, even Mr. Fanshaw was satisfied and dashed home to make a swift change in his own raiment.

In keeping with the motif of the ancients, Diantha had chosen a Grecian gown this evening, white and gathered at the throat by a stunning diamond clasp. Her curls were scooped up high on her crown, and she only hoped she did not look like one of those ladies balancing a pitcher of water on her head which she had seen once carved on a Greek frieze in the British Museum.

Susan, the recipient of this confidence, whooped with laughter, as she attached a pearl earring to one earlobe. "A pitcher of water? Oh, Diantha, you are impossible. You look splendid."

"As you do." Di returned the compliment, which was all too true. Susan was in her best looks, wearing an azure gauze over a tunic of silk. "Will Dr. Brewster be attending?"

"No. Unfortunately he is waiting on one of his patients to deliver a babe. But he bade me give him a full report."

Diantha gathered her fan, and together they descended the stairs to find Fanshaw back from his speedy trip home. The playwright was garbed sedately for a change in a black swallow-tailed coat and white frilled shirt.

Lord Sylvester and Sir Philip Forth were among the first arrivals, and Fanshaw had enlisted their help with last minute changes to the set.

"Good heavens, don't let him change anything!" Diantha whispered in Sylvester's ear. "Once he starts, there will be no stopping him. He'll change everything, with the performance slated to begin in just thirty minutes!"

Precisely at eight the curtain rang up and all present were transported to ancient Athens. Diantha declined Mr. Fanshaw's invitation to sit in the front row, explaining that she had to stand near the door to greet and seat the late arrivals. She did not intend to spend her evening holding Fanshaw's hand.

No hand holding turned out to be necessary. To Diantha's profound shock, the play was a definite hit with the audience.

Even the scene with Parliament, the one which Mr. Fanshaw had laboured over for nearly a fortnight, was deemed a gem by no less an authority than Mr. Edmund Kean, who made a belated appearance to stand in the back of the room.

"Knowledgeable, witty, and first-rate," Lady Natterly complimented Fanshaw after the performance. "You must allow me to present some of your work in my drawing room."

"It would be an honour, ma'am!" he gurgled.

Diantha bade the beaming playwright to lead her guests to the refreshment room.

As the crowd filtered through the door, Viscount Devlin uncharacteristically lingered behind. For once the lobster patties did not attract his immediate interest. Miss Atwood in her fetching white gown did.

From the minute he had set foot in the Long Gallery, his eyes had been riveted on her dainty figure. No sign of partiality had he witnessed as she greeted her guests. No one seemed inclined to sit in her pocket, other than that bag pudding Forth who was prosing on to her now. Perhaps her secret love could not attend the theatrical tonight?

On the receiving end of Sir Philip's moral lecture concerning the plight of a pair of orphans from Cornwall, Diantha found herself woolgathering.

"What do you think of my plan, Miss Atwood?"

Sir Philip's question brought her up short.

She gazed into his vacuous eyes. "I think it splendid, of course," she said promptly.

Her hand was seized and pressed between his two damp palms. "I knew I could rely on you. I shall bring them to you later in the week."

"Them?" she asked uncertainly.

"The orphans."

"Orphans!" she exclaimed as Forth hurried off. What in thunderation had she agreed to?

"Never fear. You haven't adopted the Cornish brats," a familiar voice drawled.

Diantha gazed up at Devlin's tall, imposing frame, elegantly dressed as always. She felt her heart skip a beat. Why was he so handsome?

"Devlin? Did you hear what Forth was saying?" she managed to ask calmly. "What bacon-brained scheme have I agreed to?"

He couldn't help chuckling. "Sir Philip asked if you would put the two orphans up for a week prior to their setting out for relatives in America."

"Oh. Good gracious. Well, I suppose that isn't so bad."

"Isn't so good, either. Orphans do eat a lot." He fought the urge to play with a recalcitrant curl dangling unnoticed from the side of her head.

"I shall have to make the best of it. It's my fault for not paying attention. I didn't see you come into the Long Gallery," she said, then regretted her words. That was as good as admitting she'd looked for him. What a goosecap she was. Mrs. Whorley had him thoroughly in hand.

"I came in while Parliament was in session," he replied. "The play turned out to be first-rate. Surprised?" he asked, admiring the line of her throat as she laughed her agreement.

"It quite bowled me over, sir."

"Is the playwright cast in alt?" Why were her eyes so bewitching a shade of brown?

"Very nearly there!" she agreed. "Lady Natterly has commissioned a work from him, and I believe he is about to become renowned. Even Mr. Kean came. He left immediately, but he said that he thought the play was creditable indeed."

"High praise from one so notoriously closemouthed," Devlin agreed, wishing that her own lips didn't look so full and so kissable. Who was her lover?

"You mustn't forget the refreshments tonight," she said. "I have some special treats from Gunter's." She led him out into the hall towards the refreshment room.

"What happened to your Ming vase?" he asked, stopping abruptly.

"What?"

He gestured towards the empty stand. "You had a Ming vase on this stand. What happened to it?"

The unexpected question caught Diantha off guard.

"I sold it," she blurted out.

Two blue eyes stared at her. "Why?"

Here was the very opportunity to beg pardon for having placed the guilt for Andrew's and now her father's debts at his door. But much as she tried, the apology withered on her tongue. She'd always turned cat in the pan when it came to apologizing for anything. Andrew used to tease her about it. She'd rather perform the worst penance than say the words I'm sorry.

"Why did you sell your vase?" he asked. Would she confide in him? Perhaps her desperate straits had led her to accept another gentleman's offer.

"Because it might have been broken here in the hallway," she said, wracking her brain for a suitable explanation. "You know Sylvester and his inventions."

"Yes. That's the only reason? You weren't in need of funds?" he asked sternly.

"Everyone is in need of funds these days, my lord," she said with a laugh.

"Yes. Cost of everything has gone up, hasn't it?" he agreed.

"Shockingly so. Why Susan and I went shopping to find things for a trousseau and—" she broke off, seeing the stricken look in his eyes and cursing her wretched tongue. How stupid of her to even mention Susan's trousseau to the gentleman she had spurned.

"I'm sorry, my lord. My wretched tongue."

"Pay it no mind," he said stiffly, though her words fell on his heart like blows from a hammer. So she was shopping for her trousseau, was she? "When will the announcement be in the *Gazette?*"

"Soon, my lord."

Both participants in this discussion were relieved when Lady Natterly fluttered up, claiming to have lost her fan somewhere between the Long Gallery and the refreshment room.

"I shall go off and look for it straightaway," said her hostess.

"Permit me to perform this task for you," Devlin said, escorting the older woman back to the Long Gallery. That was the last Diantha saw of him that evening.

As DIANTHA CLIMBED into her bed that night, she felt an overwhelming urge to cry. Love was nothing at all like the poets said it would be. Love was a heavy weight where her heart should have been. It made her feel so alone, something she was very sure that Devlin wasn't feeling, thanks to Mrs. Whorley. As the image of Devlin's merry widow flitted into her mind, Diantha punched a down-filled pillow with two fists. *I must stop thinking of him. I simply must,* she told herself as she fell into a long, exhausted sleep.

THE NEXT MORNING began agreeably enough with a breakfast tray and a cup of chocolate in her bedchamber, but after Diantha spread the gossip pages of the *Morning Post,* her appetite suddenly deserted her. The opening paragraph described in exhaustive detail Mrs. Whorley's reattachment of Devlin.

Unable to read another word through the blur of tears, Diantha crushed the newspaper in a fist and hurled it across the room, then she stalked over to her wardrobe and began to dress. She was still feeling cross when she went belowstairs. Because of the theatrical the night before, her Open Day was cancelled, and to distract herself from thoughts of Devlin and his merry widow she took her sketchbook and a bowl of fruit into her blue drawing room. Midway through her still life exercise, Mr. Fanshaw called, ready to begin work on his next masterpiece.

"I am afraid you shall have to stage it elsewhere, Mr. Fanshaw," Diantha said, blinking at the orange neckcloth round the playwright's throat. "Last night was the last theatrical I shall hold here. I've had my household turned top to bottom, something I am loath to go through again."

"But haven't you read the review in the *Morning Post?*"

Diantha dusted off her fingers, not wanting to be reminded about the *Morning Post* and not at all pleased with the pear taking shape on her page. Much too rounded at the bottom.

"The critic in the *Morning Post* said my work showed great promise, as great as Mr. Sheridan's in his prime," Mr. Fanshaw reported with considerable pride. "See for yourself." He thrust a copy of the newspaper at her.

Diantha skimmed the portion he pointed out to her and discovered that Mr. Fanshaw had not mistaken the matter. The reviewer had indeed called his work full of promise and audacity. Well, audacious it certainly was. "My felicitations, Hugo," Diantha said now to the promising playwright. "I'm sure you deserve all the praise."

"Thank you." He beamed. "I did work devilishly hard, as you know. And that's why you must allow me to put on my next work here."

Diantha laid aside the newspaper and picked up the sketchbook again. "No," she said firmly. "My mind is made up. My drawing room is not Drury Lane! What about Lady Natterly? I thought she was all agog over you and had invited you to put on your next performance at her residence."

"She did, but Lord Natterly had other thoughts on the matter," Fanshaw said, his head drooping even lower.

He looked so downhearted that Diantha took pity on him and volunteered to speak to Mrs. Purdy, who was the most amiable soul in London and whose drawing room was even larger than the one on Portman Square.

"She came to the play last night and was quite enamoured of it. I think I can persuade her to sponsor your next theatrical!"

"Oh, my dear Miss Atwood." Mr. Fanshaw pressed his bony fingers against Diantha's charcoal-smudged ones. "How good of you. I wish I knew how to begin to thank you. All your kindnesses. I am so obliged to you."

"Now, Hugo," she said, rather touched by this tribute. But another second brought a change in her emotion as he swept her sketchbook off her lap and planted a damp kiss on her hands. It put her in mind of having her hand licked by a dog.

"Hugo, what are you doing?"

"Oh, Diantha, how well we go on together!" he exclaimed. "My plays and your knack for knowing how to present them. Many successful partnerships have been made on such a foundation."

Diantha wrenched her hands free. "Oh?"

"That's why I hope you will consent to..." The playwright slipped to his knees, unaware that his kerseymere trousers were now firmly planted on a charcoal drawing of a bowl of fruit. "Dash it all, Diantha, we are both of the same class, even though my purse is more pinched than yours. Do let's get hitched."

"Hitched?" Diantha gaped at the young man kneeling on her sketchbook. "Are you making me an offer, Hugo?"

The playwright nodded eagerly. "Yes, of course an offer. It shall be a wonderful future for the two of us. I can live here with you at Portman Square and work on my plays at my leisure. We shall stage them together."

Diantha recoiled from this horror of a future, wondering if all the unsuitable young men who ever visited Portman Square were destined to make her offers. At least she had her previous episode with Sylvester to aid her and knew better than to laugh off the idiotish idea of marriage to Fanshaw.

"I thank you for your very kind offer," she said as gently as possible, "but I can't accept. We just wouldn't suit."

Fanshaw sat back on his heels. "Yes, we would. You are a bluestocking. I am an artist. What better match could you hope for?"

A knife twisted in Diantha's heart. The only gentleman she could hope for was enamoured of her friend and in the arms of that odious Mrs. Whorley.

"I don't know, Hugo," she said, holding her feelings in check. "I daresay it is very freakish of me. I am fond of you in a way, but I don't love you."

Much to her surprise Fanshaw accepted this without a blink.

"No, of course you don't," he agreed. "We're speaking of marriage, Diantha. A partnership, not some grand passion. You've never been that interested in love. Everything I've ever heard you say on the topic of love was to put it to scorn."

Diantha wished with all her heart she had been a shade less opinionated in the past.

"Nevertheless, I have decided I shall only marry for love. And you don't love me."

"No, I don't," Mr. Fanshaw admitted. "But that doesn't matter in a marriage."

"It matters to me." Her voice was quiet but firm. "Do cheer up, Hugo. Perhaps with your continued success in the theatre you will find another female who is more prone to accept you."

"I should still like to show you my appreciation for all you've done. I know. I shall dedicate my next work to you."

"There is no necessity to do that, I assure you!" Diantha said, alarmed at the prospect.

"It won't be any trouble," the playwright replied with a happy smile. "I want everyone to know you are the inspiration for my work!"

Diantha wondered how long she would be obliged to live on the Continent if such a thing came to pass.

"Come, let's see if Mrs. Purdy will receive us today."

As Diantha drove towards the Purdy residence on Green Street she could not help noticing that Fanshaw did not appear too dismayed by her refusal. Nothing like the way Devlin had positively glowered, the vein on his temple standing out, when she declined his offer on Susan's behalf. But then Devlin loved Susan. Fanshaw didn't love her.

"Don't you agree, Miss Atwood?" Fanshaw looked at her expectantly.

Diantha had learned her lesson from her conversation with Sir Philip Forth.

"I didn't hear your question, Mr. Fanshaw. What did you say?"

"I asked if you thought I should show Mrs. Purdy the review in the *Morning Post*."

"I think you could mention it. She will probably take pains to read it herself later."

As Diantha hoped, Mrs. Purdy was receiving callers, and she took an instant liking to Mr. Fanshaw, enthusiastically greeting his announcement of a sequel to the last play. While the enthusiasts animatedly discussed the scenes which might ensue in this new work, Diantha was able to apply herself to a plate of biscuits set in front of her.

A half hour later, her efforts were rewarded by Mrs. Purdy's commissioning Mr. Fanshaw to write a play about her family history.

"The Purdy heritage?" Diantha queried. "That has a definite allure."

"No, no!" came the vehement rejoinder. "Not Purdy's family, but mine." The silver-haired dowager thumped her ample bosom. "The McKenzies."

"Scottish blood?" Fanshaw asked, pricking up his ears.

Mrs. Purdy nodded.

The playwright's face was wreathed in smiles. "I can see it now. The heather and the heath. The sound of bagpipes, men in kilts. Spectacle of the first order."

Mrs. Purdy was utterly entranced by Fanshaw's words, not so Diantha, who began to wonder which hostess would agree to have heather placed in her drawing room. The smell alone...

"Oh, when do you think I might see something from you?" Mrs. Purdy asked, champing impatiently at the bit.

"I shall have to gather research," Mr. Fanshaw said meticulously. "Can't just dash such a thing off. Have to be sure of my facts. Speak to you at length. Establish the dates."

"Of course. My library is at your disposal. And so am I."

"Then we can begin now, if you wish!"

From this Diantha concluded that her own presence was not needed and, leaving Fanshaw in hushed consultation with his new benefactress, thankfully brought her visit to a close.

CHAPTER SIXTEEN

THE BUTLER CARRYING a silver tray down the hallway paused outside of his employer's bedchamber, a look of indecision on his usually impassive mien. Squaring his shoulders, the butler knocked.

"Come in," came the curt command.

Lindell pushed the door open. Devlin was seated in front of the fire with his coat off and his cravat untied.

"Since you missed breakfast, my lord, I have taken the liberty of preparing you a substantial lunch," Lindell explained as he put down a tray on the pier table.

"If that food came from my kitchen, I'd as lief starve," Devlin growled.

The butler was greatly relieved. If his employer could rail about the dismal creations of his chef, perhaps the situation was less serious than he had first thought.

"Oh, no. I ordered the meal from Gaston's restaurant."

"Thank you, Lindell. You are a prince among butlers. If you could only cook—"

"You will eat something, sir?" Lindell asked, suppressing a smile.

At the viscount's nod, the butler withdrew. Devlin had not intended to eat anything, but the sight of a tender morsel of lamb reminded him that he had gone without food for more hours than normal. A tentative nibble followed another until he demolished every bit of food on the plate.

After eating he felt better and took a cigar out from a box on his night table. Cigars were a new vice, and one which he indulged in only in private.

He snipped off one end, lit it and drew in the warm smoke. Would that all his anxieties could be relieved by a cigar and a hearty meal. But some could not. Like Miss Diantha Atwood.

He sank back in his Trafalgar chair and saw again the stricken look in Diantha's eyes at her slip of the tongue. Trousseau, indeed.

In love with a soon-to-be-married woman. Devlin inhaled more deeply this time. What further proof did he want that her heart was given to another? To catch her making love to the fellow?

Devlin reached absently for the copy of the *Morning Post* which Lindell had brought up with his tray. A few minutes later in a move reminiscent of Miss Atwood's, he crushed the gossip pages and hurled them into the fire. Thalia's triumph, indeed. Cupid had extracted a cruel revenge. And he was still paying the price. He scowled. He'd promised Thalia to take her for a drive in the Park at the fashionable hour.

SUSAN'S DIAMOND RING glittered in the sunlight as she held it out proudly for Diantha's inspection.

"It's beautiful," Diantha said sincerely from the bed where she had been resting with a handkerchief drenched in lilac water over her forehead.

"Angus insisted," Susan said, settling herself on the side of the bed with a hearty bounce which caused Diantha's head to reverberate alarmingly.

Susan saw her wince and was instantly contrite.

"Oh, you poor thing. You are feeling out of curl, aren't you?"

"It's just a migraine. It shall go away. I just need quiet and a dark room."

Susan bent over and stroked her friend's hand. "What a dunce I am, prattling on this way about myself. You rest. I shall keep everyone away."

At long last, Susan closed the door behind her. Diantha took off the handkerchief and dropped it into a nearby pan. She closed her eyes. But sleep eluded her, her brain teeming with images of Devlin. Devlin asleep on her library couch, Devlin eating a lobster patty. Devlin holding the reins of his Welshbreds, Devlin dancing, Devlin offering for Susan.

At this last image, her eyes flew open. What a ninny-hammer she was. She didn't even know what he felt for her. At times she knew he found her amusing, but then, she thought dourly as she reapplied the handkerchief drenched with lilac water, so was a trained pup.

In the midst of this self-examination came a soft rap on the door. Once again Susan entered.

"Diantha, I know I promised to bar all visitors. But there is someone I think you would want to see."

"Who would that be?" Diantha asked doubtfully.

"Andrew."

"Andrew!" Diantha exclaimed and sat up on her bed, her migraine forgotten.

"He's in the blue salon with Esmeraude. Will you see him?"

Diantha had already gathered up her skirts and flew out of her bedchamber. Andrew and Esmeraude were indeed waiting for her in the blue salon.

"Andrew! Thank heaven! If you only knew what a coil you left behind!" she exclaimed, stopping as she realized that her brother was supporting Esmeraude who had a splint on one leg. "What in the world has happened?"

"Broken leg, Di," Andrew said, pecking her on the cheek. "And pray don't you scold me. I wasn't driving at breakneck speed either. You can ask Esmeraude."

"It's true, Diantha," Esmeraude interjected softly. "We were nearly run down by a farmer on his cart. I broke my leg. Luckily the farmer was quite sorry about it, and insisted he put us up in a nearby posting house.''

"We never got to the Lakes," Andrew went on. "We fell to a touch of the fever, as well. The two of us."

"What a pity Dr. Brewster has just left," Susan interjected.

"Esmeraude must go upstairs and lie down." Diantha reached for the bell pull, but Susan swiftly intervened, saying that she would see to Esmeraude being settled abovestairs.

"Thank you, Susan," Andrew said. "I knew the two of you would take care of Esmeraude for me."

"Did you indeed?" Diantha said dangerously after the two other ladies had quit the room. "It appears to me that you think I should take care of more than just Esmeraude."

"Well, I could do with a plate of whatever you have in your kitchen," Andrew said, sinking into the nearest chair.

Diantha couldn't believe her ears. "Food? Is that all you can think of at a time like this? I vow you're just as bad as your friend Devlin when it comes to eating."

"I'm sorry if you feel that way. But we didn't stop for lunch. Why do you look daggers at me?"

"Because, dearest brother, I could box your ears."

On the receiving end of this threat, Mr. Atwood merely stared at his sister.

"What did you mean by marrying Esmeraude when you are already married to Miss Tribbet?" Diantha went on. "The truth, Andrew, I beg of you. I know it is bound to be awkward, but if you lie it shall just complicate things even more."

Attempting to follow the logic in his sister's tortuous recital, Andrew gave up and demanded to know if she were foxed.

"Or has Sylvester set off another invention which has addled your pretty little head?"

She paid no intention to this left-handed compliment. "Are you or aren't you married to Miss Tribbet?"

"My wife, dear sister, is Esmeraude. Esmeraude Lowell."

"Then you didn't come upon Miss Tribbet bathing in a stream and seek to do the honourable thing by her?" Diantha demanded.

"Is that what she says?" Andrew asked with a broad grin, his irritation with his sister's strange tale momentarily abated. "The chit's barking up the wrong tree. I'd remember a female bathing in a stream. And I am sorry to say I've not seen the sight you describe. Is she pretty?" he asked curiously.

"She is not only pretty, but respectable," Diantha said, delivering this facer.

Mr. Atwood turned pale. "Respectable? You've met her, then?"

"We've spoken to her at length, Devlin and I."

Andrew's eyes narrowed. "Is Devlin involved in this? By Jove, if this is one of his stupid hoaxes, I'll wring his neck. I asked him to keep an eye out for you, and look what happens. You've lost your mind!"

"Oh, Andrew, do stop talking rubbish. I should be wringing *your* neck for not telling me about Papa."

All sign of amusement vanished from Andrew's face. "Did Dev tell you that?" he demanded.

"Did he know that, too?" Diantha asked, her cheeks burning with mortification at the idea. "No, he didn't tell me. I was approached by Mr. Baillie because Mr. Lowell was not honouring the settlements."

"Why not?" Andrew asked, trying to make sense of this new embellishment to his sister's strange tale.

"Because of Miss Tribbet, you gudgeon."

"Do you mean Esmeraude's father has heard of this tale?" he said, looking alarmed for the first time.

Diantha nodded. "Lowell threatens to have you arrested for bigamy. And he's not giving your creditors the monies due them. Luckily, I was able to pay Baillie a portion of what you owe. Or should I say what Papa owed?"

"Dash it all, Diantha, you weren't supposed to know!" Andrew fumed. He raked his hair with his fingers. "I promised Father."

"So it is true," Diantha said quietly. "All this time I thought my brother a wastrel and profligate. And while it was hard to accept Papa as a gamester, accept it I must."

"Brave words," Andrew said, leaning over and squeezing her hand. "How much of your blunt did you part with to old Baillie? Our father owed him a prodigious sum."

"I paid him three thousand quid."

Andrew whistled. "How did you raise such a sum?"

"I sold a few things."

Andrew frowned, but the light dawned swiftly. "The Ming vases? Di, you didn't! You used to say the vases were the legacy of our parents."

"They were the only possession which would bring in any money. I don't repine, I assure you. The vases have gone to an agreeable collector."

"Well, I assure you that I shan't rest until I return them to you," Andrew said, squaring his jaw. "The debt was Father's and now mine. You have nothing to do with it."

"He was my father, too," she reminded him. "And as such I have a perfect right to settle all his debts if I could, which I can't completely," she admitted frankly. "The total must be well outside of my league."

"Outside of mine, too," Andrew said with a laugh. "I can't believe this. I leave London thinking that I have finally paid off all Papa's debts and return to find that I'm supposedly married to another female, my debts have not been paid and my father-in-law is ready to clap me into prison. Where is this Miss Tribbet? I'd like to face her down. I'm no more married to her than to the Queen."

"At the moment she is at Roddy and Emily's," Diantha replied.

Andrew beetled his brow. "Roddy? Does he know this absurd story?"

She shook her head. "No one knows except myself and Devlin and Lowell, and of course Miss Tribbet."

"Then why is she staying at Roddy's?" Andrew asked.

"Devlin persuaded them to employ her. Her name there is Miss Marsh."

"Miss Marsh? I thought you said her name was Miss Tribbet," Andrew asked, looking more and more confused at the tangled tale his sister was spinning.

"Andrew, pray don't be a simpleton. She adopted the name Marsh for her employment at Roddy and Emily's. The mother is an eccentric and they quarreled and Devlin thought it best to keep Miss Tribbet hidden away."

Andrew rose from his chair. "I shall go to Roddy's straightaway and see her."

His announcement did not impress Diantha. "Under what pretence, pray? She is supposed to be Harry's governess."

"Harry?" Andrew wrinkled his brow, wondering who this Harry could be.

"The babe. Oh, you wouldn't know. Emily was delivered of a baby boy and Miss Marsh—Tribbet—actually is the governess. It will look odd if you went round demanding to see her. Besides, if Lowell sees you on the street, he will have you arrested for bigamy. That reminds me, you must persuade Esmeraude not to see her father. She hasn't yet, has she?"

"No. I told her we could call on him later."

"You must keep her here," Diantha ordered. "Esmeraude mustn't see her father until we have straightened things out. And perhaps we shouldn't tell her about Miss Tribbet, either."

Andrew stared down his nose at his sister.

"You wish me to deceive my wife, Diantha?"

"Good gracious, I'm only thinking of her feelings. How do you think she would feel if she knew a tale was circulating which implies you might have married someone before her? She might believe it.''

For a minute she wondered if Andrew would baulk at her suggestion, but he eventually consented to say nothing to Esmeraude.

''I'll invent some way of keeping her here and not allowing her to see her father.'' He threw Diantha a rueful smile. ''Sweet sister, I find myself wishing I'd never left my posting house.''

''Everything will be fine, now that you are here,'' Diantha said encouragingly. ''I shall write to Miss Tribbet, asking her to call here tomorrow morning. One look at you and she will know that you are not the man she wed.''

''Write to Devlin and ask him to call, too,'' Andrew said. ''I want to hear the story from his lips.''

''Very well,'' Diantha said, her heart lifting then sinking at the prospect of having Devlin under her roof once again.

AT THAT VERY MOMENT Devlin was driving his highsteppers in the Park with Mrs. Whorley sharing the seat on his high-perched phaeton. The day was balmy, and the widow looked quite jaunty in a new green riding habit, but her mood was far from pleased. The viscount crying off from Alice's soirée had not set well in Mrs. Whorley's dish. Learning that Devlin planned to attend a boxing match on the Heath this evening increased her dissatisfaction a hundredfold. What was the point in attaching a prize like Devlin if he was never seen with her? He should be dangling after her, not attending silly pugilistic exhibitions.

''You have been most disobliging. First last night crying off from Alicia's soirée and now tonight.''

''Do keep your voice down, Thalia. The quizzes will say we have fought, and that will be on the gossip pages for everyone to read about.''

Mrs. Whorley tossed her head back. ''Let them. We *are* fighting.''

"No, we are not." Temper flared briefly in the viscount's blue eyes. "I haven't the inclination. Don't be a peagoose, Thalia. I have matters to attend to. I can't be dangling after you every second. You *wanted* my patronage, as you call it. You have it, as well as that ruby necklace from Rundell's."

This pointed reminder was lost on Mrs. Whorley.

"I want you to pay attention to me." Her thin lips pouted.

"Am I not hanging on your every word now?" he asked.

"No, you're not!" she exclaimed. "You may be here but your mind is miles away. Who are you thinking of? That odious Miss Tribbet, perhaps? You positively flinch each time I kiss you. You are in love with some other. And I shall find out just who."

"Be still!" His tone was so ominous that Mrs. Whorley actually fell silent. Further proof that her words had hit their mark. Devlin was famed for his civility. To render him out of countenance meant that he really did have his mind on another female. Mrs. Whorley seethed. She would find out just who it was if it were the last thing she did.

IN ANOTHER PART OF London, another young lady rose from her comfortable bed, her nap at an end. Miss Tribbet was feeling quite the happiest she had ever felt in recent years.

This she knew was owing entirely to one Lord Sylvester. She had not much experience in romantic dealings, but Sylvester was so earnest, so sincere in his appreciation of her that she could not help but be affected. And yet, how would he receive the news that she was married to Andrew Atwood?

As she mulled over this dilemma, Emily knocked on the door.

"Oh, my dear!" She fluttered in, wringing her hands. "You must come quickly. You have a caller. It's a female. Quite an odd creature, and so insistent about seeing a Miss

Tribbet. I told her we had no such person here. Then she asked to see the young lady who is my guest. I never heard of such a thing. But when Fergus would escort her out, she turned quite nasty and stuck him with her hat pin."

"What?" Miss Tribbet exclaimed.

Emily nodded. "Yes. Just a minor prick, but it turned him quite white. I never knew before that he turned sick at the sight of blood, particularly his own. So then I asked her to leave, but she wouldn't budge. If she would turn a hat pin on a butler, what would she turn on me?"

Miss Tribbet made no immediate reply, her own thoughts racing every which way.

"It did occur to me to call in the Authorities," Emily said softly.

The Authorities! "Oh, you don't want to do that."

"I quite agree. The Authorities will just make a great mull of things. So I thought I might come and ask you to speak to her. You are the only young lady under our roof."

When the two ladies entered Emily's drawing room a few minutes later, Miss Tribbet's worst fears were realized. Her mother in a purple dress and matching hat clucked and smiled at her.

Before Mrs. Tribbet could speak and give away the game, her daughter turned to Emily and begged for a moment of private speech with her caller.

"Are you sure you will be all right?" Emily asked anxiously. "She still has that hat pin."

"I don't think she will hurt me," Miss Tribbet said. "She is an old neighbour."

"Very well. But if you need any assistance, don't hesitate to call out."

After Emily had gone, Mrs. Tribbet circled her daughter, chuckling. "Well, well, so it is you. Old neighbours, are we? Become mighty high in the instep all of a sudden, haven't you?"

"How did you find me, Mama?" Miss Tribbet asked.

Her mother winked one heavily painted eyelid. "I have my ways. I've known important gentlemen in my salad days. I can command a favour or two still." She strolled over to the mantel and picked up one of Roddy's snuff boxes. "Very pretty..."

When she put it down her daughter let out a breath. "What are you doing here?" she asked.

"Come to find out how you were. Heard any more of that husband of yours?"

Miss Tribbet stared down at her hands, trying to find the best way to phrase her request.

"Mama, the situation is very complicated. You must go back to Topping Green. You don't understand—"

"I don't understand. Me? At three-and-forty I've known more gentlemen than you'll shake hands with. *I* don't understand. You're the innocent. That's what landed you in the suds."

"Mama, please!" Miss Tribbet implored. "Lord Devlin is helping me to locate Andrew."

"Devlin, is it?" Mrs. Tribbet snorted. "I don't know why you would put your trust in that one."

"Well, I do... and since you've all but turned me out—" she left the sentence unfinished.

"Words spoken in haste, my dear Maggie," Mrs. Tribbet said. "Flesh is flesh, is it not? And you be flesh of my flesh."

"What are you doing in London, really?" Miss Tribbet asked, half afraid to know what her mother was up to.

"Looking for you, of course, my dear. And since I'm here I might pay another call on Mr. Lowell."

The mention of Lowell caused the blood to drain from Miss Tribbet's face. Oh, why had her mother appeared now, when things were going so swimmingly for her? For once in her life she had met a gentleman who liked her, Sylvester. *Sylvester!*

"You mustn't see Lowell, Mama. You'll ruin everything," she said hastily now.

"*I'll* ruin everything!" Mrs. Tribbet said, eyes kindling. "It's not my reputation and honour that have been trifled with."

"If it's money you want, I'll send you what I've been paid."

Her mother bridled, then a crafty look stole into her eyes. "How much?"

"Fifty pounds."

Mrs. Tribbet scoffed. "The merest trifle."

"I'll send you more," Miss Tribbet promised. "Just please do not call on the Lowells."

"I shall do what I like!" Mrs. Tribbet announced and sailed out of the drawing room.

Emily came in almost at once. "My dear, you've got rid of that dreadful woman. What did she say to you? You look in such queer stirrups."

"I am fine. Pray excuse me," answered Miss Tribbet before fleeing up the stairs to her bedchamber. What would her mother do? Miss Tribbet knew only too well her mother's fickle nature. Alone, she might have been able to explain to Sylvester about the circumstances of her marriage to Andrew, but if her mother was determined to pursue her course, how could she ever again face Sylvester?

CHAPTER SEVENTEEN

"GOOD MORNING, MY LORD."

Devlin handed his hat and gloves to Lindell.

"I trust you had a good evening, my lord?"

The viscount grunted, seeing no need to relive his evening and a good portion of the morning, which had been spent first on the heath watching Black Bart demolish the Dutchman and then later in the card rooms of White's and Watier's.

"Lindell, I shall have you dismissed with ignominy if you continue to hover over me," he warned.

"You misunderstood, my lord," the butler said, following him up the staircase. "I was merely anxious that you receive this message from Miss Atwood." Lindell held out a cream-coloured note.

"This arrived yesterday afternoon, just after you set out on your drive in the Park with Mrs. Whorley," he said without a blink.

Wordlessly, Devlin picked up the note and continued up the stairs to his sitting room. Had Diantha changed her mind about his offer? He shut the door quickly and broke the seal. Instead of the love letter his imagination had sketched for a fleeting instant, there was just a civil request to call at Portman Square at ten in the morning. Andrew had returned.

Devlin held the note between two fingers and inhaled. No scent of any kind teased his nostrils. Good. He was tired of lilac-scented missives.

So Andrew had returned, and high time, too. Devlin wanted to be free of the entire tedious business of Andrew and Miss Tribbet once and for all. When that was done he could give Mrs. Whorley her congé again. Then he'd be free to do as he wished.

He rubbed a finger idly against the writing on the note card. As he wished. And just what did he wish? Blast it! He was no schoolboy wishing on stars. He wanted Diantha as a wife. He slammed his right fist into the palm of his left hand. That was it. And by Jove, he had to win her.

He'd had enough of her unknown lover! Stripping the cravat from his throat, he stalked to the door.

"James!" he bellowed for his valet.

He'd need a shave and a bath. He could not win Miss Atwood's hand in marriage by appearing in all his dirt.

"REALLY, ANDREW, you are treating me like an invalid!" Esmeraude protested in their bedchamber at Portman Square. "Aside from my leg, I am perfectly stout."

"But your fever," he said. "You'd do better to rest."

She kissed him on his cheek. "I am perishing from boredom. Just let me go belowstairs."

"No!" Andrew declared. "I absolutely forbid it." It was eight o'clock and no telling how long Esmeraude might linger below. She might be there when Devlin or Miss Tribbet called.

Esmeraude's eyes widened as she drew away. "You forbid it?" she asked. No one had ever forbidden Esmeraude to do anything before, and never before had Andrew sounded so authoritative.

Andrew cleared his throat, unhappily aware that his future as a married man hung precariously in the balance. "Yes," he said, anxiously scanning the painted ceiling for help. "I don't want you to stumble and break the other leg."

Before Esmeraude could thwart this pessimistic view of her walking ability, a knock sounded on the door. Diantha swept in, carrying a breakfast tray.

"I hope you slept well and are hungry," she said, putting the tray down with a flourish on a small pier table.

"I am famished," Esmeraude said. "But you shouldn't have brought a tray. I have just been trying to coax Andrew into letting me go belowstairs. Now that we are sisters you must lend me your support on this issue."

"But you don't want to go below," Diantha protested. "The breakfast parlour is so drafty. Up here it's so much cosier. And I also brought some lending-library romances that you are so partial to."

"Capital notion," Andrew said, picking up a fork and preparing to spear a slice of ham.

Esmeraude, however, did not follow suit. "Diantha, pray don't think me ungrateful, but I don't see why we must stay here with you."

"Andrew, didn't you tell her?" Diantha chided.

Andrew chewing on the ham shot her a dagger look. "Indeed no, dear sister. Why don't you explain things?"

"Very well," Diantha said with aplomb. "Andrew had commissioned me when you were on your trip to make sure the workmen he hired completed the repair of the roof of his residence. However, being a rather shatterbrained creature, I forgot all about it until just a few days ago. I soon discovered that no work had been done. By now of course they are working feverishly to finish the roof. Nothing would be more vexatious for you than to endure that pounding. Since it was all my fault, you must be my guests."

"If such is the case, we can go and stay with Mama and Papa," Esmeraude said, clapping her hands. "I am longing to see them. I have missed them so."

"No, we can't," Andrew said.

"Why not?"

"Because you're my wife, and I say no," he said, driven to the wall.

This second autocratic order from her husband brought a frown to Esmeraude's brow. Diantha stepped in quickly to heal the breach.

"What Andrew means is that he doesn't want to intrude any more on your father's generosity," she said.

Esmeraude smiled. "Oh, Andrew, you and your precious pride. Papa won't mind."

"I'd just feel better staying with Diantha."

"Oh, very well," Esmeraude said, beginning to sip her coffee. "But do send word to my parents that we are staying here, won't you, Di?"

"I will send word to them this afternoon," Diantha said. By that time, she fervently hoped that Andrew's marriage to Miss Tribbet would be sorted out.

OVER AT CAVENDISH SQUARE Miss Tribbet eyed herself uneasily in the looking glass. She had received Diantha's summons yesterday and had spent the entire night tossing and turning.

Now less than an hour from the appointed time she pulled a tortoiseshell hairbrush through her tangled locks. Her heart was besieged with doubts. She wanted to go to Portman Square and settle things. Yet another part of her didn't want to face Andrew again.

Becoming aware that her hand was shaking, Miss Tribbet put down her hairbrush. She thought momentarily of not answering Miss Atwood's summons. Perhaps then nothing would come of it. But she immediately gave up that notion. No doubt Miss Atwood would bring Andrew to see her at Cavendish Square.

And then there was the problem of Mama.

Resolutely, Miss Tribbet knotted the ribbons of her blue chip bonnet under her chin.

Miss Tribbet had no sooner crossed the hall to the door than she halted. Sylvester had just come in. A broad smile crossed the inventor's face when he caught sight of her.

"Good morning, Miss Tribbet," he said. "Permit me to say how lovely you look in that blue dress."

Miss Tribbet felt the colour rise in her cheeks. "Thank you, my lord."

"Are you on your way out?" he asked, deducing as much from her hat and the gloves she was now drawing on.

"I have some errands I must run," she explained.

"Permit me to escort you," he said, turning and leading her out the door.

The last thing in the world Miss Tribbet wanted was Sylvester to accompany her to Portman Square.

"No, that won't be necessary," she said hastily.

He continued to follow her down the steps. "Do you have a carriage?" he asked.

"I planned to catch a hack."

Sylvester shook his head. "No, don't do that. They are so dirty. Permit me to drive you."

"No, really, my lord. I'd as lief walk."

"Where are you bound for?" Sylvester said, falling into step with her.

"I thought I'd stop and see Miss Atwood."

"Diantha?" He halted. "But she lives at Portman Square. In this wind you'd better allow me to drive you."

"No, really I cannot." Miss Tribbet said, feeling increasingly agitated.

Sylvester took her by the elbow. "Come into the carriage," he ordered, leading her to his vehicle. "Now," he said, when they were both settled against the velvet squabs, "you will tell me what the problem is so that I can assist you."

"You can't. No one can," Miss Tribbet said in accents of despair. "You are so good, Sylvester, truly. And I wish..."

Her tear-filled eyes gazed up into his. Sylvester held her hands tightly in his.

"What has overset you so much that you are crying?" he asked. "Dear Miss Marsh, tell me."

"My name's not Miss Marsh," Miss Tribbet said.

"It's not?" His freckled face wrinkled momentarily in thought.

"It's Tribbet."

"Tribbet. Well, that's a perfectly fine name. I don't understand why you prefer Marsh—"

Miss Tribbet wrung her hands. "I told you it was a muddle. You might not want to speak to me when you hear the whole story."

"I shall always want to speak to you," the inventor declared. "In fact, I came over today expressly to speak to you. I know that we haven't known each other long, Miss Marsh—"

"Tribbet . . ." she murmured.

"Tribbet, then, but I knew instantly that you were the woman I was meant to marry. Would you, could you, see your way to having a husband such as myself?"

Far from looking gratified by such a proposal, Miss Tribbet burst into tears.

"Good heavens," Sylvester said, alarmed by this transformation of his companion into a watering pot. She dug into her reticule and brought out her handkerchief. "Miss Marsh, I mean Miss Tribbet. What a fool I am. Devlin warned me that you were country reared and I should go slowly. I am sorry if I've terrified you with my offer."

"You haven't terrified me," Miss Tribbet said, drying her eyes on the handkerchief. "You've done me a great honour. I should be happy. But I can't be. It's because of Andrew," she said thickly.

"Andrew?" Sylvester sat back. "Andrew Atwood?"

"Yes. I'm married to him."

Sylvester pushed back his beaver felt. "What nonsense is this? You can't be married to Atwood. He wed Esmeraude Lowell not a fortnight ago."

"I know, so everyone says. But I married him a month earlier."

"You did? But why? You don't love him, do you?"

"No!" Miss Tribbet said from the depths of her being. "It is a long story," she said. "It will probably give you a disgust of me."

"It will never give me a disgust of you," he said. "But I own to considerable confusion."

She sighed. "You see, it all started when I went bathing one day in a stream by our house. . . ."

"And Andrew's back now?" Sylvester asked when she had finished her tale.

Miss Tribbet nodded. "So his sister's note to me indicated. I was to present myself at Portman Square at ten today."

Sylvester consulted his pocket watch. "Then we must head there without further delay."

"But I don't want to go," Miss Tribbet said, hanging her head.

He put down the reins he had just picked up. "Why not?"

"Because what if it is Andrew and he wants me for a wife? I certainly don't want him for my husband."

"You don't?"

She shook her head. "I want you, Sylvester," she said shyly.

A smile suffused Sylvester's face, and he clasped Miss Tribbet to his chest, not caring who might see them. "My dear, you don't know how happy you have made me. But we must go and see Andrew."

"What if he doesn't want to divorce me?" Miss Tribbet asked, clinging to his coat of olive superfine. "What if he wants to keep me as his wife?"

Sylvester dropped a kiss on her head. "If he married Esmeraude, it stands to reason that he didn't wish to be married to you," he pointed out. "Dashed silly of him. I can't fathom anyone letting you get away from him."

"I have no fortune," Miss Tribbet said, continuing to nestle against Sylvester's coat. "Miss Lowell is a great heiress."

"That's so," Sylvester said, accepting this matter-of-factly.

She pulled away. "Does that not concern you, my lord? My lack of fortune?"

"No. I'm no Golden Ball, but my pockets aren't to let, and I don't care a fig about your lack of a dowry. So we must see Andrew and settle this mess once and for all." With that he set the horses off.

Midway to Diantha's, Miss Tribbet ventured to broach the subject of Mrs. Tribbet.

"There is another thing, Sylvester. My mother."

The inventor cocked his head at her. "What about her?"

"You may not like her."

He smiled over at her. "Impossible."

"She's loud and coarse and prone to saying whatever she wants—" Miss Tribbet said then held her breath. What would Sylvester say to such a mother-in-law?

"Aunt Agatha."

"I beg your pardon?"

Sylvester grinned. "Your mother sounds exactly like my aunt Agatha. Now there was a griffin. I'm sure your mother could be no worse than my aunt who is rumoured to have been even an actress at one time in her life."

"Mama hasn't been an actress, but I think she was a Cyprian."

Sylvester laughed. "Good. I know Aunt Agatha would take her under her wing. You see, my dear, I have relatives that put me to the blush, too."

"You don't know how happy I am to hear that," Miss Tribbet said.

DEVLIN ROUNDED THE CORNER at Portman Square just as Sylvester's carriage was pulling up on the flagway. He waited for a few moments, unaware that another carriage carrying Mrs. Whorley had been following him from Berkeley Square.

Mrs. Whorley was not the type of woman to let the grass grow under her feet. Find Devlin's new lover, she had promised herself, and that she would do. It had been child's play to lay in wait outside the Square and follow his distinctive carriage. Whoever his new love was, she'd be surprised to learn the truth about the viscount. Mrs. Whorley was in no hurry. She would allow Devlin a few moments with his loved one. Then she'd spring the surprise. An entrance. Yes. She would definitely make an entrance.

UNAWARE OF THE PLANS which Mrs. Whorley was busy hatching, Devlin exchanged greetings with Sylvester and Miss Tribbet.

"How do you go on this morning, Miss Marsh?" he enquired.

She smiled shyly. "You needn't bother with calling me Marsh, my lord. Sylvester knows the name is bogus. He knows everything about me."

"He does?" Devlin dealt his friend a speculative glance.

"Didn't heed your advice, Dev, sorry. I took my fences with a rush."

"Hasn't appeared to have hurt you any," the viscount replied, as the two faces beamed back at him.

"No, it hasn't. Tried to wait, Dev, but thought it best to follow my heart."

Out of the mouths of babes. Perhaps he should take a cue from the inventor, Devlin thought as Hughes led them into the blue drawing room where Diantha sat with Susan, the two ladies working on their stitchery.

For a second Diantha seemed unaware of her guests. She sat, smiling down as she worked the stitches on her tambour frame. Devlin watching felt a tightness in his throat. He would not let her wed another. As though she felt the intensity of his gaze, she glanced up and quickly laid her embroidery aside.

"So good of you to come," she said, shaking hands with Miss Tribbet.

"I wanted Sylvester with me," Miss Tribbet said to explain the inventor's presence.

"Of course," Diantha said, shaking hands with the inventor.

But when she laid her hand in Devlin's palm, instead of shaking it, he lifted it to his lips. She felt a definite thrill travel from her fingers to her heart. She glanced quickly at Susan, who was greeting the others in the group.

"Where is Andrew?" Sylvester asked.

Diantha turned with relief to the question. "Above-stairs, trying to coax Esmeraude into staying in her room.

I ordered Hughes to fetch him the minute that you all arrived. He and Esmeraude were involved in a carriage accident. Unfortunately she broke her leg, forcing them to abandon their plans for the Lakes.''

''Was he driving?''

''I knew you'd ask that, Dev,'' Andrew Atwood said, coming in and clapping his friend on the shoulder. ''And the answer to that is yes, I was driving but it wasn't my fault. You know how horrid country roads are.''

''Seems I've heard that excuse before.''

''It's the truth. I'll take you back to the village and show you.''

''What interesting things you do devise for me to do, Andrew. I can find fewer things more scintillating than to stare at a rutted country lane.''

''That's enough talk about your driving,'' Diantha said. ''I didn't bring everyone together to discuss that.'' She pulled Andrew away from the viscount and led him towards Miss Tribbet, sitting on the couch with Sylvester.

Miss Tribbet rose from the couch, eyes riveted on Andrew. The cheery smile on Mr. Atwood's face faded under her intense scrutiny.

''Is this your brother?'' Miss Tribbet asked Diantha.

''Yes.'' Diantha said as Miss Tribbet circled Andrew.

''I've never laid eyes on him before in my life,'' Miss Tribbet declared.

''Thank God!'' Sylvester ejaculated, jumping up and sweeping her into his arms.

Diantha felt a surge of relief in her veins. She'd always known Andrew wouldn't be such a blackguard as to marry one woman while married to another. Here was the final proof she sought.

Andrew for his part was staring just as intently at Miss Tribbet through a quizzing glass.

''Are you the female I'm supposed to have seen bathing in a stream?'' he asked.

Miss Tribbet blushed. ''Yes.''

"Be careful of your tongue, Andrew," Sylvester said dangerously. "Miss Tribbet is going to be my wife."

Andrew laughed. "Good for you, Sylvester. All I was going to say was that I'd never seen her before. Surely I'd remember and I don't." He turned to his sister. "It's all a hum, Diantha, I told you that before. The only one I've ever wed was Esmeraude."

"That will be a great relief to all, particularly Esmeraude," Susan said, "who doesn't want to remain above-stairs much longer."

"If Miss Tribbet would be good enough to tell Mr. Lowell that she didn't marry Andrew," Devlin said, "all this fuss and botheration will be over." And he could get down to the real challenge of persuading Diantha to marry him.

"But it isn't over for me," Miss Tribbet said, pulling away from Sylvester's embrace.

"Of course it is," the inventor soothed. "Are you thinking about what Lowell will say? I shall come with you. Or if it's your Mama who worries you—"

"That's not the problem."

"You're not married to Andrew," Diantha said. "He and you both agree to that."

"Perhaps not, but I did marry someone who took the name of Andrew Atwood in our wedding ceremony. And if it's not the real Andrew, just whom did I marry? And how can I ever find him and persuade him to get a bill of divorcement?"

"Oh, good heavens, I never thought of that," Diantha said.

Miss Tribbet cast an imploring gaze from face to face. "You do see, now I am in a greater fix than before."

CHAPTER EIGHTEEN

"Zounds, she's right!" Andrew exclaimed. "Who is the fellow, if not me? I'd like to get my hands on him myself. Rum bit of business, besmirching my good name."

"It's impossible," Miss Tribbet said. "We'll never find him." She drooped in her chair like a forlorn child.

"Not so," Diantha said. "You saw him and must know what he looks like."

"Perhaps you could sketch him," Susan added.

"I don't know if I could," Miss Tribbet protested. "I've never been much good at sketching."

"Then you must describe him, and Susan shall sketch him," Diantha replied.

Before Miss Kirkpatrick could gather her sketching materials, an altercation resonated from the hallway with a loud voice demanding entrance.

"I know Devlin is in there. I wish to see him now!" Mrs. Whorley burst into the drawing room with a stern Hughes at her heels.

"I am sorry, Miss Atwood," the butler said, "this person would not heed my request to wait."

"It's all right, Hughes," Diantha said, beset by the liveliest curiosity concerning Devlin's chère amie. Why was she seeking him out in this public way?

"You thought you could get away from me, didn't you, Ollie?" Mrs. Whorley advanced on the viscount.

"Perhaps we should discuss what's on your mind in private, Thalia," Devlin said calmly.

Mrs. Whorley's teeth flashed as she laughed. "You would like that, wouldn't you? Then the woman you love wouldn't know what a blackguard and loose screw you are."

Diantha glanced immediately to her left at Susan, who gazed placidly at the scene now under way.

"Be quiet, Thalia," Devlin said, taking her by the arm. "I won't have you making a cake out of yourself this way."

"Making a cake out of myself!" Mrs. Whorley pulled herself out of his grasp. "You mean making a cake out of you. Would these same friends now with you be willing to keep your acquaintance if they knew the truth about your taking ruthless advantage of an innocent woman?"

Diantha eyed Mrs. Whorley dubiously. Woman she certainly was. But innocent?

Standing by the mantel, Andrew coughed. "Are you the innocent involved?" he asked.

Mrs. Whorley sniffed. "Of course I am not. Although Ollie did treat me less than civilly. That man—" Mrs. Whorley fixed a rigid finger at the viscount "—seduced and then tossed aside a young, gently bred female from the country. When it became evident that she would bear his child, he banished Miss Tribbet to a nunnery."

For a moment no one spoke, then Sylvester leapt to his feet, shaking his fist.

"I have heard enough," the inventor roared. "You, ma'am, are a curst bagpipe. I find your slanderous remarks intolerable."

Mrs. Whorley put up her chin. "You are a friend to Devlin, of course."

"Miss Tribbet is not in a nunnery," Sylvester declared hotly.

"How do you know?" Mrs. Whorley sniffed.

"Because I am Miss Tribbet, ma'am," Miss Tribbet replied in her quiet way.

"And this—" Diantha waved her hand about the drawing room "—is certainly no nunnery."

Mrs. Whorley gaped. "But I heard. That is to say, I know—" she fumbled for words.

"I beg your pardon, ma'am, but you seem to know very little," Miss Tribbet said. "And as for my bearing Devlin's child..." She blushed, unable to complete her thought.

"But then why did you submit to my threats?" Mrs. Whorley demanded of Devlin, who was standing to one side, observing the scene with great interest. "When I threatened to speak earlier in the week you were all atwitter."

"My reasons are none of your concern," Devlin said, inhaling a pinch of snuff.

"You treated me shabbily, Oliver," Mrs. Whorley railed. "You intended all along to humiliate me in this fashion."

"Good heavens," Diantha burst out, unable to keep still. "'Twas you who insisted on making your preposterous accusations in public."

"But he knew it wasn't true and should have stopped me." Mrs. Whorley stamped her foot.

"Acquit me of this latest error in my judgement," Devlin said. "I seem to be committing many of late. You mustn't repine, Thalia. You have the ruby necklace. That's what you wanted from me, anyway. And if you are quick, you can perhaps reattach Sir Arthur."

With two spots of colour high in her cheeks, Mrs. Whorley stalked out of the room.

"What the devil did you ever see in her, Dev?" Andrew asked.

"I don't know," the viscount replied irritably.

"I hope she didn't go about telling people I was *enceinte*," Miss Tribbet said.

Devlin immediately reassured her.

"How can you be so certain?" Sylvester asked, raising a sceptical brow.

"The ruby necklace."

Confusion was writ large on the inventor's face.

"I bought her silence with the necklace," Devlin explained. "I knew that if she started to kick up a fuss, it would bring more botheration onto everyone."

"But such a necklace must have cost an enormous sum."

"I would have paid much more to be finally rid of her, which now I finally am."

"You are too modest, my lord. I owe you much," Miss Tribbet said.

He shrugged off her thanks. "Nonsense. Only did what a gentleman should. I apologize for her unseemly conduct."

"And now I believe it's time for sherry," Diantha said, ringing for Hughes.

Her butler, however, took longer than usual in replying to the summons.

"I beg pardon for the delay, Miss Atwood," he said when he finally appeared.

"Sherry and whatever refreshments Henri can concoct for my guests, Hughes."

"To be sure. I'll get the sherry straightaway." He lowered his voice an octave. "Sir Philip Forth has arrived with the orphans."

"I expected them next week." Now she would have them as well as Esmeraude and Andrew underfoot. "Are they very tired? Why don't you bring them in and then ask Henri for some lemonade and cakes."

"Very good, Miss Atwood."

A few minutes later a beleaguered-looking Sir Philip Forth entered the drawing room, holding a scruffy schoolboy in either hand.

"Say good morning to your hostess, you pasty-faced brats," he muttered.

"Good morning, ma'am," the two angelic-looking boys chorused.

Sir Philip released his hold on their necks.

"Good morning." Diantha smiled at the children.

On the other side of the room Miss Tribbet murmured softly, "Andrew."

Mr. Atwood cocked his head at her. "Yes, Miss Tribbet?"

But her large eyes were trained not on Mr. Atwood but on Sir Philip standing with the orphans.

She rose from her chair. "That's Andrew!" Miss Tribbet said. "Oh, yes, it is. I'm positive."

Sir Philip blanched as he beheld the woman crossing the floor towards him.

"Do you know Miss Tribbet, Sir Philip?" Diantha asked, staring intently at the baronet now running a finger between his neck and collar points.

"I don't believe I've made her acquaintance."

"How can you say that?" Miss Tribbet exclaimed. "You came upon me when I was bathing..."

"Shush." Sir Philip waved an agitated hand, pointing to the orphans. Diantha hastily summoned a footman to take the boys to the kitchen.

"Now, Sir Philip, the truth," Diantha demanded.

"There's nothing to her story."

"You married me. You must remember that!" Miss Tribbet said, her veracity under attack. "In March in Hertfordshire."

"Never been to Hertfordshire in March," Sir Philip said stiffly.

"Au contraire," Devlin interposed. "I distinctly remember you prosing on about a speech given at some remote village there. And the month mentioned was March."

"You must be thinking of someone else," Sir Philip said. "Obliged to you for seeing to the orphans, Miss Atwood. But I must go."

Devlin reached out a lanky arm. The muscles of his forearm bunched as he held Sir Philip fast. "I'm afraid, Sir Philip, that I must detain you until we have discerned the truth once and for all," he drawled.

"Really, Devlin." Sir Philip squirmed like a helpless rabbit in the grasp of a lion.

Devlin gazed blandly across at Diantha. "Miss Atwood, may I use your library? I would like to exchange a few words in private with Sir Philip."

"If anyone has a few words with him, it will be me." Andrew crossed to Devlin's side before his sister could speak. "Abusing my good name."

"You may have him after me," Devlin said graciously.

"I want a few words, too," Sylvester said, brandishing his boomerang, the sight of which caused Sir Philip to capitulate.

"Don't beat me with that club!" he begged. "Very well. I admit it. I did come across Miss Tribbet bathing in a stream. Quite by accident and not design, I assure you. And I didn't look at her, really."

"You perpetrated this dreadful hoax on Miss Tribbet!" Diantha exclaimed. "You, with all your fine talk of moral decay in our society. For shame, sir."

"It wasn't a hoax. I was in a fix," Sir Philip said doggedly. "If any word got out about what occurred, my reputation would be in tatters."

"And what about Miss Tribbet's reputation, pray?" Sylvester asked, continuing to look dangerous.

"I *did* think about her reputation. Why do you think I married her? So she wouldn't be ruined."

"What twaddle. You're already married!" Devlin said.

"What?" Miss Tribbet interrupted the interrogation. "Is that true?"

Sir Philip hung his head. "Yes, I know it was very bad of me. But it wasn't a real wedding, anyway," Sir Philip said as Sylvester embraced the tearful Miss Tribbet. "I knew the vicar was laid up with the gout. So I hired a man at a posting house to pretend to do the ceremony."

"Do you mean to say the marriage was all bogus from the start?" Sylvester exclaimed, one arm round his beloved's shoulders. "I should beat you."

"And I will assist you," Andrew said, rubbing his hands in anticipation. "Embroiling me in this reprehensible scheme."

"No, you mustn't," Miss Tribbet intervened. "Because he was trying to protect me, in his own fashion."

Andrew snorted. "Trying to protect himself. And what possessed you to give my name to Miss Tribbet?"

"I've always been a bad hand at thinking on my feet," Sir Philip said. "Needed a name and I thought something with A for the alphabet, you know. Well, then of course I thought of Andrew, and Atwood just seemed made to order."

"But what is to be done about righting this wrong?" Susan asked, a voice of reason in all this Sturm und Drang.

"I think Sir Philip should beg Miss Tribbet's pardon and Andrew's, too, for using his name," Devlin said. "Then he must swear that no one will hear about this ever again."

"Oh, I swear. And I am so sorry, Miss Tribbet, and I beg your pardon, too, Andrew."

"And we present in this room must undertake a similar pact not to mention this again."

"Agreed."

"But is that all?" Diantha said after everyone had chorused their agreement and the sherry had been distributed. "What about the wedding certificate that Mrs. Tribbet is brandishing about?"

"It's a bogus one," Sir Philip said. "Had the man at the posting house sign it."

"I wouldn't fret about Mrs. Tribbet. Before too long she will be brandishing a legitimate one, won't she, Sylvester?" Devlin asked with a quizzing look.

"Yes, by Jove, she will," Sylvester said, kissing Miss Tribbet on the cheek.

"Well, then, you see. Everything has fallen into place." Devlin held his sherry glass out to be refilled.

"It still seems a bit havy-cavy to me," Andrew said, pouring the sherry from a decanter.

"Perhaps you're right," Devlin said after a judicious sip. "I believe I know how this can be remedied once and for all. Sylvester ought to elope with Miss Tribbet!"

"Elope? You mean to Gretna Green?" the inventor asked, agog at the suggestion.

"Why not? You have your vehicle outside, don't you?"

"Yes."

"And I feel sure that Sir Philip would advance you the sums necessary for a stay in Scotland, would you not, Sir Philip?" Devlin asked.

The baronet could take a hint, particularly when it was delivered by one of Gentleman Jack's prize pupils. With a sigh he reached into his coat pocket and pulled out his purse. "Whatever you say, Devlin."

Sylvester gazed over at Miss Tribbet. "What do *you* say, my dear?"

"I believe an elopement is in order, my lord."

AN HOUR LATER the blue drawing room was empty save for Diantha and Devlin. Sylvester and Miss Tribbet were on their way to the Lowells to explain everything to Esmeraude's father. From there Sylvester and Miss Tribbet would go on to Scotland. Andrew and Esmeraude were removing to their residence on Albemarle Street. The orphans were in the music room with Susan learning a song to delight their new relatives in America.

Diantha glanced across at the viscount. By all rights he should have left long ago. Why did he linger? she wondered. Then she glimpsed the clock on the mantel, and a smile crossed her lips. Luncheon would be served soon.

"What a morning this has been," she said.

"Enough comings and goings for one of Mr. Fanshaw's plays," he agreed.

"I'm glad it's all settled."

"Not everything." He crossed the room and sat down on the couch next to her.

Diantha felt her heart beat faster.

"Sylvester and Miss Tribbet are bound for the border to be married. Sir Philip is back in the bosom of his own family. Andrew's good name will be restored and his debts settled. What is left to settle?"

He tapped himself on the chest with a finger. "Me."

She looked away from him. "I don't think it will be hard for you to find a new chère amie after Mrs. Whorley."

A dark frown descended on his face. "I am not talking about a chère amie. I've had my fill of them. Never want another one. I am talking about a wife."

"Oh, Devlin. I wish you would not persist in those foolish thoughts," she said. What a good thing Susan was out of the room. "It will only bring you continued distress."

"Distress? It has brought me more than distress, my dear Miss Atwood."

"Devlin, please, say no more," she implored. She couldn't stand to see him in such agony.

He held her hands tightly in his. "Look at me," he commanded.

Reluctantly, she obeyed his order. His eyes were a clear crystalline blue. How she hated to inflict pain on him.

"Tell me one thing?" he growled. "Who is the lucky fellow?"

Diantha swallowed hard.

"Dr. Brewster," she said softly.

"Egad," he exclaimed. "That quack? You must be bamming me."

"Dr. Brewster is not a quack. He is a most excellent doctor. I know he cannot hold a candle to you in rank or fortune or looks, but he's quite respectable, and—" Diantha licked her lips "—Susan loves him."

He gazed down at the soft lips and the dark eyes blinking back tears. "Susan, did you say? Miss Kirkpatrick is going to wed Brewster?" he nearly shouted at her.

"Oh, Devlin, pray, don't take it to heart. I know you have wanted Susan for your wife from the start. But in time you might find someone else to love."

Devlin held his hand to his face. To hide his anguish, no doubt, Diantha thought.

"When I spoke to you the other day about an offer of marriage, you thought I was offering for Miss Kirkpatrick?" he asked.

"Naturally. Anyone could see the way the land lay. You met Susan at Hookam's and the next week you were haunting our residence. I can add one and one."

"Can you, indeed, my lovely bluestocking?" Devlin said, putting his hand down and revealing blue eyes brimming with laughter. "Then give me leave to say that you have led me an awful dance."

"Me? What do you mean?"

"I wasn't offering for Susan, minx. I was offering for you!"

"For me!" She flushed. "Pray, if this is a joke, sir, it is not funny."

"It is no joke. I've never proposed to a woman before. Am I doing it wrong?" he asked earnestly. "Perhaps I should go down on bended knee."

Diantha laughed as he suited action to his words. "Do be serious, my lord. You can't really want me for a wife. I am a bluestocking, not an out and outer."

"I am well aware of what you are, my dear Diantha," Devlin said, looking down at her with a look which nearly took her breath away. "If you think I can live without you as my wife you are as foolish as Sir Philip. Cupid shot me with his arrow the first time I glimpsed you at Andrew's wedding. And if you agree we shall soon be walking up the aisle together."

"But you can't love me," Diantha protested.

"I can't. Why not? Do you have another lover in mind?" he asked, looking dark. "If you do I'll have his name and beat him within an inch of his life."

She choked on a laugh. "Would you do that, for me?"

"More," he said, sweeping her into his arms and kissing her the way he'd yearned to from the start.

For a breathless moment Diantha felt perilously close to swooning. So this was love, the way her pulses raced at his touch, the way her hands twined at his neck, pulling his mouth closer, the way her heart felt close to bursting just as the poets had described it. And even better than they said it would be.

"You haven't said you would marry me," Devlin reminded her breathlessly ten minutes later.

"Haven't I?" she asked, resting her hand against his comfortable shoulder. Her lips felt rather bruised from his kisses, but in a delightful way.

"No, you haven't. Don't keep me on tenterhooks, you flirt."

"I do hope your offer is sincere, my lord, and not just a ploy to get my chef."

He sat back, a bemused expression on his face. "Now, what an excellent notion that is. I hadn't even thought about all those dreary meals I won't be obliged to consume anymore. You must marry me. That way I will get your chef, and you will get your Ming vases back."

"Do you mean to say you were the wealthy collector Hathaway sold them to?" she asked, astonished.

"I am," he acknowledged. He pulled her back into his embrace. "We can talk later about vases and chefs. But now I must tell you how I love you, my lovely bluestocking. Will you put me out of my misery and marry me soon?"

"As soon as you wish, my lord," she said and lifted her face up to be kissed again.

Celebrate the most romantic day of the year with
MY VALENTINE 1992—a sexy new collection of four
romantic stories written by our famous Temptation
authors:

GINA WILKINS
KRISTINE ROLOFSON
JOANN ROSS
VICKI LEWIS THOMPSON

My Valentine 1992—an exquisite escape into a romantic
and sensuous world.

 Harlequin Books ®

HARLEQUIN'S "BIG WIN"
SWEEPSTAKES RULES & REGULATIONS
NO PURCHASE NECESSARY TO ENTER OR RECEIVE A PRIZE

1. Alternate means of entry: Print your name and address on a 3" ×5" piece of plain paper and send to the appropriate address below:

In the U.S.	In Canada
Harlequin's "BIG WIN" Sweepstakes	Harlequin's "BIG WIN" Sweepstakes
P.O. Box 1867	P.O. Box 609
3010 Walden Ave.	Fort Erie, Ontario
Buffalo, NY 14269-1867	L2A 5X3

2. To enter the Sweepstakes and join the Reader Service, scratch off the metallic strips on all of your BIG WIN tickets #1-#6. This will reveal the values for each Sweepstakes entry number, the number of free books you will receive and your free bonus gift as part of our Reader Service. If you do not wish to take advantage of our Reader Service but wish to enter the Sweepstakes only, scratch off the metallic strips on your BIG WIN tickets #1-#4. Return your entire sheet of tickets intact. Incomplete and/or inaccurate entries are ineligible for that section or sections of prizes. Torstar Corp. and its affiliates are not responsible for mutilated or unreadable entries or inadvertent printing errors. Mechanically reproduced entries are null and void.

3. Whether you take advantage of this offer or not, on or about April 30, 1992, at the offices of D. L. Blair, Inc., Blair, NE, your Sweepstakes numbers will be compared against the list of winning numbers generated at random by the computer. However, prizes will only be awarded to individuals who have entered the Sweepstakes. In the event that all prizes are not claimed, a random drawing will be held from all qualified entries received from March 30, 1990 to March 31, 1992, to award all unclaimed prizes. All cash prizes (Grand to Sixth) will be mailed to the winners and are payable by check in U.S. funds. Seventh Prize will be shipped to winners via third-class mail. These prizes are in addition to any free, surprise or mystery gifts that might be offered. Versions of this Sweepstakes with different prizes of approximate equal value may appear at retail outlets or in other mailings by Torstar Corp. and its affiliates.

4. Prizes: (1) ★ Grand Prize $1,000,000.00 Annuity; (1)First Prize $25,000.00; (1)Second Prize $10,000.00; (5)Third Prize $5,000.00; (10)Fourth Prize $1,000.00; (100)Fifth Prize $250.00; (2,500)Sixth Prize $10.00; (6,000) ★ ★ Seventh Prize $12.95 ARV.

   ★ This presentation offers a Grand Prize of a $1,000,000.00 annuity. Winner will receive $33,333.33 a year for 30 years without interest totalling $1,000,000.00.

   ★ ★ Seventh Prize: A fully illustrated hardcover book published by Torstar Corp. Approximate Retail Value of the book is $12.95.

   Entrants may cancel the Reader Service at any time without cost or obligation (see details in Center Insert Card).

5. This Sweepstakes is being conducted under the supervision of D. L. Blair, Inc. By entering this Sweepstakes, each entrant accepts and agrees to be bound by these rules and the decisions of the judges, which shall be final and binding. Odds of winning in the random drawing are dependent upon the number of entries received. Taxes, if any, are the sole responsibility of the winners. Prizes are nontransferable. All entries must be received at the address on the detachable Business Reply Card and must be postmarked no later than 12:00 MIDNIGHT on March 31, 1992. The drawing for all unclaimed Sweepstakes prizes will take place on May 30, 1992, at 12:00 NOON, at the offices of D. L. Blair, Inc., Blair, NE.

6. This offer is open to residents of the U.S., the United Kingdom, France, Germany and Canada, 18 years or older, except employees and immediate family members of Torstar Corp., its affiliates, subsidiaries, and all the other agencies, entities and persons connected with the use, marketing or conduct of this Sweepstakes. All Federal, State, Provincial, Municipal and local laws apply. Void wherever prohibited or restricted by law. Any litigation within the Province of Quebec respecting the conduct and awarding of a prize in this publicity contest must be submitted to the Régie des loteries et courses du Québec.

7. Winners will be notified by mail and may be required to execute an affidavit of eligibility and release, which must be returned within 14 days after notification or an alternate winner will be selected. Canadian winners will be required to correctly answer an arithmetical, skill-testing question administered by mail, which must be returned within a limited time. Winners consent to the use of their name, photograph and/or likeness for advertising and publicity in conjunction with this and similar promotions without additional compensation.

8. For a list of our major prize winners, send a stamped, self-addressed ENVELOPE to: WINNERS LIST, P.O. Box 4510, Blair, NE 68009. Winners Lists will be supplied after the May 30, 1992 drawing date.

Offer limited to one per household.

© 1991 Harlequin Enterprises Limited   Printed in the U.S.A.

BWH192

HARLEQUIN
PROUDLY PRESENTS
A DAZZLING NEW CONCEPT IN ROMANCE FICTION

One small town—twelve terrific love stories

Welcome to Tyler, Wisconsin—a town full of people
you'll enjoy getting to know, memorable friends and
unforgettable lovers, and a long-buried secret that
lurks beneath its serene surface....

JOIN US FOR A YEAR IN THE LIFE OF TYLER

Each book set in Tyler is a self-contained love story;
together, the twelve novels stitch the fabric of a
community.

LOSE YOUR HEART TO TYLER!

The excitement begins in March 1992, with
WHIRLWIND, by Nancy Martin. When lively, brash
Liza Baron arrives home unexpectedly, she moves
into the old family lodge, where the silent and
mysterious Cliff Forrester has been living in seclusion
for years....

WATCH FOR ALL TWELVE BOOKS
OF THE TYLER SERIES
Available wherever Harlequin books are sold

TYLER-G